Kissed by Darkness

D1520065

Kissed by Darkness

THE SUNWALKER SAGA, BOOK ONE

Shéa MacLeod

 Montlake
Romance

First edition © 2011 Shéa MacLeod
Montlake edition © 2012
All rights reserved.
Printed in the United States of America.

Published by Montlake Romance
P.O. Box 400818
Las Vegas, NV 89140

ISBN-13: 9781612185620
ISBN-10: 1612185622

For Bonnie,
Cousin and Beta Reader Extraordinaire

Chapter One

Moonlight glinted off yellow fangs dripping with blood as the vampire spit at me like a cornered cat. Her bloodshot eyes watched my every move, her body coiled and ready to strike.

"You did not just hiss at me," I spit back.

The vamp snarled, hovering over her meal, which happened to be a teenage boy—one of the emo kids who hung around Portland's Pioneer Courthouse Square to smoke weed, drink too much expensive coffee from the Starbucks on the corner, and wallow in dark emotions. Probably, she'd lured him away from the square with her perky blonde ponytail and her little blue-and-yellow cheerleading outfit, now smeared in blood. No doubt he went to angsty teen vampire movies and thought the undead were cool. Bet he was having second thoughts about that now.

She was young and strong and newly turned, no more than a year or two old. I could feel her age like a tickle at the base of my skull. That little party trick, feeling the age of a vamp, along with a few other nifty abilities, were all thanks to the vampire attack that changed my life three years ago and made me perfect for what I had become: a vampire hunter.

I loosed a knife from my wrist sheath, the nearby streetlamp turning the silver-edged blade a golden bronze. I needed to do this fast: The boy was bleeding profusely, and if he didn't get help…well, being overly emotive would be the least of his problems. Fortunately for him, I was faster and stronger than your usual human.

"OK, Miss Thing. Let's dance." With a flick of the wrist, I sent my blade slicing through the air so that it lodged to the hilt in her chest—just to the right of her heart. Dammit.

With a shriek of anger, she sprang over the boy's prone body, her bony fingers curled like claws. I dodged out of the way, but one of her long, dirty nails caught my cheek, slicing it open. Great. All I needed was another tetanus shot.

She hit the sidewalk in a tangle of limbs, the rough pavement lacerating her skin. Droplets of dark, diseased blood oozed sluggishly from the cuts. This was going to be a bloody mess. Literally. My fingers curled around my UV gun. One shot from that to the heart and it would be bye-bye vampire.

With a scream of anger, she pounced again. This time she sent me crashing into the brick building behind me, knocking the gun out of my hand and the breath from my lungs. Little black dots danced in front of my eyes.

"Shit." It came out more a wheeze than anything. The gun was too far away for me to grab, and my sword was still strapped across my back. I could feel the sheath digging into my spine where I was plastered up against the cold brick wall.

The vamp coiled to pounce again, the muscles in her hindquarters tensing as she braced herself. I had seconds. Maybe.

I dropped down to a crouch and snagged my little silver dagger from my boot sheath. It wasn't much, but the silver would keep the vamp from healing quickly. It would be enough. Hopefully.

She sprang at me again with a feral scream, and I let her come. Her arms and legs wrapped around me as she went for my throat. I could feel her warm, thick blood soaking into my clothes.

As her breath hit hot against my neck, I plunged the dagger home. She stilled, eyes wide, as the blade slid between her ribs and struck her heart. Between one breath and the next, she exploded around the dagger, leaving nothing behind but a small pile of ashes and dust.

2

I hurried to the prone boy, pulling out my cell as I went. As I pressed a compress to his neck with one hand, I sent Kabita a quick text with the other. His pulse was so weak I doubted he'd make it to morning. If he turned, which wasn't likely, there was no saving him. The number of people who'd survived a vampire attack without turning numbered exactly one: me. Kabita would contact the SRA so they could post someone at the hospital to make sure. The thought made my heart ache, but there was nothing I could do about it.

Then I made a phone call.

"Nine-one-one, I need to report an animal attack..."

∽

"You're dripping blood on my carpet. Again." The voice was as expressionless as the face. Only a slight glint behind deep-brown eyes betrayed the fact that Kabita Jones, my boss, best friend, and natural-born witch, was *extremely* peeved.

I could sort of see her point. Last time I'd come to the office covered in blood she'd had to replace the carpet. This time the blood only went up to my elbows, and it was mostly dry already. There were just a couple of drips. It wasn't like she couldn't get the place steam-cleaned.

"That's what you get for calling me in right after a hunt." I dropped into one of the two chairs in front of her massive mahogany desk. She scowled at me. She didn't like me soiling her fake-leather chairs, either. Bad for business, having a client sit down in a pool of vampire blood.

"Here." She tossed me a box of wet wipes—only semi-effective, but certainly better than nothing. I grabbed a wipe and scrubbed at my arm. That was when I noticed a few drops of blood in my cleavage. *Gross.*

Kabita leaned back in her chair, early-morning light spilling over her dark hair. "I have a new job for you."

3

I tried to raise an eyebrow at her, but I was no Mr. Spock; both went up. "What kind of new job?" I held back a wince as I shifted in my chair. Despite my more-than-human strength, the vamp had really done a number on me. I'd need a tanker truck of Epsom salts after this.

"As in an 'up your alley' kind of job. Fun, supernatural weirdness."

Ah, she meant bloodsuckers. Nightwalkers. Minions of darkness. Otherwise known as vampires.

Except, calling it "weirdness" is like saying that baking bread is an odd job for a baker. For Kabita and me, vampires aren't weird. They are normal, everyday stuff. Or maybe I should say every-night stuff.

Kabita runs a private investigation firm that specializes in hunting down things the government likes to pretend don't exist—creatures that would give most people nightmares. There are lots of these little firms all over the country. Technically, we work for a branch of the government called the Supernatural Regulatory Agency (SRA), bringing down the bad guys who leaked through the weak spots between worlds, but there is the odd civilian who hires us for ordinary jobs, like surveillance and tracking down lost loved ones. It's how we keep our cover intact.

It's not exactly that civvies aren't allowed to know about the "supernatural." It's more that they don't *want* to know. People like to believe that they understand the world they live in. That it's safe and ordinary. They don't like knowing there are monsters on every street corner or portals to other dimensions that could open up and swallow them at any moment. For some people, no matter how many times the obvious is thrust in their faces, they'll never believe the monsters truly exist.

The government is fine with that. So the politicians focus on fighting crime and the war on drugs, and turn the real monsters over to people like us. We get excitement and fortune, if not fame. The human race is kept safe and in the dark (mostly). The government gets plausible deniability. We all go home happy.

"How is this weirder than any other 'up my alley' case?" I asked as I cleaned off the last of the blood.

Kabita pushed a file gingerly across the desk. Despite being one of the best demon-spawn hunters in the business, she finds vampires extremely distasteful, not to mention creepy. Go figure. "It's not an ordinary vamp," she said. "It's a sunwalker."

"A sunwalker?" I checked to make sure my jaw wasn't lying on her desk. Nope, still attached to my face. "You're kidding, right?"

"Brent Darroch, our new civilian client, wants us to hunt this sunwalker and kill him, but more important, he wants us to retrieve something the sunwalker stole from his family. He'll fill you in on the details. You're to meet him at this address." She shoved a piece of paper across at me while carefully tucking a strand of long, ink-black hair behind her ear.

Despite edging on forty, she doesn't have a single strand of gray. I haven't quite hit thirty yet—twenty-nine, to be exact—but I hope I look half as good as she does at forty. I have my doubts. My job isn't exactly the kind that keeps one young.

I shook my head. "This is insane. A sunwalker? As in vampires who can walk in sunlight? You do know they're not real, right? Sunwalkers are just a myth."

It's one of those things whispered about in our business. I have no idea where or when the rumor got started, but there isn't a hunter alive who doesn't know the stories: vampires who are ten times as violent, without any of the weaknesses of normal vamps, like being mortally allergic to sunlight. Fortunately, no one has actually seen a sunwalker—which is a good thing. If they were real, a single sunwalker could do a hell of a lot of damage.

"There is no way I'm going after a sunwalker. Are you crazy?"

She gave me a look. She was good at "the Look." "Excuse me, oh Great Slayer of Vampires, but you don't have a choice. Not if you want to keep your job."

Which I did, and she knew it. It's sort of a running joke: I bitch. She threatens to fire me. Both of us know it'll never happen. I love my job. There is something so immensely satisfying about going to work and hacking someone or something's head off. They don't usually let you do that at, say, a pharmaceutical company or the post office, even if that someone really deserves it. They kind of frown on it, actually. I also get to wear jeans and really cool kick-ass boots every day.

Kabita would never give me anything I couldn't handle, no matter how much I bitched and moaned about an assignment. I am damn good at killing vamps. A sunwalker would just be a little…trickier. Not only are they not supposed to exist, but how are you supposed to find a vampire who can walk around in daylight? Heck, he probably even has a nice tan.

"Jesus, Kabita. What have you gotten me into this time?" I snatched the paper off the desk. "Wait a minute. This guy is private, right? How does he know about sunwalkers?" Heck, how'd he know about any of this?

She shrugged. "He's connected. Friends in high places. Apparently, he's some kind of rich eccentric who travels the world searching for proof of magic and whatnot."

What most people don't realize, despite the knowledge being there for the taking, is that "magic" isn't real. Not in the abracadabra sense, anyway. It is all about quantum physics, which means it is way more *Star Trek* than *Lord of the Rings*. I think it was Arthur C. Clarke who once said that any sufficiently advanced technology was indistinguishable from magic. That's quantum for you.

"Fine. I'll meet Darroch after I take a shower."

"Good idea."

I just glared at her. Sarcastic witch.

Her return smile was annoyingly beatific.

I crossed my legs and leaned back in my chair, trying desperately not to look like I wanted to crawl out of my skin. Kabita must not have met our new client in person. He was giving me the heebie-jeebies big-time. Granted, when it comes to humans, my Spidey senses aren't so accurate, but there was something a little off with this guy.

It was just past noon, but the room we were meeting in was draped in perpetual twilight. Dark wood paneling and big leather chairs, plush wine-red carpet and even plusher drapes turned the room heavy and almost grim. He even had matching hired muscle standing at attention on either side of the door, plus a few more scattered throughout the property. All very manly. All very overbearing. And the client? Well, he was just as bad.

Sure, he was good-looking and suave. Definitely suave, but in a creepy Julian Sands kind of way. Like, you wouldn't be surprised to see this guy hanging out with royals or schmoozing with the rich and powerful, but you sure wouldn't want to meet him in a dark alley. He very much suited the lavish home in Portland's posh West Hills. He made my skin itch.

Then again, maybe I was wrong. After all, Kabita had vetted the guy, and Kabita was never wrong. *If* she'd met him in person. Dear gods, I hoped she'd met him in person.

"So, Mr. ah…" Not Sands. Bloody hell, what was it? I sneaked a glance at the file. "Mr. Darroch. How can I help you, exactly?"

He gave me a smile that made me feel like I needed another shower. "Please, Ms. Bailey, call me Brent."

"Right." I forced a smile. "Brent. How can I help you? I hear you have a slight problem with a sunwalker?"

He quirked a smile at that. Not so smarmy this time. In fact, he seemed genuinely amused. "I know. Sounds insane, doesn't it? Rich businessman chasing after a mythical sunwalker." He leaned forward earnestly. I was surprised; he did earnest pretty well. "Then again, until a few years ago, *you* believed vampires and lycanthropes and demons were pure fiction, did you not?"

He had a point. Once upon a time, I'd thought the monsters that dwell among us were just a myth, just like everyone else in the civilian world does. But that had changed the night of my attack. It's why I became a hunter: to protect others like me from going through what I had. Except, how did Brent Darroch know about that? How did he know about me? But before I could ask him, he plowed on.

"Sunwalkers *are* real, Ms. Bailey. Or at least *one* of them is real." He leaned back and steepled his fingers together in an excellent Dr. Evil impression.

"Excuse me? Did you say *one*?" Images of the *Highlander* flooded my mind: *There can be only one.*

Darroch nodded. "Yes. According to legend, there were more, once upon a time. Dozens of sunwalkers lived among us, if not hundreds. Now there is just one left."

"How do you know all this? And what does this sunwalker have to do with this object you want us to retrieve?"

There was a coldness in his eyes that belied the smile on his lips. "Do you honestly think you hunters are the only civilians who know the truth about our world? The government isn't *that* good at keeping secrets." He crossed one leg over the other in a very European way. "As to the object, it is a family heirloom. A necklace. Not particularly valuable except, perhaps, to collectors of the arcane."

My ears perked up. "The arcane?" Oh, juicy. I do love a good magical twist. Keeps things interesting.

He nodded. "According to family legend, the necklace was created by an ancestor of mine who dabbled in the magic arts. Of course, back in the day, people did not understand the difference between 'magic' and physics. In any case, my ancestor created the necklace, a simple amulet on a chain, as a sort of ward with magical symbols and so on. I don't know if it ever held any power over the quantum, but it certainly doesn't now. However, it might be of interest to a collector or a museum as a curiosity more than anything."

I always find it interesting when a client is willing to kill to get back an object he claims has no value. In my experience, the object usually has a great deal of value to someone, somewhere; otherwise, killing someone for it isn't worth the risk.

Granted, in this case, it was a sunwalker the client wanted me to kill, so there wasn't exactly any risk involved. At least, not to Brent Darroch. The only risk was my getting my ass handed to me.

"About twenty years ago," Darroch continued, "this particular sunwalker stole the necklace. I believe he thought it would give him some sort of power." He laughed, but the laugh sounded forced. "I'll bet he was surprised to find it a useless hunk of metal. In any case, it has sentimental value and I want it back."

"Do you have a photo of the amulet?"

"Of course." He slid a small photograph across the desk. It was the sort of photo you'd take for an insurance company. The amulet lay against a dark background, a ruler laid next to it for scale. It was a small metal disc about two and a half inches in diameter, faint etchings scratched in its surface. In the very center was a round dark-blue stone. Sapphire, maybe.

"It's quite beautiful. Why'd you wait so long?" It was a pretty obvious question, as far as I was concerned.

His eyes bored into me like twin icicles. "He disappeared, of course. I've been tracking him for the last twenty years. I finally traced him here, to Portland. I don't know where he is, exactly, but I know he is in this city." He leaned forward. "Once you find the amulet, you must destroy this sunwalker. He is extremely dangerous. One of these creatures in the world is bad enough, but should he begin to perpetuate his kind again, the world as we know it will be destroyed, as it almost was once before."

Part of our purview at the agency is to hunt and kill any and all supernatural creatures that pose a threat to humanity. Vampires are certainly in that category—and so are sunwalkers, if they are real, as Darroch claimed. These things have no souls, no conscience. There's no curing them of the disease that made them turn in the first place. The only way of stopping them is death. That's my job. The thought of killing the last sunwalker gave me pause, but only for a moment. We weren't talking Bengal tigers here; we were talking unstoppable killing machines. Still, Darroch might be the client, but I was the one dealing the deathblow.

"All right, Mr.…Brent. I'll see what I can do. But the final solution? That's my decision to make, understood?"

I could tell he didn't like it, but he nodded anyway. "Understood."

"Have you any idea where the sunwalker is now? How I can find him?"

"Sorry. Like I said, I tracked him to Portland, but I've been unable to find his lair."

Lair? Seriously? "All right. I need to contact a few informants. I'll keep you posted."

"Go carefully, Ms. Bailey." He leaned back gracefully, his leather chair creaking slightly, and steepled his fingers together again.

"I always do."

ﬡ

I had one place to start, but since nightclubs in Portland didn't open until late, I decided to call it a day and head home for some much deserved sleep. It was way past my bedtime. But first I wanted to drop in on Kabita's cousin, Inigo Jones.

Don't ask. I have no idea why a person would name their child after an architect from the 1600s.

Inigo is a clairvoyant, or something of that nature, and into all kinds of unusual stuff, like hanging out with necromancers and vampire wannabes and channeling spirits. Not that you can actually channel spirits in the traditional sense. Ghosts aren't really entities in and of themselves, but more leftover energies. It's another quantum thing.

Maybe Inigo could point me in the right direction. He has worked with Kabita and me at the agency ever since our move from England to Portland a little over a year ago. When he isn't helping us, he works in freelance IT. He is ridiculously smart—not to mention hot. But I try not to think about that. After all, he *is* Kabita's cousin, and I'm pretty sure there's something in the Best Friend Rules that states that best friends can't date each other's cousins. Even if there weren't, the guy is in his early twenties—practically a kid. A really hot kid, but a kid nonetheless.

Granted, twenty something is only a few years younger than my own twenty-nine, but I feel a lot older than my years most of the time. The job sort of does that to you.

Inigo lives in the funky yuppie Northwest District of Portland, just a short drive from Darroch's. I love the area because the shops remind me a lot of Europe and the vibe is super chill. Inigo's fifth-floor apartment is in one of the mellow old brick buildings built at the turn of the twentieth century. It has secure entry, so I paused at the snazzy brass plate lined with little black buttons.

Three rings later, Inigo buzzed me in, and I hoofed it up to his floor. He stood in the open doorway wearing a pair of red silk pajama bottoms and nothing else but a pair of geeky glasses, which I found ridiculously sexy. His shoulder-length gold-and-toffee hair was artfully tousled, and his usually brilliant blue eyes were heavy lidded with sleep.

Get your hormones under control, girl. It had obviously been way too long since I'd had a boyfriend.

He bared his teeth at me, and not in a nice way. "Whaddya want?" came out more a growl than a question.

"Sorry to wake you, Sleeping Beauty." I stepped past him into the dim living room, which was just a touch too warm for my taste, and flopped down on his comfy brown couch. Kabita, Inigo, and I had watched more than one John Wayne movie on this couch. "But I need your help with a little project."

"At"—he hesitated and squinted at the wall clock hanging above the television, its arms glowing faintly in the darkness— "one in the afternoon?"

"Sorry, but Kabita's got me working for this new client. He wants me to kill a sunwalker."

Inigo blinked. "Uh-huh. As in the mythical creatures that don't exist? Those sunwalkers?"

"Yeah. You see anything?" I didn't mean in the physical sense.

He shook his head. "Nah. Not before coffee. And I'm not drinking any, 'cause I'm going back to bed the minute you leave. Which will be…?"

"Soon," I assured him. I crossed my arms under my chest and gave my already impressive cleavage a subtle boost. I am such a bad girl. "I just need your help tonight. There's this woman, Cordelia Nightwing. I've used her a couple times as an informant. She just started working at a club called Fringe. You know it?"

He grinned, his eyes on my chest. He knew exactly what I was doing, and it was pretty clear he was enjoying the view. "Yeah, I know it."

"I take it that this is one of those weirdo clubs where the supernatural set hangs out, or something like that."

"Yeah, something like that."

"Well, I need to talk to Cordelia, and that's where she's working these days. Can you go to the club with me so I can chat with her and find out if she knows anything about this sunwalker?" It wasn't that I needed his help so much; it was that, at clubs like Fringe, I stick out like a sore thumb.

"Yeah, sure, if you promise to leave me in peace and let me sleep. Unless you want to join me?" His grin was pure naughtiness as he reached out to stroke a single finger down my cheek.

I batted away his hand. "As if." My phone gave a jingle and I pulled it out to glance at the text. It was Kabita with a lead from one of her sources on a vamp I'd been tracking. "OK, I'll pick you up at ten tonight. I've got another hunt. I'll try to get it done before then." I headed for the door.

"Make it midnight," he called. "The weirdos never come out before then."

I tossed him a look over my shoulder. "Obviously."

Chapter Two

Before the vampire attack that changed everything in my life, I'd always been sort of a victim. A victim of circumstance. A victim of bad boyfriends. A victim of verbal and emotional abuse from boyfriends. I'd never stood up to anything, ever. Maybe that was why, once I had the strength to fight back, I'd done so with a vengeance. Slaying vampires lets me make up for all those years of victimhood—not just for me, but for everyone like me.

I once had a conversation with a monk who told me the Catholic Church still prefers old-school slaying: wooden stakes and holy water. That's all well and good for a six-foot monk with enough muscle to bench-press a Volkswagen, but trust me, shoving a wooden stake into someone's rib cage is no easy task, and the holy water is just for show. A metal stake through the heart kills a vamp just as dead as a wooden one. Not to mention you can get the point a lot sharper on a metal stake, so it goes in a heck of a lot easier.

I find rather perverse enjoyment in slaying. I sometimes wonder if that doesn't make me just a little bit sick and twisted. Or maybe a lot sick and twisted, but it isn't like I go around killing animals and taking candy from children. That would just be…wrong. I only enjoy killing things that go bump in the night. Nasty things that turn humans into victims.

Terrance was one hell of a nasty bump in the night. With a name like Terrance, you'd expect leather patches on his tweed-jacketed elbows and smoke billowing from a pipe. You didn't expect one of the meanest, wiliest vampires in the city. It wasn't that he was particularly powerful, just psychotic—the guy was a serious piece of work. His latest foray into the "real" world was prowling for an after-dinner snack in a sorority house.

Most vamps don't give a shit what's for dinner, as long as it's human and breathing. But I'd been hunting Terrance for a while, and I knew he had a particular taste for college girls, preferably ones with big boobs and long blonde hair. I'd had to kill more than one of his snacks after they'd ended up turning vampire.

Fortunately, Terrance also went for girls who were less than smart, so hunting them once they'd turned was fairly easy. Intelligence, or lack thereof, seems to carry over into the undead. I don't need to come up with a cover story for their disappearing; that's Kabita's job. It's amazing how many unsavory boyfriends suddenly appear overnight in the missing girls' lives.

The night before, Terrance had pretty much gone through half the girls in one of the sororities at PSU, and the dean of the university—a supernatural himself, one of the nonviolent shape-shifters called therianthropes—wasn't real happy about it. It didn't look so good when your entire cheerleading squad got eaten by the undead. He'd hired us to get rid of his problem, which meant he really hired *me* to get rid of his problem, me being the only one of the three of us who actually killed vampires for fun and profit.

According to the text Kabita had sent me, Terrance had recently taken up residence in the basement of an old apartment building in southeast Portland. Nice and dark, and only tiny little windows high up in the walls, blocked by a few sheets of plywood. The neighborhood was the polar opposite of Inigo's—not exactly dangerous or seedy but definitely a bit worn around the edges, with smaller houses and hardworking blue-collar families.

If I didn't catch Terrance now, he'd be on the move. Then it was anyone's guess how many more lives would be wasted before I caught him again.

The building had a security entrance, but that wasn't exactly a problem. I used to live in one of these old places. I didn't bother pushing any of the buzzers; I just waited until someone came out, then grabbed the door and walked in like I belonged there.

The door to the basement stairs was on the right. I took them fast, using the handrail to propel me downward.

The basement was cold and dank. Under the odor of mildew and laundry soap was another, darker smell: the stench of the undead.

I can't really explain that smell, because it isn't actually real. Vampires don't generally smell any different from living humans. If you were to dance with one in a nightclub, you wouldn't know the difference, except that a vamp would possibly be a lot paler and maybe try to chomp on your neck. But I can smell them— something to do with my abilities and more a metaphysical smell than a physical one. It's one of my least favorite side effects of the virus that changed me, but a very handy talent to have when hunting down vampires.

Terrance's hideaway was the old maintenance man's room from back when they used to hire guys full-time to live in the basements of apartment buildings to keep the boilers going. Nowadays, they either turn them into storage or rent them cheap to people who like living in caves. Vamps love them.

A thick metal door marked *B* stood between Terrance and me. Definitely a dead bolt or twelve. It was daytime, so I knew he'd be in that undead state of sleep that's closer to death and wouldn't sense me or hear me, no matter how much noise I made.

The basement was deserted. I got out my tools and went to work on the dead bolts. I'd rather have just gotten out a gun and blasted the door open, but despite what they show in the movies, that is actually a really stupid idea. Bullets have a tendency to bounce off things like metal doors and cement walls and wind up places you don't intend for them to go. Like your own leg. Or head. Not exactly the best way to get into a locked room. Plus, it upsets the neighbors.

So I took the slow and boring route, opening the door like any normal person would—with a locksmith's tools.

I popped the last lock, packed away my tools, and then, with UV gun in hand, slowly swung the door open. It was black as pitch inside the room, the only light coming from the tiny windows outside in the hall. I didn't bother with a flashlight. This way I could let my eyes adjust somewhat in case I had to fight.

I could feel Terrance across the room, still deeply asleep. A vamp won't usually wake during the day. As long as the sun is up, he's out cold, unless he's incredibly old or incredibly strong. I could tell from the tingling grip at the back of my skull that Terrance was neither, so I figured I was pretty safe.

I was wrong.

I approached the camp bed, gun drawn, when a hand shot up and wrapped around my throat. I struggled to breathe, but the hand was too tight and squeezing tighter. That's when I realized the vamp on the bed wasn't Terrance. I didn't have time to wonder about it, though; I was too busy fighting for my life as his other hand gripped the wrist of my gun arm so I couldn't shoot him.

The gun dropped to the floor with a dull thud as my hand went numb. Spots were dancing in front of my eyes. I knew I was going to pass out and be vampire lunch if I didn't do something. So I did the one thing I could think of: I went limp. Dropped like the proverbial stone.

Unfortunately, the vamp dropped with me—dead on top of me, in fact. Fortunately, he let go of my wrist and loosened his hold on my throat. I felt him go for my neck, felt the teeth sink in. Hurt like hell, but it distracted him just enough. I planted my knee in his groin—hard. Even undead guys still get unhappy when you plant a knee in their family jewels. Death—or rather, undeath—doesn't change that particular physiological fact.

He reared back, teeth ripping out of my neck, and grabbed his crotch. He fell to the ground screaming. "You stupid bitch!" he howled.

"That's hunter bitch to you." My hand closed around the UV gun. "Now, who are you, and where the hell is Terrance?"

"I dunno, man."

He was young and obviously terrified as hell. I could work with that. "Tell me where Terrance is, or I dust you here and now."

If vampires could urinate, he would have wet himself for sure. "He's off helping Kaldan with some shit. He's just letting me crash here."

Kaldan.

Every vampire clan has a master: either the creator of the clan or another vamp strong enough to take them on if their creator is dead. Kaldan is the master of the biggest local vampire clan, and I'd bet anything he and Terrance were up to no good. I placed my booted foot over the vamp's groin and pressed down nice and firm, giving a little twist. "What kind of shit is he helping Kaldan with?"

The vamp let out a high-pitched screech. "I told you I don't know. He didn't tell me anything. Shit, that fuckin' hurt!"

"Yeah, well, this is gonna hurt even worse." My fingers tightened around the UV gun, and with a precision born of three years of hunting vamps in the dark, I pointed the gun at him and pulled the trigger.

He let out a horrific scream as the UV ray sliced through his stomach to his upper chest and found his heart. Within seconds he'd caught fire, then flashed to dust.

Nobody knows why vamps dust instead of leaving a body like humans. Some hunters claim it is the dispersal of the quantum energy holding the vamps together, others that the earth is claiming back the blood they stole. Not terribly scientific, but there aren't a lot of scientists out there studying vampires.

I pulled myself up off the floor and staggered to the door. I could feel the blood dripping down my neck and sliding under the collar of my jacket, soaking my T-shirt and trickling into my bra. *Ew.* Fortunately, the very virus that had once nearly killed me not only made me immune to a vampire bite, but it would also heal the wound quickly enough that I wouldn't bleed out. Probably wouldn't even have much of a scar.

I staggered up the steps and gently pushed open the door to the hall. A quick glance told me no one was around, so I hurried out through the front door to my car. I usually keep a spare set of clothing in the car, but laundry day was way overdue. I fumbled in the glove box for an old pashmina I keep there and then carefully wrapped it around my neck so it draped across my front. It looked like I'd watched one too many DIY makeover shows. Not that I cared—I've never much been one for fashion.

I sent Kabita a quick text to tell her what had happened, then started the car and drove gingerly up 148th and onto Stark Street. I probably shouldn't have been driving. I was weak and shaky—more from lack of food than from actual blood loss. I needed something to eat. Fast. Preferably something with high sugar content.

I swung through the next drive-through and ordered a large orange juice and three boxes of cookies. The girl didn't even blink. In fact, I wasn't entirely sure she was awake. Could zombies work a drive-through?

My little craftsman cottage was just a fifteen-minute drive away, but I'd eaten all three boxes of cookies and downed the entire cup of OJ before I reached home. I was feeling much better.

I spent thirty minutes in the shower before tumbling into bed. I didn't bother with pajamas. Too tired. I just dragged the duvet over my head and was asleep before I could think to set my alarm clock.

∽

Something woke me. I felt disoriented and slightly feverish, the result of my body healing itself, no doubt. But what had woken me? I lay still, letting my sensory ability to smell and feel the undead play over the room and through the house. No vamps, nothing threatening at all. And yet…

"Inigo, what the hell are you doing in my bedroom?" It wasn't the first time he'd sneaked into my house without knocking. It's a little game he likes to play. So far, he is the winner, but only because I've never bothered to return the favor.

The streetlight pouring into my window caught and flashed in his toothy grin. "I was hoping to catch you naked."

"Bloody idiot," I grumbled, shoving hair out of my eyes.

"Plus, you're late."

I squinted at the clock. 12:05 a.m. Dammit. I sat up, clutching the duvet to my chest. My very naked chest. "Sorry. Forgot to set the alarm."

"Yeah, I know." He stood up and handed me my robe. Not the nice, thick terry one I generally like to hang around in, but the silky one I keep for when I have someone over. I hadn't had anyone over in longer than I cared to recall…But one must be prepared for these things. You know, just in case.

I threw him a glare, grabbed the robe, and hauled it around my shoulders before heading to the bathroom and slamming the door. I looked a fright. My hair was sticking up in about a hundred different directions, giving the appearance of a red nimbus around my head. My skin was pasty white from blood loss, with dark circles under my eyes, and my green eyes were fever bright.

I splashed cold water on my face, brushed my teeth, and ran a comb through my hair. Didn't work. I grabbed some hair gunk and used it to muss up my hair some more so it looked like I intended the whole light-socket look. I patted some cover-up under my eyes, swiped on some mascara and lip gloss, and added just a bit of blusher to my cheeks so I didn't look like a member of Vampires "R" Us.

I gave myself a critical look. Probably not enough makeup, but there wasn't time for full war paint. The right outfit and I'd probably blend into the crowd at Fringe OK.

By the time I went back to my room, Inigo had vacated it. Thank the gods. I didn't have time to deal with both his hormones and mine.

I grabbed a pair of jeans and a black tank out of the closet and yanked them on over a black bra and panties. I don't do thongs. Trust me, when you're kicking vampire ass, the last thing you want is a scrap of cloth climbing up into your nether regions.

The tear from the vampire's fangs was nearly healed now, leaving a bright-pink mark on my neck. I grabbed a black-and-white choker, which covered the mark pretty well, and then threw on a sheer black top that I keep around for just such occasions. Not that I spend a lot of time in clubs, but my job takes me strange places.

I finished off the outfit with my black combat boots and my weapons holster tucked neatly under my leather jacket. I have a special federal license to carry anything capable of killing vampires, but I didn't want to advertise that I was packing. No sense causing problems at the club if I could avoid it.

Inigo gave me the once-over as I strode into the living room. If the expression on his face was anything to go by, I looked just fine. I was really glad I wasn't a clairvoyant because I was pretty sure whatever he was thinking would make me blush big-time.

"Come on, pretty boy, let's go hit the town."

He laughed. "Your wish is my command, oh Vixen of the Dark."

I snorted. "Idiot." Why, oh why, did he have to be Kabita's damn cousin?

21

The club was pulsing with hard, eerie music. It was almost alive and incredibly sexual. Heated. Full of desire and passion and very naughty things. The heavy bass settled into my chest like a heartbeat.

Portland has a lot of nightclubs for a small city. There is everything from salsa clubs to a reggae bar. We even have a fairly famous musical revue that showcases some brilliant female impersonators. How's that for cosmopolitan? Nothing, however, had quite prepared me for the weirdness that is Fringe.

We pushed through the front bar area, which was heavily populated with vampires. Not real ones, of course. These were sanguine vampires, people who lived vampirism as a lifestyle and a religion but weren't actually vampires in the physical sense. I'd never seen so many tattoos, piercings, and fake fangs in one place in my life.

There were a couple of beings working the crowd who sent my Spidey senses zinging, but not because they were vamps. Although they looked perfectly normal to ordinary humans, to my mind's eye they glittered and glowed, their features constantly shifting in the dim light. I had no doubt these were members of the Glittering Throng.

One of them caught my gaze and his/her purple eyes sparkled with unholy glee. My mind shied away from seeing him/her, but I yanked it back. I was the mistress of my own mind and no sidhe glamour was going to change that.

I started right back at him/her, watching as his/her face shifted and molded through several incarnations. Again, it isn't something an ordinary human can see, but ever since the attack, I can. With a smirk, the sidhe tipped an imaginary hat in my direction and disappeared into the crowd. I held back a shiver. Messing with a member of the sidhe is not a good idea. In fact, it is best to stay below their radar altogether. They tend to get their kicks from the suffering of other beings, both mortal and supernatural—usually suffering they've created. Fortunately, this one had a sense of humor.

Inigo led us to the main dance floor and bar, where there was a giant fish tank along one wall with an honest-to-gods mermaid inside. I'd never seen a live one before, but this was the real deal, right down to the rainbow-hued fish scales and hair the color of dark-green seaweed. Nobody in the club batted an eyelash. Probably since nearly every person there was a supernatural (except the sanguines, who probably thought the mermaid was just a girl in a fish suit). People have an amazing ability to see what they expect to see. I was starting to feel like I'd fallen down the rabbit hole.

The moment he walked in, all eyes were on Inigo, even fish-tank girl's. Not that I blamed anyone. He was unbelievably hot in a dark suit and silver shirt. His shoulder-length hair gleamed gold and honey in the dim light of the club, and his eyes were such a luminous blue they practically glowed. I was pretty sure that wasn't just an effect of the lighting. I had my suspicion that somewhere in Inigo's genetic background was a little bit of fey blood or something, even though Kabita didn't seem to show any such affinity. It would account for a lot of things.

Like the way every woman in the bar had stopped dancing and was frozen in place with her tongue hanging out. Most of the men too, if truth be told, which was a good thing for me. No one would remember I was there, even if I did have hair practically the color of a fire truck.

I slid up to the bar and caught the bartender's attention after about the third try. He was good-looking, if a bit on the slender side, but no match for Inigo. He swallowed hard, dragging his eyes away from Inigo. "How can I help you, my lady?"

My lady. How quaint.

"I'm looking for someone. Cordelia Nightwing. You know her?"

He pointed toward an alcove on the other side of the dance floor. The silky blue curtains had been drawn to ensure privacy. "She's doing a reading, but she should be done soon."

I threw him my best smile and a ten-dollar bill. "Thanks." He didn't respond. His eyes had already returned to Inigo, who had strutted to the middle of the now-still dance floor and started grinding his hips. I hid a smirk. Inigo could be a real peacock sometimes.

I strolled casually along the edge of the dance floor toward the curtained alcove, scanning the crowd. All eyes were on Inigo. No one paid me any attention, which was fine by me, at least for tonight. When I wasn't around Inigo, it was a different matter. Bloodred hair, porcelain skin, and moss-green eyes sort of leave an impression. The skin and eyes I can't lay claim to. Genetics, you know. But the hair is completely deliberate.

I waited by the shimmering curtain for Cordelia's client to come out. I've known Cordy for several years now on one level or another. She is one of the few people who is still in my life from before the attack. Most of my old friends slowly faded away, uncomfortable with the changes they'd seen in me, though they didn't understand them.

Before I moved to London, I'd consulted Cordy for a tarot reading. Just one of those fun things you do and don't take seriously. She'd told me that if I moved across the sea, my life would change in unimaginable ways.

I'd taken her a lot more seriously after that.

When I returned to Portland, I looked her up. She'd known immediately that I'd changed, and ever since, she's been a sort of confidential informant, if you will. She is also a friend, someone I can talk to when my life gets a little too overwhelming.

The club had returned to what appeared to be its usual manic writhing. I was pretty sure the couple in the corner was having sex with their clothes on. Either that or he was a doctor inspecting her tonsils. Due to the serious pelvic grinding that was going on, I was sort of guessing it was the former.

A dark-haired man hurried from behind the curtain and disappeared into the crowd. I figured it was Cordy's client, so I slipped into the alcove. The shimmery curtain hid a pocket door, which I slid shut, cutting off most of the club noise.

Cordelia Nightwing sat at a small round table draped with midnight-blue velvet, a crystal ball sitting in front of her. It was so clichéd I nearly burst out laughing.

A pair of bright-blue eyes laughed up at me from behind a fringe of dark-brown hair. She is easily in her late forties, but the sparkle of energy surrounding her and the smile pulling at her lips belied her age. She is beautiful, no doubt about it. But it is the kind of true beauty that only comes with age, wisdom, and honestly knowing oneself. It's no wonder I'd warmed to her instantly the first time we'd met.

"Nice ball."

Her smile widened. "It's for the clients." Her hand waved over the crystal ball. "Makes them feel like they're getting their money's worth. I tried it without the ball, and I swear I had a guy nearly in tears over it." Her laugh spilled out, light and bright. It reminded me of Christmas, for some odd reason.

She tilted her head, dark hair spilling about her shoulders. She was wearing a silk kimono, for gods' sakes. "You're looking good, my darling. Come give me a hug."

I grinned and edged around the table for a hug before sitting back down.

"So, how can I help you?" One dark eyebrow cocked up.

"I need your help, Cordy. I'm doing a job for a guy named Brent Darroch."

Her face hardened. "What do you know of Brent Darroch?"

"Nothing, really," I told her. What was with the attitude suddenly? "He just hired my firm to find someone."

"Who?"

I cleared my throat, wondering how she was going to react to what I had to say. "It's a bit odd; that's why I thought you might be able to help. But...uh...It's a sunwalker."

She looked at me for a long moment, her gaze inscrutable. "And what will you do with this sunwalker once you find him?"

I had expected more of a reaction from her, but she didn't flinch, let alone question me about it. "I'll retrieve the necklace he stole from Mr. Darroch, and then I'll kill him, like I would any vampire."

She didn't bat an eye. She only held out her hand. Without thinking, I placed mine in hers. "Remember, Huntress, things are not always as they seem, and there are two sides to every tale. Before you slice off the sunwalker's head, you might want to hear what he has to say."

Riiiight.

She let go of my hand and reached into a voluminous bag beside her chair. She placed a business card in my hand. It read, *Eddie Mulligan, Majicks and Potions.* The address was in the funky, bohemian Hawthorne District, not far from where I lived.

"I don't know this sunwalker," Cordelia told me, "but I have heard the legends. If anyone can help you find what you're looking for, it's Eddie. Tell him I sent you. Tell him I said it was OK to help you."

"Right. OK. Thanks."

She smiled enigmatically. "Not a problem. You know where to find me if you need me."

I turned to go.

"Remember"—her voice stopped me—"look beyond the obvious. Not all of those who walk the dark path are evil."

I glanced back at her before sliding open the door to reenter the writhing mass of bodies in the main club. "They are in my world."

Chapter Three

Inigo joined me outside the club. He had lipstick smeared on his collar, and his lips looked a bit swollen.

"Lucky bitch," I said, giving him the once-over.

He threw his head back and laughed. "Gee, thanks, Morgan. You'd probably get some too, if you bothered to stop and smell the roses once in a while."

"Whatever." I don't like to think about my lack of success in relationships with men. It is pathetically Freudian and I know it. Absentee father (or in my case, dead), cheating ex-fiancé, lack of trust, yada yada. Didn't need to go into a whole song and dance about it. "Sense anything, lover boy?"

He shrugged. "Not much. Just the usual fun at Fringe. But your girl gave me tinglies on the psychic plane."

I blinked. "Excuse me?" My mind was suddenly going places it really shouldn't go. At least not with Inigo.

"Good ones. Cordelia gave me a good vibe. I like her."

I shook my head. "Don't bother. Doesn't take a clairvoyant to see you're nothing but a flirt."

He chuckled. "Ouch. But she's not clairvoyant. Well, not exactly. She's a lot more than that. She's sort of a…a mystic, I think."

"Whatever." I pulled the business card out of my pocket and handed it to him. "She said this Eddie guy can probably help us find the sunwalker. It looks like he runs some kind of magical mumbo jumbo shop."

"You're a fine one to talk about mystic mumbo jumbo." Inigo raised a brow at me.

"True. But I'm not about to start burning incense and dancing naked in the moonlight."

He gave me one of those head-to-toe gazes that men give women they find particularly tasty. "Too bad."

"Pervert."

"Tease."

"Can we be serious for a minute? We need to talk to this guy, find out what he knows, even if he is a loon," I insisted.

"OK, but you'll have to go alone. I know this place. It's a strictly daytime operation. And you know how I feel about getting out of bed before six p.m."

"Right. I'll hit the shop tomorrow, then, while you're getting your beauty rest."

He reached out and caressed my cheek. Sent a shiver all the way down my spine. Now I was the one with the tinglies. "You should think about getting some yourself. You're looking a bit tired."

"Gee, thanks," I said dryly. "Just what every girl wants to hear—some young stud muffin telling her she looks tired."

He smirked. "So, you think I'm a stud muffin, huh?"

"Oh, shut up. Kabita would kill me if she heard us having this conversation."

"What Kabita doesn't know won't piss her off." He grinned. "C'mon. I got plenty of room for two." He waggled his eyebrows at me.

I couldn't help but laugh. "Inigo, you are way too young for me."

"Twenty-four is not that young. I'm certainly old enough for what counts." His grin turned unbelievably lascivious, and my mind went straight to some very naughty places.

Great, just what I needed: out-of-control hormones in the middle of a hunt. And it wasn't Inigo's out-of-control hormones I was worried about. "Oh, yes, I'm sure you're very…ah…good in that department. But I'm very busy and important and don't have time for your nonsense," I said loftily, and I stomped off down the street. When in doubt, a grand exit is always appropriate. Especially when one is trying desperately not to jump one's best friend's cousin's bones.

∽

It was just past 2:30 a.m. when I got home. I stripped down to my underwear, yanked on a T-shirt, and crawled into bed. I was starting to think I was getting way too old for this shit.

Granted, twenty-nine isn't that old. It's like the new nineteen, right? But I've been hunting vampires for three years now, and it never gets any easier. In fact, it seems like the more of these things I kill, the more new ones pop up.

I jerked the fluffy duvet up to my chin and stared at the ceiling. If sunwalkers do exist, then how on earth does one kill them? And why would a centuries-old vampire who can walk around in daylight steal a worthless necklace from some rich guy? I was starting to think there was a lot about this case that wasn't going to make any sense.

I let out a sigh. Sometimes I wish I were back living my old life, before the vampire attack that changed everything. Just doing the day-to-day thing at a regular nine-to-five job in a regular office. Having drinks with the girls after work. Sunday lunches with Mom. Going about life doing all the normal, ordinary things that normal, ordinary people do, even if I do sometimes long for something more…exciting.

Then again…naw! I wouldn't miss this for the world.

I fell asleep with a smile on my face.

∽

I was up to my armpits in dirt. Digging was hot, dirty work, plastering strands of long, dark hair to my stubbled cheeks. I swiped a forearm across my sweaty brow. Two of my fellow knights worked beside me, their dark eyes gleaming with excitement in the torchlight.

We were all convinced there was something under the temple, something of great value. Some said it was the Ark of the Covenant. Others whispered rumors that it was the lost writings of Mary Magdalene. Whatever it was, if we could find it, it would change everything and bestow on our order power greater than that of kings and even the Church.

My shovel went through the floor, chunks of dirt falling through to another level below. There was a cavern under there. I gave a shout to my brother knights, and we all began digging furiously. "Bring a light!" Torches were brought, and the three of us clambered down into the cavern below, leaving our falchions behind in our haste.

It was a small, naturally formed cave. The walls were painted with brightly colored murals depicting, at a brief glance, a terrible battle. The cavern was otherwise completely empty except for two corpses in the middle of the room.

I cautiously approached the bodies, followed by my fellows. The two bodies lay sprawled across the floor, one cradling the other like a child. One was nothing but bones, ancient beyond belief, and dressed in some sort of armor. The other...

The other looked as though he'd died just hours ago. His body was perfect, though his clothes were rotted nearly to dust, and he cradled the bones of the dead warrior like a child. In his hands, he clutched an amulet. It appeared to be made of gold, but dulled by age and dust. One of the others leaned down to pick it up. Some part of my brain screamed at me.

"No, stop!"

It was too late. The corpse became horribly and suddenly alive, fangs I hadn't noticed before sinking deep into my brother knight's neck. The living corpse dropped the nearly dead knight and grabbed the next, rearing back to strike again. The screams were hideous and chilled me to the marrow.

I ran for the ladder leading up to the entrance to the cavern and my sword, but it was too late. I felt the fangs enter my neck like needles of red fire, the blood draining from my body as surely as my life drained away. Strangely, at the same time my life left my veins, I felt something enter and begin growing inside me, a living thing.

As panic surged through me, I tried again for the cavern entrance, but my body had no strength. I slumped to the floor, and the world went black.

$$\sim$$

I sat bolt upright in bed, fighting with the duvet, which had managed to wrap itself around my legs. *Shit, shit, shit.* I touched my neck with the tips of my fingers. Smooth skin. No blood. Gods, it had felt so real.

I glared blearily at the clock—4:00 a.m. Way too early. I flopped back down on my pillow.

It was like reliving my own attack. Except that wasn't how it happened. I hadn't been digging in an underground tunnel by torchlight. There hadn't been two corpses, only the one vampire. And I'd never held a falchion sword in my life. I certainly wasn't male. Or a knight.

I rubbed my nose. Just a dream, that was all. A really strange dream. I shut my eyes and willed myself back to sleep. Unfortunately, sleep refused to come. I couldn't escape the memories dredged up by my dream. They chased through my brain, reminding me of all I'd lost. All I'd gained.

That one moment in time had changed my life so profoundly I no longer recognized the person I used to be.

Chapter Four

When I first moved to London, I loved it with a passion that only those who have lived there could ever understand. My family certainly couldn't. My grandmother was sure I'd be raped and murdered by bandits and redcoats. She wasn't terribly up on the modern world. I tried to explain that the UK and the US were on friendly terms and had been for a number of years now, but I don't think it sank in.

My mother was just worried I'd end up married and having babies with a Brit, which was, as far as she was concerned, a fate worse than rape and murder at the hands of redcoats. I was supposed to get married and have babies and move into a house next door to her so she could see her grandbabies anytime she wanted. My moving halfway around the world hadn't exactly been factored into her plan.

But I was head over heels in love. I had met Alex at a local coffee shop. He was on a business trip to Portland for a British antiques company and was in between client meetings. I'd sneaked out to grab a quick latte after my boss at the textile company where I was working had berated me once again for something she'd done wrong.

Maybe it was his sexy British accent or the way he acted as if I were the only woman in the room. He'd said all the right things, done all the right things. I hadn't had many boyfriends, so I fell for his charm hook, line, and sinker. I was sure it was "happily ever after." So when he asked me to move to England and marry him, I did it. I moved to London, and there I stayed—even after

I'd caught the bastard in bed with another woman. Alex had the gall to tell me that he didn't love me anymore and that, in fact, he didn't even particularly like me. If there'd been signs, I'd been too naive to see them. Or maybe I'd seen them but had been too afraid to confront him. In any case, I was devastated.

For a long time, I stayed in London because I didn't know what else to do. I guess I thought if I didn't go home, Alex might realize he'd made a mistake and change his mind. But he didn't. Eventually, I made friends, built a life, and enjoyed every minute of every day I lived in that most magical of cities. And I forgot about Alex.

Mostly.

The night that changed my life was such an unbelievably ordinary one. It was a Thursday, and I'd just gotten off the bus after a long day at work as an office administrator for an energy company in the city. It was nearly dark out, and the late-October evening held a distinct chill.

Leaves crunched softly underfoot, and the faint scent of wood smoke tickled my nose as I headed home, enjoying the crisp night air. I could hear the steady hum of traffic up on the Headstone Road, but my street was quiet, all my neighbors shut up in their homes for warm dinners and an evening in front of the telly. I snugged my scarf a little higher around my throat and tucked my hands deep into the pockets of my wool coat.

I walked a little faster. My flat would be nice and warm, and an evening of sci-fi and crime shows sounded fantastic. I could spot the red-and-white brick of my building through the bushes. I fumbled for my keys, which had managed to lose themselves once again inside the depths of my handbag.

Something heavy slammed into my left side. I flew through the air, smashing into my neighbor's stonework wall. I actually heard my own ribs snap. The pain made me gag.

I never even saw him coming, and my mind struggled to make sense of the fact that I was now lying on the freezing cold ground feeling like I'd been rammed by a truck. Making a little mewling sound in my throat, I groped for my handbag. Everything had spilled out across the pavement. My fingers skittered across lipstick tubes and pens. My phone. Where was it? I needed to call…someone.

I saw it lying about a foot away. I tried reaching for it, but the pain in my side was overwhelming. I couldn't even cry I hurt so badly.

I glanced up and down the street, looking for help, and realized my vision had gone a bit fuzzy and I tasted blood in my mouth. I reached up and touched my right temple and cheek where I'd hit the wall. My fingers came away sticky with my own blood. My stomach pitched.

Gods, what had hit me? A car, maybe? But all the cars along the street were parked and empty. I couldn't see anything else, just an empty street in front of me and the cold stone wall behind me.

"Help." It was hardly more than a whisper. I tried again. "Help!" It didn't come out much louder, but someone heard me because behind me there was a low laugh in response. My blood ran cold. Fear clawed at my insides, screaming at me to get up and run.

"No one gonna help you, bitch. No one gonna hear you." The speaker moved around and crouched down beside me.

I blinked to clear my vision and wished I hadn't. Nightmares were prettier. His face was hollow looking, waxy pale skin sunken against his skull. Yellowish fangs extended past his lower lip like a freak out of some kind of horror movie.

I thought I must have hit my head harder than I realized. I tried to push myself to my feet, but I cried out as another wave of pain hit me.

He laughed, and when he did, those long fangs flashed in the amber light of the streetlamp. If it weren't for the agony, I would have thought I was dreaming. They didn't exist. Vampires weren't real.

I felt the fangs go right into my jugular. It hurt more than anything. The pain ripped through me worse than the broken ribs or the head trauma. I would have screamed, but I had no breath. My hands fluttered against him, trying to beat him off, but I had no strength. His clawed hands squeezed my throat shut, and he slammed my head into the wall again.

There was only the sound of my heart beating slower and slower and slower. Then it stopped. The world went black, and there was no more pain and no more blood and no more fear.

When I woke up, it was to a world of hard, bright white. The sheets beneath my fingertips felt cool and smooth and smelled faintly of bleach. The light stabbed viciously through my head, lodging a violent ache behind my eyes.

It was obvious I wasn't dead.

I ran a quick mental check. Other than the headache, nothing hurt, which could be a good sign or a very bad one. I subtly started flexing muscles, bending joints. Mostly everything worked, except for one thing: I was strapped down to the bed with thick leather cuffs. That baffled me. I was the victim here. Didn't they know that? Why was I tied down?

I must have made a noise, because a face came into view, hovering over my bed. Dark eyes and honey-kissed cinnamon skin, a mark of her Indian descent, an expression far too serious for a face meant to smile at the world. "How are you feeling?" The woman's voice held an accent that wasn't quite British, but close.

"Um, OK, I think. How long have I been out?"

"Three days. You were banged up pretty bad." Her voice was cool, detached, her eyes watchful.

My mouth tasted of roadkill and felt stuffed full of cotton. "Thank god. I thought I died."

Her smile turned strangely tender. "Yeah," she said softly, "you did."

My whole body froze. "I don't understand." My voice came out a raspy whisper. "Why am I cuffed to the bed?"

"Just in case." She pulled a chair up next to my bed.

"In case of what?" My voice was getting a little shrill. Fear clawed at the back of my throat. I wanted to believe that I'd imagined the creature that had attacked me, but I knew I hadn't. What I'd seen shouldn't exist, but it did. I knew what I saw was true.

I remembered the fangs ripping into my throat, the pain, the blood, the sharp stink of fear. My fear. I'd felt my life ebbing away, leaking out onto the cold pavement. I should have been dead. The refrain kept pounding through my head: *I should be dead.*

"In case you turn." Her voice was flat.

"Turn? Turn into what?" Panic tried to take hold, but I fought it down with a fierceness I didn't know I had.

"A vampire." She wasn't kidding. "We tied you down in case you turned into a vampire." I could tell by her expression that if I had turned, I wouldn't have lasted long.

"I didn't turn." I wanted to feel relieved, but I didn't. Not yet. Not until I was sure. "Wait. Vampires are real?" What I'd seen already told me they were real, but I wanted someone to tell me I wasn't crazy, and she was the only one there in that cold, bright room.

This time her smile was pure and true. "Yes, vampires are real. So are a lot of other nasty things you've probably never heard of."

I didn't even want to know what she meant by "other nasty things." I was still trying to get over the fact that vampires were not only real, but they weren't the dazzling, beautiful creatures of Hollywood. The creature that had attacked me had been anything but sexy. "Why didn't I turn?"

She shrugged. "I still don't know. If you were going to turn, you should have done it within the first twenty-four hours."

I breathed a sigh of relief. "Thank the gods."

"Yeah, you should definitely be thanking somebody. Nobody survives a vampire attack like that without turning. Nobody. Every single attack victim we've found has turned. You're the first who hasn't, and we don't know why. Do you?"

"No. I don't." Why would I?

She looked me over as though I were an interesting new specimen. Despite my fear and bewilderment, I stood my ground and refused to squirm.

"Good, you'll do." Her expression went from cool curiosity to warm approval that fast. It threw me just a little, but it also made me feel kind of warm and fuzzy inside. Acceptance always feels good, even when you don't really know why you're being accepted.

I gave her a baffled look. I was feeling decidedly confused and a little bit lost. "Do for what?"

She stripped off the binding on my wrists, then stuck her hand out. I took it gingerly, and she gave my hand a firm shake. "I'm Kabita Jones, vampire hunter and demon slayer. Welcome to my world, Morgan Bailey."

Chapter Five

Early that evening, I headed over to Eddie Mulligan's shop. Majicks and Potions is on the northeast side of town, not far from me, and fits perfectly into the hippie boho-chic vibe of the community, sandwiched in between a used-car lot and a burger joint. It's a ramshackle building with a huge Third Eye painted dead in the middle of the wall above the entrance and arcane symbols in Day-Glo colors scattered around the rest of it. It looks like it barely survived an attack by spray paint.

The bell above the door jangled merrily as I entered the shop. Row upon row of shelves lined the room, jammed with crystals, colored glass bottles, bowls of candles, and gods knew what else. I found the hodgepodge strangely appealing.

The place reeked of incense, and the stereo system was playing something I was pretty sure was a pan flute and wind chimes. Maybe even a gong in there somewhere. Chinese-Andes fusion gone horribly wrong. I like fusion music, but I wasn't sure you could call this music. I winced as a dulcimer was added to the mix.

The shop was otherwise empty. No customers and no Eddie. Not even a bell to ring for service, so I decided to wander. There was a second room toward the back. It, at least, looked somewhat normal for an occult shop. Books, mostly, and a few packs of tarot cards, some CDs, DVDs, and other knickknacks. The books were all on various spiritual and magical topics. I picked one up. *Sex Majick: Majickal Spells and Potions for a Fulfilling Sex Life.*

Hmm. Now, there was something that might come in handy, if I actually had someone to have a sex life with. I slid the book back onto the shelf.

Maybe there was something in here about sunwalkers. Doubtful, but one never knew. I quickly scanned the shelves. There was an entire section on mythical creatures. Lots of stuff on vampires. Most of it utter rot, no doubt. Nothing at all on sunwalkers. Too bad.

There were two doors along the wall to my right. I turned the knob on the first and pushed the door open carefully. Toilet. Always good to know where the nearest toilets are.

The second door led to a storeroom. Instead of the antique wood shelves out front, back here they were cheap metal and filled with boxes of unpacked goods. There was a proper work desk stacked high with books and papers, nearly drowning a PC that looked at least ten years out of date.

Still no Eddie. I was starting to get a little concerned. People don't just open up their shops and then leave. So either Eddie was bloody stupid or something was wrong. Maybe he knew I was there and was hiding or something. Yeah, right. I was so scary.

I cleared my throat. "Ah, Mr. Mulligan? Eddie Mulligan? Cordelia Nightwing sent me. Eddie, are you here?"

A head popped down from the ceiling. I nearly let out a yelp. Fortunately for my sense of self-respect, I held it back.

"Oh, hey," said the head. "Didn't hear anyone come in. Can't always hear the bell in the attic. Cordy sent you, huh? Haven't seen her in a while. Crystal ball must be working for her. Be right down." The head disappeared before being replaced by a pair of feet, followed by legs, and then the rest of what I presumed was Eddie Mulligan.

He scaled his way down the ladder, then turned to face me, dusting his hands off on his trouser legs. He was short—a good five inches shorter than me, and I wasn't exactly tall. A fringe of

curly gray hair surrounded a cherubic face, set off with a bur-
gundy bow tie at his throat, which unfortunately clashed with his
mustard-yellow vest and olive-green pants. He was either color-
blind or he liked to make an impression.

"Mr. Eddie Mulligan?"

"Yep, that's me," he said, holding out his hand.

I took it. His grip was firm but not hard. The grip of a man
secure in himself and at one with the world. Cordelia was right: I
could sense the gift in him as surely as I'd sensed it in her. Eddie
Mulligan was no ordinary human.

"So, how can I help you? If Cordy sent you, it must be important," he said, leading me out to the front of the shop.

"It is," I assured him. "I'm looking for...well, a sunwalker." I
was embarrassed to even say it out loud.

He went utterly still for a moment, then let out a little laugh.
"Good one. Sunwalkers are extinct."

"So, they did exist, then?"

"Oh, yes, indeed. Once upon a time." He waved me to the
front counter before ducking behind it.

"Can you tell me about them?" I asked as he popped back up.

His gaze was sharp on me, measuring me, judging me.
Then with a little nod, he lifted a package wrapped in silk from
behind the counter. He carefully unwrapped it to reveal an
ancient book complete with leather cover and brass fittings. It
was kind of what I always imagined the *Doomsday Book* would
have looked like.

"All right," he said with a gentle smile, opening the cover, "let's
see what this little baby has to say about your sunwalkers."

He flipped through the pages, sending dust flying everywhere. I sneezed. "Oh, sorry." He gave me an apologetic smile. "I
don't consult the book too often. Most people are more worried
about your average, run-of-the-mill vampires, werewolves, that
sort of thing. Not much call for sunwalker info." I wondered just

exactly what sort of clientele Eddie Mulligan catered to. It is very rare that I run across a civilian who knows such creatures are real. One who isn't bat-shit crazy, anyway.

"OK." He stopped at a page with a sketch of a handsome, muscular man. He looked human, but it was obvious he wasn't. The fangs sort of gave it away.

"That's a sunwalker?" He looked suspiciously like the guy I'd dreamed about last night, the knight with the ocean eyes.

"Yes, indeed." He grinned up at me. I noticed his eyes were a slight almond shape. Might explain the huge section of books on Chinese folklore and dragons. I really hoped I wouldn't need his help with any dragons.

"What does it say?"

His fingers ran down the page. "All right, according to legend, the sunwalker is essentially a vampire who is able to withstand daylight."

Great. I knew that much.

He continued. "It also says they are descendants of an ancient race that was destroyed long ago."

"Does it say who they were? The ancient race, I mean."

He shook his head. "No, it says nothing about this ancient race. Very interesting. I wonder…In any case, it says the last of the sunwalkers was killed during the thirteen hundreds, when the king of France slaughtered the Knights Templar."

I blinked. That was not something I'd expected. "Excuse me? Did you say Knights Templar?" I swallowed hard. Surely my dream about the knight was just a coincidence.

"Yes, apparently the knights were in league with the sunwalkers. Protected them, something like that. The gods only know. In any case, when the Templars were killed off, so were the sunwalkers. Not a single one has been seen in more than seven hundred years." He shut the book with a thump, sending up another dust cloud.

I sneezed again. "But I thought some of the knights survived the purge?" They certainly never mentioned sunwalkers when they were talking about the Knights Templar in history class.

He shrugged and wrapped the book back up in its silk covering. "That's the rumor, but no one really knows. It was such a long time ago. Records have been lost; truths have been covered up." He frowned as he stuffed the book back under the counter. "I would have thought, though, that this book would tell the truth. It usually does." His face brightened. "Then again, it has a mind of its own, most days."

"Sure. But theoretically, if some of the Knights Templar survived, a sunwalker could have survived too, right?"

He gave me a rather shrewd look. "Theoretically, yes. If any knights truly survived, it's entirely possible a sunwalker could have survived as well, though one would have thought that there would be rumors of such a thing."

"You don't think he would have gone underground for seven hundred years?"

He laughed. "I wouldn't have thought so." He grew thoughtful. "Then again, the bloodlust could have been disguised as a vampire attack, if sunwalkers have such a thing as bloodlust. And if he'd been careful not to turn anyone, then it would be less noticeable. No one's exactly sure how the sunwalker ability was passed, or if it could be passed. Some think they were an entirely different species from vampire, though the book says otherwise."

I sighed. "Right, so how do I find this guy, if he exists? Look up sunwalkers in the Yellow Pages? Take out an ad in the *Oregonian*—better yet, the *Willamette Week*?"

He threw his head back and laughter spilled in waves. There was almost a magic to it. Certainly nicer on the ears than whatever he was playing on the stereo. "Now, that would be interesting, but no, I don't think it works that way."

"What, then?"

He stroked his lower lip. "Well, you obviously won't be able to count on the usual vampire haunts, seeing as how, if he exists, he can walk around in daylight." This guy really knew how to state the obvious. "Your idea might not be that bad, after all."

"What, taking out an ad?"

He chuckled. "Maybe not that exactly, but something similar. Imagine you are an ancient, mythical creature that's been able to hide out for centuries without detection. Then some nosy person comes along and starts blabbing all over about looking for you. You might get a little nervous that her investigation would be heard about in certain circles, putting your very existence in jeopardy. What would you do about it?"

"Shut her up."

He grinned. "Exactly."

Great. I was about to go out and piss off a centuries-old sunwalker. Some days I just want to quit my job and take up professional doughnut eating.

ဢ

My next stop that night was Inigo's. It's a good idea to take backup along when going to piss off ancient, mythical creatures.

Fortunately, he was between IT jobs at the moment and Kabita didn't have him doing anything, so he was free to play bodyguard.

"Where to?" Inigo asked as we headed to my car.

I sighed. "Not sure. Basically, I need to blab to the mythical underworld that I'm looking for a sunwalker. I have no idea where to start. I mean, I'm usually going to kill somebody in the mythical underworld, not have a chat over coffee."

Both eyebrows hit his hairline. "Excuse me? Are you *trying* to piss this guy off?"

"Yep. Pretty much."

He heaved a sigh. "You must be positively suicidal."

"Cordelia's contact—really interesting guy, by the way—seems to think it's the only way to draw him out."

"Yeah, I'm sure he does. He's not the one who's been appointed cannon fodder," Inigo growled. I didn't like it when Inigo growled. Or rather, I liked it a little too much. It did things to me.

I cleared my throat. "Anyway, we've got to find the best place to start spreading the word. You know a good mystic bar or something?"

"Graveyard."

I blinked. "Excuse me?"

"Graveyard. You'd be amazed at who you can find in a graveyard."

"Is this one of your clairvoyant things?" He's always coming up with unusual ideas that he conveniently blames on his abilities.

"No, this is one of my commonsense things. Best way to get word out to your sunwalker is to hit the supernatural grapevine, and the most gossipy members of the grapevine have a bizarre tendency to hang out in cemeteries."

"Fine. Graveyard, it is. And he's not my sunwalker."

"Sure, if you say so." His wolfish grin told me he wasn't buying. "I'm thinking Lone Fir."

I started the car and pulled out into traffic, heading toward Twenty-Sixth and Morrison, the oldest cemetery in the Portland metro area. If you're going to go creepy, you might as well make sure it's really old creepy. Too bad we weren't still in London. They know how to do creepy old graveyards properly in London. I should know. I almost ended up in one.

∽

Moonlight bounced off white marble headstones, giving the place an eerie glow as we got out of the car. Despite the warmth of the evening, there were tendrils of mist swimming about the bases of trees and swarming over graves.

"All right," I said to Inigo, placing my hand on the grip of my UV gun, not that it would do any good unless we ran into some vampires. "Now what?"

Inigo shrugged. "I dunno. This is your gig."

"You're the one who insisted we go to a graveyard," I pointed out with flawless logic.

"Gods, would you two stop arguing; you're giving me a headache." We both started as a dark shape rose from behind one of the stones. I would never admit it, but I very nearly yelped.

I yanked my gun out of the holster and pointed it. The shape barked out a laugh. "Are you nuts? A UV won't do diddly squat against anything but a vamp."

"Well, I know that," I snapped back. "But since I can't see you, you might just be a vamp."

The shape stepped into the moonlight and became a man. A very tall man with silvery hair pulled back in a ponytail and an honest-to-gods black cape. Not a vamp. Necromancer, probably. They were more common on the East Coast, but there were a few of them wandering around Portland. It was either that or just some weirdo who liked hanging out in cemeteries dressed up like a bad Dracula stand-in. I shoved the gun back into the holster.

"Sorry. Habit." I gave him what I hoped was an apologetic smile, but felt a lot like a grimace, and flashed my ID. "Morgan Bailey. PI." Gods, that sounded dopey. Who'd I think I was? Magnum? I had no idea what made me add "PI." I don't usually bother.

"No problem. So, what's a cute couple like you doing hanging out in a cemetery on a lovely night like this?" He reached into a pocket in his cape. For a second, I thought he was going for a weapon, and I wrapped my hand around the hilt of my dagger, but instead, he yanked out a bag of caramel popcorn, which he proceeded to munch. Not that caramel popcorn was weird. I love caramel popcorn. It's just that eating it in a cemetery in the middle of the night seemed a little…well, strange. Especially when one was dressed in a black cape.

I would have loved to say so many things, but I settled for, "We're looking for a sunwalker."

"Aren't they make-believe?"

I exchanged a glance with Inigo. "Apparently not. Have you seen one?"

He blinked. "At night?"

"Well, maybe he's trying to blend." I shrugged.

"With what? Corpses? Ghosts, maybe?"

Was that sarcasm? "Well, you never know."

"Right." He gave me a look not unlike one you might give a madwoman.

"Inigo," I hissed, "back me up here."

Inigo cleared his throat. "We were thinking that, quite possibly, he might be…ah…living here. In a crypt. Like a vampire. Maybe. You know, so no one suspects he's *not* a vampire."

Way to go, Inigo. Smooth. I was starting to think he'd been spending too much time with me.

"Aha. Well, no sunwalkers here. I would know. I have an affinity for the dead. And the undead." His smile was more than a little disturbing.

Well, that settled it. Necromancer. Maybe even a necromage. I always wonder how much truth there is to the stories about necromancers raising the dead or necromages powering their magic with the energy of ghosts, but it seemed rude to ask.

"You're sure you haven't seen a sunwalker?"

He munched on his popcorn. "Pretty sure. What you want him for?"

"He stole something from a client of mine. I've been hired to get it back."

"Oh, well, good luck with that." He seemed completely uninterested.

"Thanks for your help." I gave him a little wave as Inigo and I backed up and headed quickly for the car. The necromancer, or whatever he was, continued to munch on his popcorn. I swear some days I am surrounded by weirdness. You know, more than the usual.

As I pointed the car back down the hill toward the sparkling lights of the city, I glared at Inigo. "Well, a fat lot of good that did."

Inigo gave me an enigmatic smile. "Oh, that did exactly what we needed it to do."

It took me a moment. I could be a little slow sometimes. Then it hit me: a guy who hangs out in graveyards eating popcorn is probably the type of guy who has friends in strange places, friends whom he'd be sure to tell all about the cute couple in the cemetery looking for sunwalkers. "Well, damn."

∽

The rest of the week passed slowly. No sunwalkers popped up on the radar, but I dusted four more low-level vampires and helped Kabita seal a hellhole. Not bad for a few days' work.

Friday night I had a date.

I hadn't had a date in quite a while, so I admit to being a bit nervous. OK, a lot nervous. Despite the fact that deep down I'd really love to be in a relationship, dates are so not my thing. I don't do well. I mean, small talk is bad enough to begin with, but how on earth does a vampire hunter answer questions like, "What do you do for a living?"

It had been months since I'd been on a date at all, and I hadn't had a full-fledged relationship since Alex. In every other area of my life I'd managed to get over being a victim. I'd moved on, gotten stronger, braver. But in this one area? Not so much. Which is probably why my mother took matters into her own hands. No doubt she was convinced I'd never give her any grandbabies if left to my own devices.

I'd once made the mistake of telling her I don't meet guys in my line of work. Which isn't entirely true. I do meet guys. They just aren't generally human. My mother, however, doesn't know that. She thinks I am a night manager at the Benson Hotel downtown. It's the only thing I could think of that would explain my hours.

Ever since then, my mother has been on the prowl. Not for herself—perish the thought—but for me. My mother has been trying to pawn me off on some guy or other—with zero success. She's the one who dug this guy up—someone she met at a charity event she'd worked during one of her volunteering stints. I swear she has a new cause every week. Apparently, she thought we'd make a "cute couple."

Sure, until the first time I kill a vampire in front of him. Gods save me from my mother and her matchmaking.

I hadn't realized my hands were shaking until I tried to put on my lipstick and nearly smeared it across half my face. Like I said, I don't do so well with dates. Not since London. It's easy to be tough when you're chasing down the bad guys. Not so easy when your heart is liable to get smashed to itty-bitty pieces.

This was ridiculous! I kill vampires without breaking a sweat. Or at least not much of one. How could one stupid date turn me into such an incredible mass of nerves? I didn't even know the guy, for crying out loud!

I took a deep breath, found my center, and tried again. The lipstick went on OK this time, but I was still a bit shaky. The mascara was a little trickier, but I got it on eventually without poking out an eye or ending up with a black streak on my cheek.

I gave myself a critical look in the mirror. The neck wound had healed nicely, leaving only the faintest trace of a pinkish scar.

No half-decent guy would comment on such a thing. The green dress I'd chosen for the occasion was simple and a good color and cut for me. Showed off the curves, one of my few vanities.

Well, this was as good as it was going to get. I grabbed my black bag off the dresser and headed for the door, ignoring the fancy beaded evening bag my mom had given me on my last birthday. There was no way I was going out unarmed, and evening bags just weren't built for carrying UV guns or silver-tipped knives. So I wouldn't exactly be stylish—nothing new there.

I was ten minutes early to the restaurant. I hate being late. It always seems so rude. By the time I walked through the doors, the butterflies were having a disco in my stomach.

The restaurant was one of those soothing and somewhat posh places you find in downtown Portland, with low, cushy booths, dim lights, and an open fire in the middle of the room. There was even a real live pianist plinking out something hauntingly romantic by Bach. I knew it was supposed to be calming, but it just made me even more nervous. I hoped the glasses weren't real crystal. With my jitters, that was the last thing I'd needed. More than likely, they'd end up in little shards on the floor.

I stepped up to the desk. "I'm looking for Richard Winters."

"I'm sorry, madam, but the gentleman has not arrived yet," the maître d' said with an affected British accent. That almost got my mind off my stomach. Almost. After living in London for a few years, I knew the real thing when I heard it. His accent was most definitely *not* it. "Would madam like to sit in the bar and have a drink?"

"Oh, yes, madam most certainly would." I think the sarcasm went completely over his head, as he gave me a vacuous smile and waved me down the hall toward the bar.

The bar was even cozier than the restaurant, all dark wood and rich auburn carpet, heavy drapes on the windows and old-school jazz on the sound system. A group of businessmen had their jackets slung on the back of their chairs and were laughing over bottles of microbrew. The couple in the corner was too busy making eyes at each other to drink their cocktails.

Half an hour and two glasses of wine later, my date finally showed up. Normally I wouldn't have waited, but I admit to being slightly tipsy—plus, he'd sent me a very nice apologetic text. He'd had a flat, but he promised he was on his way.

Still, I was feeling a bit irritated by his lateness—but that was nothing compared to how I felt after he gave me a very obvious once-over. But then he flashed me a charming smile complete with dimples and held out his hand. His handshake was a little limp and his palm rather moist, but maybe it was nerves. "Hello, you must be Miss Bailey. Richard Winters. Your mother has told me so much about you."

Miss Bailey? Was he kidding? My mother tries, really she does, but I was starting to think my bad judgment in men is genetic. Still, he had a nice smile, he'd actually apologized for being late, and he did charity work. That was good, right?

I gave his hand a good, hard shake. "Morgan. Nice to meet you." At least the butterflies in my stomach had calmed down. Maybe this wouldn't be so bad. Maybe he was a truly decent guy.

Fifteen minutes later, I was praying for a hellhole to open up and swallow me. Or preferably him. I hadn't been able to get a word in edgewise. He'd been droning on about his work as an accountant. An accountant! I'm sure it's all very fascinating stuff, but honestly, I kill the undead for a living. The vagaries of number crunching somehow just don't interest me all that much.

My eyes were just about glazed over by the time the waiter finally came for our order. "We'll take two of the veal," Richard ordered.

Oh, no, he didn't. No, he didn't.

"Excuse me," I said in my most saccharine-sweet voice. "*We* will not take the veal. *I* will have the eggplant parmesan." I am not a vegetarian, but I find perverse pleasure in ordering vegetables in front of self-obsessed people like Richard Winters. Especially ones who order veal. Even more so for ones who order veal for me like I'm some helpless, brainless twit.

I gave Richard another fake smile and took a sip of wine for fortification. I had a feeling I was going to need a lot of fortification before this date was over.

He did not smile back. In fact, he looked extremely put out. Fine. Let him get his panties in a bunch. What was my mother thinking?

The meal dragged on with Richard yammering nonstop about his job, his car, his health club, his money. Frankly, I tuned him out after the first twenty minutes and focused on enjoying my food and ogling the bartender. He wasn't really my type, but he had a seriously nice pair of guns.

"So then I told him that while he could deduct the hotel bill, he could *not* deduct the three porn movies…"

I stopped with my fork halfway to my mouth. Had he just said *porn* on a first date?

He plowed on: "Well, I don't know what you do, but in my line of work…" It was obvious he didn't think I did anything interesting and that he really didn't care. His eyes were scanning the dining room while he fiddled with his lapel.

"I kill vampires."

I didn't mean to do it. It just sort of came out.

He blinked and shoved his glasses up his nose. "Excuse me?"

I took a big gulp of wine. I'd stepped in the shit now. Might as well go all the way. "Vampires. You know…the bloodsucking undead. I kill them. For a living. Demons too."

For the first time that evening, he looked unsure. Maybe even a little scared. I could just imagine the tales he'd have for the office come Monday. I was a little worried he might tell my mother, but she'd never believe him anyway. Despite my breach, I couldn't help a grin.

"You kill vampires."

"That's what I said." I smiled sweetly and took another quick gulp of wine.

He looked frantically around the room, probably for our waiter. Or maybe a straitjacket. "Um…right. OK. That's great. And how is that working out for you?"

"Love it!" I chirped merrily. This was kind of fun. The poor guy was starting to sweat. "It's a really great workout too, lots of cardio. Keeps me fit."

He gave me a startled once-over but managed to refrain from saying anything. I gave him points for self-restraint.

It isn't that I am fat, exactly. I'd say average with plenty of curves. Not exactly what one might call "fit" from Hollywood's viewpoint. Certainly not buff, which you'd think I would be with all the exercise I get. But no, I am built more like America Ferrera than Keira Knightley. I blame it on my mother. Thank you, genetics. My extrahuman strength certainly isn't down to weight lifting or workouts. It's purely down to freak science.

I gave Richard my brightest, most innocent smile. I think I might have even batted my eyelashes at him. That was when he grabbed a wad of cash out of his wallet and threw it on the table. I guessed we were leaving. I snagged my coat and followed him out the door.

I felt it the minute we stepped out of the restaurant onto the quiet side street. It started with a tingling at the base of my skull, gripping harder and harder as I got closer to the undead. Well, shit.

The only other person in sight was a well-dressed man with short blond hair. He nodded to Richard and me. Richard nodded back. I registered his identity seconds before he hit us.

Terrance.

Before I could react, he flung Richard into the brick wall of the restaurant and grabbed me around the neck.

Out of the corner of my eye, I saw Richard slumped on the ground, shaking his head and looking a little dazed. Good. He wasn't hurt, at least not badly. That meant I could focus on my job instead of whether or not my date was bleeding to death.

I couldn't break Terrance's grip, so I snagged my stiletto dagger out from where it nestled in my cleavage. One of the perks of an ample chest is a convenient place to store weaponry. Unfortunately, he was way too fast for me, and the blade went in just to the left of his heart, enough to hurt, but not enough to kill.

Terrance hissed at me, flashing fang, and I noticed his eyes were red. Strange. Vampires usually had the same color eyes in death as they had in life, just faded. But I didn't have time to belabor the point. I raised my hands in between his arms to break his hold on my neck while at the same time stomping my heel into his instep. There are times when three-inch heels come in handy.

He snarled, but didn't let go of my throat. Dammit. Only one thing to do. Up came the knee right into his family jewels. He doubled over in a bellow of rage and pain, breaking his hold on my throat.

I lurched away from him, but he was too fast. Before I'd gone more than a step, he'd grabbed me again. This time I smashed the heel of my hand right into his nose and then used the force of his backward stagger to drag the stiletto out of his chest. I swiped at him, but he moved too quickly and the blade just managed to cut a line across his pecs, ripping open his shirt and leaving a thin trail of dark blood.

He snarled again and slapped me across the face with his open hand. The force sent me reeling into the wall, my head connecting to the brick with a good, solid thunk. The world spun out of control. Squinting against the pain and dizziness, I lashed out again with the knife, opening up another cut, this one along his biceps.

Terrance grabbed my wrist, giving my hand a good, hard shake. His fingers were so tight I could feel my carpal bones grinding against each other until my entire arm went numb. My knife dropped from nerveless fingers. I didn't have any other weapons I could reach, and even my extra strength was no match for his vampire power, so I did the one thing I could think to do: I took a page from the Three Stooges and poked him in the eyes with two stiff fingers.

With a howl, Terrance dropped my hand, and then he was gone too fast for even my eyes to follow. Dammit. Now I was going to have to go on the hunt again. It was so much easier when I could dust them the first time around.

I turned back to my date, expecting to find horror in his eyes. I didn't. Instead, he looked a little too overexcited for my taste. "Oh my god. Vampires are *real*. You really *do* kill them for a living. That's hot."

Oh, crap. He's one of those weirdos who gets off on vampires and violence and stuff. *Ew.* "Don't be ridiculous," I told him, wincing as I parroted the government's line: "Vampires don't exist. Even the president says so."

He laughed. "Come on. I saw the fangs. That guy was way too strong and fast to be human. Everyone knows the government is only trying to hide their existence from us."

Great. He's some kind of conspiracy nut, and I'd practically handed him living proof that vampires are real.

"I have no idea what you're talking about." I started toward my car.

"Why didn't you kill that one?" he demanded.

I kept walking. "He wasn't a vampire. He was a mugger. I plan on filing a police report. You should too. Though I suggest you don't mention vampires. They might just decide you need to be locked up for your own safety."

That stopped him. But only for a moment. "So, hey," he said eagerly, trotting along behind me, "I had a really great time. I'd love to take you out again. How about tomorrow?"

I unlocked my car door, hopped in, and slammed it behind me. He knocked on the window, so I rolled it down.

"So, how about it? Are you free?"

"Sure I am. When hell freezes over."

∽

"So, how was your date?" Kabita slid into the booth opposite me at our favorite restaurant, Urban Turban. It's the only Indian restaurant in my part of town, and the owners are somehow distantly related to Kabita, so shoptalk is safe enough. As such, it has become practically our second home. The bhangra music thumping away on the stereo in the kitchen made me a little homesick for London.

I gave her an exasperated look and reached for a chapati. "Don't ask."

She raised her brow.

"OK, fine. It was just some idiot accountant who thought he was superior to me until I kicked a little vampire ass right in front of him."

"Shit. You did not. You know better than to hunt in front of civvies. Please tell me you made up a good cover story."

I shrugged. "Couldn't be helped. The vamp attacked me. I had no choice. I tried to convince my date the vamp was just a mugger, but now he thinks I'm the best thing since Xena."

Kabita snorted. "Look out, world; Morgan, warrior princess, has arrived." She reached for the bowl of poppadoms and snapped off a piece.

"Shut up. Anyway, he's called me five times since last night even though I told him I'd rather be eaten alive by fire ants than go out with him again."

One silky black eyebrow rose toward her hairline so high it nearly disappeared under her hair. She stopped munching on the poppadom. "You actually told him that?"

I shifted uncomfortably. "Uh, no. Not exactly."

"What exactly did you say?"

I let out a sigh. "I told him to go forth and multiply," I mumbled around a mouthful of curry. It was a clever little Britishism that was essentially the same as telling someone to fuck off. Unfortunately, it didn't translate well on this side of the Atlantic.

"Morgan," she groaned, "we're not in London anymore. You can't tell American men that. They take it too literally."

Well, duh. I didn't need her to tell me that. And I definitely didn't need her to know that he'd doubled the number of calls *since* I told him that. Some people just don't get sarcasm.

"I'm hoping if I don't call him back, he'll get the point." It sounded totally chickenshit, even to me.

I wondered if a person's eyes could actually roll right out of their head. I might find out pretty soon if Kabita didn't stop rolling hers. "*Morgan Bailey!* You are horrible. You are a wuss. You are...you are..." She glared at me. "How on earth can you go around slicing and dicing the undead and yet be completely incapable of dealing with ordinary mortals?"

She had a point. Except that it isn't all mortals. It's just mortals of the male variety. I simply have no idea what to do with them. They...befuddle me. If they were undead, I could kill them. That's easy. If they were related or friends or clients, I could handle that. When it comes to actually dating them, I am completely useless.

I didn't spent a lot of time around men growing up, since my dad had died before I was born; maybe that was part of it. But the truth is that I loved once and had it thrown back in my face. I just don't get how someone can tell you they love you one minute and then next act like you are so much garbage. Surviving that vampire attack might have given me super speed and strength, but it didn't fix my heart or take away that fear. And the fear has turned me absolutely useless around men.

My face heated. Maybe I could pretend it was the curry. I hate blushing. Badass vampire hunters do not blush. It is so completely mortifying—the absolute curse of the fair skinned. Kabita took pity on me. "Honestly, Morgan," she said as she stabbed at an onion bhaji with her fork, "we need to sign you up for lessons or something."

"Why? We both know I'd just embarrass myself."

Kabita smirked. "That's very true."

I glared at her. "Gee, thanks a lot."

"Eat your curry and I'll buy you an ice cream."

"Oh, goodie! Thanks, Mom!"

Kabita just gave me the Look.

"By the way, I should probably mention that the vampire who attacked me last night was Terrance, and he was…different. He had red eyes. That's a little weird, right?"

"That is weird." She sat lost in thought for a moment. "I'll have to go through the files and check, but I don't recall coming across anything about vampires with red eyes before."

"It's got to mean something."

"Probably. I'll let you know if I find anything. Anyway," Kabita said in a rapid subject change, "I need your help tonight. This one's a bitch."

I blinked. Kabita using a swear word, well, it's rather like hearing the pope advocating pole dancing. It just doesn't happen.

"What are you not telling me, Kabita?"

She didn't even have the grace to look shamefaced. "I've got a demon problem to deal with. They're nesting. And they're Zagan demons."

"Well, shit." I hate Zagan demons. They slip through from the demon realm, and once they are on our turf, they breed like crazy. The adults are vicious, ripping humans to shreds and eating out their soft innards. They are nearly impossible to kill. Even worse? They spit slime. It is totally disgusting, not to mention lethal. The acidic goo can melt your face off.

She nodded. "Yeah, tell me about it."

How Kabita can kill those things without blinking yet get all squeamish over vampires is beyond me.

"Fine, what time?"

"Say, about ten tonight, in front of the Bagdad Theater. The nest isn't too far from there."

"Gotcha." I stood up, grabbed my jacket, and threw a twenty on the table. "But, girlfriend, you *so* owe me. I'm gonna collect big-time one of these days."

Kabita glared at me over a forkful of curry. "Oh, yay. Can't wait."

∽

I wasn't entirely sure what else I should be doing to piss off the sunwalker. I mean, Inigo seemed convinced that bandying my motives about a cemetery in the middle of the night was sufficient, but Brent Darroch was paying the firm good money to find his amulet and take out the sunwalker, permanently. It didn't seem very professional for me to sit around doing nothing. Not to mention that I've never been particularly good at waiting.

I decided to take a walk in the Park Blocks to clear my head. There is something so bizarrely soothing and at the same time energetic about the Park Blocks. They are simply a narrow strip of park running through the middle of downtown Portland, filled with the usual parky sort of things: grass, footpaths, roses, really weird art, and the occasional bum sleeping on a park bench.

But to walk through the Park Blocks is to step out of oneself, out of time, and travel a different path. The juxtaposition of nature with city lulls one into an almost hypnotic state. Or at least it's that way for me. Nobody else seems to wax particularly poetic about it.

Today the blocks were quiet. A few bees hummed busily about, and sunlight warmed the roses, sending heady perfume into the air. I strolled slowly, eyes half closed, reveling in the solitude. University classes hadn't started yet, and so this section of the Park Blocks was nearly empty.

As I walked, I shoved my hands into my pockets. I needed some kind of direction. Somewhere to look. Frankly, I had no idea what I was doing. Hunting vampires and demons is one thing. A sunwalker is something else entirely.

Then a thought struck me. Cordelia Nightwing's apartment is right near the Park Blocks. She might not be able to help me with the sunwalker any more than she already had, but there was always the chance she'd "seen" something since I talked to her last. And she is a good person, and those are hard to come by in my line of work. Why not pay her a visit?

A warm shaft of sunlight through the trees felt good against my back. Obviously, I was spending way too much time in the dark. I pulled a pair of sunglasses out of my black shoulder bag and shoved them onto my nose.

Cordelia's building is one of the old brick ones built in the early part of the twentieth century that lines the north side of Park Blocks next door to the Portland Art Museum, with its artistic water features and creative lighting. Its art deco style is very funky and a bit bohemian. Not to mention ridiculously expensive. Having a view of the park adds a hefty chunk of change onto the monthly rent. Crystal balls must pay well.

Personally, I prefer my own house in the Hawthorne District. For the same amount of money, I get my own four walls *and* a garden and all the boho goodness I can stand. I pressed the button on the intercom and waited until Cordelia's voice chimed out. She sounded excited to have me there, and buzzed me in.

The lobby smelled vaguely of an odd combination of mildew and new carpet. No amount of refurbishment ever completely covers the scent of age in these old buildings. I wrinkled my nose and desperately resisted a sneeze, but it got the better of me.

I skipped the elevator and took the stairs. I used to live in one of these old buildings and know from experience their elevators are in no way to be trusted, despite their cool Perry Mason vibe.

In all the years I've known Cordelia, I've never been to her home. We've always either chatted on the phone or met where she worked, all dolled up in fortune-telling gear for her customers. This was my very first visit, and I admit to a great deal of curiosity. I rapped on her door, which swung open a moment later.

For a moment, I just stood there and blinked. I had to admit to some relief at the absence of flowing Chinese robes and chopsticks in her hair. Instead, she was wearing jeans, which showed off her slender frame, a pretty blue sweater, and bare feet. Her hair was up in a ponytail and she had reading glasses perched on the end of her nose. She looked so…normal.

"Welcome, Morgan. What a pleasant surprise! Come in, come in! Living room's that way."

"Hi, Cordelia. Thanks."

I followed her pointed finger down a narrow hall lined with bookshelves. The shelves were full to overflowing with all manner of books and knickknacks. It was vaguely claustrophobic, but in a nice way. Not unlike those really old bookshops, like Cameron's downtown, that have been cramming books into every nook and cranny since 1972, so you have to step over piles of vintage copies of *National Geographic* to get at the poetry section.

The hall emptied into a living room that was, if possible, even more jammed with stuff than the hall had been. I was only slightly startled to see a pair of golden cat eyes glaring at me from under a mound of multicolored pillows. I've never been much of a cat person. It closed its eyes in a haughty manner and went back to sleep. Obviously, I was beneath its notice.

Cordelia waved me to the couch, which was half lost under pillows, throws, and books. I shoved a few things aside. The cat's eyes opened and he glared at me some more before they drifted closed again. Freaking cats. I noticed there were already two cups and a teapot steaming away on the coffee table.

I raised both eyebrows. "Expecting someone?"

She laughed, that bright music spilling its way up and down the scales. "Of course. You."

"You said it was a pleasant surprise."

"Well, of course I did. And it was. Until about ten minutes ago."

Ten minutes. Just about the time I decided to go see her. "So that's how your gift works. You can't actually *see* anything until somebody makes a decision that sets them on a particular course. Then you can see the outcome." If she were really talented, she might be able to see possible outcomes of other possible decisions as well. For instance, what would have happened if I'd decided not to visit or if I'd stayed longer at the restaurant? But her gift was rare enough as it was.

She flashed me a brilliant smile. "Yes, exactly!"

I smiled back.

"You're still worried about the sunwalker. Among other things." It was a statement, not a question.

I blinked at the abrupt change of subject. Creepy how she did that. "Well…" I hesitated, "not about him so much as how to find him. I'm not really sure what I should be doing. I feel like I should be doing *something*, but I just can't come up with anything clever." That was the understatement of the century. "I visited Eddie, like you suggested. Did what he said, but now I think I'm a little lost."

She poured a cup of tea and dropped in two lumps of raw sugar and a splash of milk, just as I liked it. She handed it to me and poured another for herself. "You seem quite capable to me."

I laughed wryly. "Well, sure. I mean, vampires are pretty straight-forward, you know. They've got patterns. They're not exactly subtle."

"So you follow the pattern to find the vampire you're hunt-ing," she said with a nod, sending a swath of dark hair tumbling out of its binding and swishing around her face. "Like reading animal tracks in the wild."

"Exactly, then you stake it, take its head if it doesn't dust right away, and you move on to the next one. Easy." It seemed so weird to be chatting about killing monsters while sitting in her bright, cheery living room with Igor the Cat glaring at me with his beady little eyes.

"She."

I blinked again. "Excuse me?" I was starting to think she really was a mind reader.

Cordelia smiled gently at me. "The cat is a she. And her name is Bastet."

Of course. Who else to name a cat after but the Egyptian goddess of war?

"OK. Bastet. She's very…intense."

"She likes you." Cordelia's smile was warm. "I knew she would. She's very particular, but she always knows a good person when she meets one. She especially likes your kind."

I could only assume that by "my kind" she meant hunters. I can't imagine she meets many of us, but you never know. "Uh, yeah, right." I could so totally tell. You know, what with the evil cat eye and the glaring and all. She'd pretty much done everything but hiss at me. "So, about the sunwalker?"

"Relax." Cordelia waved her left hand around, coming dangerously close to dislodging a stack of tarot cards from their precarious perch on the desk behind her chair. "Everything is in motion. You'll meet him soon enough, when the time is right. Now, enjoy your tea and tell me all about your date."

"My date?" How'd she know about that?

"Bet it was a doozy. I can still see the negative energy clinging to your aura. Come on. Spill."

∽

The Bagdad Theater is a relic of the roaring twenties, with an interior like something out of Arabian Nights. The theater is central to life in the Hawthorne District. I've enjoyed more than one movie there over a glass of wine and some pizza.

"You bring extra salt?" Kabita asked when I met her as planned.

I nodded. I was armed to the teeth with holy water, salt, and other demon-hunting accoutrements. While holy water doesn't do a thing to vampires, it does cause Zagan demons some serious grief. It's more or less the equivalent of pouring sulfuric acid on human skin. It's nasty, but effective—and seems fair to me, considering their face-eating slime.

Kabita had her thick black hair pulled back in a ponytail tight enough that not a single curl dared escape. She was in her demon-hunting uniform of black cargo pants, a black long-sleeved tee, and black steel-toe boots. She is nothing if not eminently practical.

"The nest is down there," Kabita whispered, nodding toward the alleyway that ran behind the theater. "You stand guard while I cast the circle."

"Got it."

The alley was weakly lit by a streetlight half a block away and littered with empty boxes and sacks of garbage. The tang of old urine stung my nose and sent my gag reflexes into overdrive. I struggled to ignore the stench as I scanned the shadows for anything that moved. Nothing did, not even a rat. Smart rats.

The nest was tucked away at the back of the alley. The old cardboard box looked like any other makeshift shelter the homeless erected around the city. Only, this box housed something a little less harmless than an old man needing a bath and a run of good luck.

While I stood by with machete and holy water at the ready, Kabita cast a circle with the salt. She is better at spell-casting, or energy manipulation, than me. My vampiric abilities are a result of some kind of virus, not anything mystical or quantum, and they make it hard to focus. Not that I've ever been any good at focusing anyway. But Kabita is a natural-born witch. Anyone can channel energy or work magic or whatever you want to call it in order to manipulate the physical world, but natural-born witches are the only humans who can do it without breaking a sweat.

"Salam kepada penjaga," she whispered as she walked the circle around the nest. It sounded like Hindi or something, but then, I'm not very good with Asian languages, and she is multilingual, so it could have been just about anything. The words aren't technically necessary, but it's the focus and intent behind them.

The minute Kabita finished casting the circle, the young Zagans felt the spell hit and spilled out of the nest, snarling for all they were worth. They were so young they weren't even secreting slime yet, though they were fortunately old enough that the adult demon that spawned them had already left them to their own devices. If mama had still been around, we'd have been in serious trouble.

A single swipe and Kabita took the heads off two, while I went after a third. Machetes work wonders on young Zagan demons, their slimy hides not having completely hardened yet. I felt the blade as it slid into the soft tissue behind the skull, then scraped through spine, parting it like a knife through hot butter. Its head popped off and rolled across the alley.

We were finished in less than ten minutes, and I didn't even get spattered. I pulled out my bottle of holy water, sprinkled some on the bodies, and watched them melt. In seconds, there was nothing left but smoking stains among the multitude of other stains on the grimy cement.

"Well"—Kabita smiled, wiping demon goo off her machete— "that was a good night's work."

I wrinkled my nose at the foul stench from what little was left of the Zagans. "I definitely prefer vampires. Not nearly as messy."

"Just be thankful they weren't spitting slime all over the place. That stuff is seriously nasty. You want a ride home?" She waved at her pride and joy, a vintage 1941 Harley-Davidson, which she'd parked a good block and a half down the street.

I shuddered. I am not a big fan of motorcycles. Plus, she drives like a bat out of hell. "Thanks, but I'll walk." I live just a few blocks away, and the fresh air would do me good.

She shrugged. "Sure. Be sure to drop by the office tomorrow morning. We need to send Darroch an update on your sunwalker adventures, and you are behind on your paperwork."

Paperwork. My favorite thing. "Yeah, sure." Right, my nonexistent sunwalker adventures. My little jaunt to the cemetery had yielded absolutely nothing so far.

The moon was bright, nearly full, and the night air had just an edge of crispness to it. I love walking at night. Sometimes, in the dark and quiet, it feels like I am the only one left in the whole world.

Right after the attack, I was terrified to walk alone at night. But as Kabita began training me to be a hunter and my extra abilities began to show themselves, I slowly began to recover my sense of security, my love of the dark. I'm not afraid anymore.

I turned down Fortieth, which was a little darker than the main street. A high stone wall ran along the sidewalk. I could smell the roses and honeysuckle in the garden behind the wall. I stopped for a minute, just to breathe in the heady scent and let the night seep into my soul.

That was when it happened.

He came out of nowhere, slamming me up against the wall with enough force to rattle my teeth. I didn't even feel him coming. I was not exactly a lightweight, yet he picked me up like I was no more than a child. I went for my stiletto, but he snagged my wrist in a viselike grip. Panic surged through me, taking me straight back to the moment of my attack three years ago. Oh, damn, I was in trouble.

Chapter Six

H e leaned forward slowly. His eyes were aquamarine, like the Pacific Ocean on a hot summer afternoon. Little gold lights flickered in their depths, dancing like dust motes in the sun. For half a second, I forgot I was in mortal danger. His eyes were that mesmerizing. His scent, a heady mix of spice and man, swirled around me, sending my already overactive libido into overdrive.

My heart beat hard in my chest, my blood hot and thick. Desire pooled low in my belly. All I wanted to do was breathe in his scent, wrap myself up in it until I drowned.

Which was more than a little odd, seeing as how I'd been panicking a moment ago. My whole reaction was definitely not normal.

I tried to distract myself by staring at his mouth. Bad move. He had the most delicious mouth I'd ever seen: full lips, soft as velvet, absolutely perfect for all sorts of naughty things. I gave myself a mental head slap. Obsessing over the enemy's mouth was so not a good idea.

Then he leaned even closer. Shit. He was going for my throat, and I couldn't even move. Didn't want to move. And that worried me. Vampires aren't supposed to possess that kind of power. Vampiric mind control is another myth Hollywood drummed up. Vamps don't need mind control to subdue their victims. The only power they need is strength and speed. They just grab and bite.

But he didn't bite. Instead, his breath caressed my ear, my neck. He was *sniffing* me. Then I felt his lips move gently back and forth over my skin, just above my carotid artery. He was *tasting* me, for crying out loud. Those lips of his were made for sin, and they were most definitely doing really sinful things against my throat. My legs went a little rubbery, and I actually had to grab on to his rather impressive biceps in order not to end up on my ass.

This was ridiculous—and it was scary, which pissed me off. Badass vampire hunters do not go all gooey over a vampire, no matter how sexy he is, which is a weird concept, since vampires are, by nature, not at all sexy.

When he spoke, his voice was melted chocolate with the faintest hint of an accent I couldn't quite place running like caramel ribbons all through it. "Little girl," he breathed, sending shivers up and down my spine. Vin Diesel had nothing on this guy. "You do not know who you are messing with."

I struggled to maintain some sense of decorum, but I was pretty sure I squeaked. I cleared my throat and tried again.

"Sure, I do. You're just another pathetic vampire hopped up on junkie blood." Vampires are strong and fast, but not as strong or as fast as this one. Junkie blood was the only thing that explained it.

He pressed that rock-hard body of his up against me and laughed softly in my ear. His laugh did things to me down low, and my thighs clenched. My libido did a happy dance. Something it was definitely *not* supposed to do in the presence of a vampire. Come to think of it, my vampire radar wasn't going off at all.

What in blazes is this guy?

I thrust my chin out, hoping I looked tough and macho instead of the quivering mass of Jell-O I actually was. "You're no vamp." My eyes narrowed. "*What* are you?"

He grinned in a way that I was pretty sure was illegal in at least fourteen different states, then leaned forward to sniff me again before whispering in my ear, "Darlin'"—his rich voice was the stuff of dreams—"you've just found your sunwalker."

Well, hot damn.

∽

After making me promise not to try killing him until we'd had a chance to talk, he led me to the nearest coffee shop. It was pretty clear that, promise or no promise, I wasn't going to take him easily, if at all. And despite my assignment, I found myself intrigued. This guy—this sunwalker—was no ordinary vamp.

Common Grounds is a uniquely Portland experience and one of my favorite places to relax with a cup of coffee. It's stuffed full of comfy couches and mismatched mugs and smells of roasted coffee beans and fresh grilled toast. Best of all, it's open from 5:00 a.m. to midnight. It would be even better if it were a twenty-four-hour place, but sometimes you just have to take what you can get.

Fortunately, the place was nearly empty, and we found a table far enough away from everyone that we wouldn't be overheard. I couldn't imagine what the other patrons would think of our conversation. Though, it *is* the Hawthorne District.

I was beginning to doubt my original plan to get the amulet and dust him was going to work. In fact, I wasn't sure I *could* dust him. He was far too strong and fast, and that weird mind-control thingy had me worried.

Nothing about this guy was anything like I'd expected. I'd imagined him as another run-of-the-mill bloodsucker, only one who could walk around in daylight. This guy was *nothing* like any vampire I'd ever seen.

The sunwalker wasn't a creepy monster that hung around in dark corners. This guy *owned* his space. I eyed his broad shoulders, muscular frame, and deliciously tight backside as he paced the room in front of the bank of windows overlooking the street.

Oh, yeah, I bet he owned anything he wanted to. An opinion no doubt shared by the barista who was ogling his butt. Poor girl was practically salivating. I surreptitiously checked to make sure I wasn't doing the same.

The strangest thing of all was that he felt familiar. I didn't recognize him, so I knew I'd never seen him before. I never forget a face. But it felt like I knew him, or that I *should* know him.

"OK." I straightened my shoulders. No way was I letting this… *sunwalker* get to me. "So, Mr. Sunwalker, have you got a name?"

He glanced up from his pacing, startled, and then gave me a grin, flashing a pair of canines that were slightly longer than strictly necessary, but nothing in the realm of vampire. "Jackson. Jackson Keel. You can call me Jack."

Jack? A sunwalker named Jack? I guess I thought a sunwalker should have a more exotic name. "Morgan Bailey. Nice to…uh… meet you." *Right. Let's go with that.* "OK, Jack, why don't you sit down and explain to me why you found it necessary to scare the shit out of me. And while you're at it, you might as well tell me why you stole my client's property."

I tried to give him a severe look, à la Kabita, but it wasn't working. It was that mouth. Sweet baby Jesus, he had such a mouth. It made me want to do very bad things.

I cleared my throat and stiffened my spine, dragging on my professional vampire hunting aura with all the willpower I could muster. I folded my hands primly in front of me and waited. This is also a Kabita trick. Unfortunately, she's a lot better at it than I am.

He just smirked at me, the big fat jerk. "First off," he said in that voice that should have been outlawed, "I wanted to make sure you understood just how difficult killing me would be."

"Uh, yeah. I get that. And secondly?"

"Secondly"—he finally sat down—"I didn't steal the amulet from Darroch. He stole it from me."

I blinked. "Yeah, right," I scoffed. "Likely story. Let me guess. You inherited it from your grandmother."

His eyes darkened. "It was entrusted to me by a friend a long time ago." A muscle worked in his jaw. "I swore to protect it. I failed. I've been tracking Darroch for the last twenty years."

"You're telling me that, in twenty years, you haven't been able to find him? Get the amulet back?" I honestly couldn't imagine this guy, this sunwalker, failing at anything. My mind was reeling with questions. If I were honest, very few of them at that moment had anything at all to do with the amulet, and everything to do with the sexy creature sitting across from me.

I sucked in a breath. The strong aroma of roasted coffee beans grounded me somewhat. I felt a little more solid. I took a sip of my latte and then tightened my fingers around the ceramic coffee mug, letting the heat seep into my hands. My silver ring cut into my finger just a bit. This was all feeling a little surreal.

"Darroch has special…skills," Jack said.

"Skills?"

"At moving. Hiding. I always seem to be two steps behind him. Until now."

I curled one leg under me and sank back deeper into the comfy couch, mug clutched to my chest. "So, this amulet…Why would Darroch claim you stole it and hire me to get it back from you if he's the one who has it?"

"I would have thought that was obvious." His voice dripped disdain. I wasn't sure if it was for me or for Darroch.

OK, right. Obvious. Now, normally I was reasonably good at obvious, but unfortunately, in this case, my brain had apparently turned to mush.

"He wants me dead." Jack's voice was completely flat. No anger, no fear, no nothing. *Just the facts, ma'am.*

"Why would he care?"

He shrugged. "He's afraid I'll get the amulet back. I'm all that stands between him and absolute power."

"Absolute power. Seriously? Melodramatic much?"

He paused to give me a glare before jumping up to continue his long strides back and forth across the dark tiles of the coffee shop. I caught the barista drooling again. He pitched his voice low enough so that, despite his pacing, I was the only one who could hear him. "He probably also thinks he has a score to settle; taking the amulet from me wasn't enough." He raked his fingers through his dark hair.

I shook my head. No matter their species, males always get hung up on their macho bullshit. "OK, fine, whatever. So he wants you dead. That still doesn't prove the amulet belongs to you."

"Then maybe this will." He strode across the floor and leaned over, right in my face. I wasn't sure whether I should hold my ground or run like hell. What I did know was that, despite everything, I suddenly had the irresistible urge to plant a big, sloppy kiss right on that mouth of his.

From the looks of things, a very similar thought had just crossed his mind. Oh, man, was I in trouble. He shook his head slightly, then slapped his palm on the scarred wooden table. In his hand was a photograph.

Now, I've seen nineteenth- and early twentieth-century photographs. In fact, I used to collect them as a kid. I'd look at them for hours on end, imagining the lives of the people in them, making up stories about their adventures. What can I say? I've always been a little odd.

The sunwalker's photo was definitely nineteenth century, mid-nineteenth century, from the looks of it. I could tell by the style of clothing. Only, instead of some random long-dead person staring back at me, the face was an exact replica of Jack's.

I gaped from the sunwalker to the photo and back again. It didn't just look like Jack; it *was* Jack—right down to the tiny scar on his chin. I wondered vaguely what could cause a scar on a sunwalker. Do they have the same healing abilities as vampires? Or did Jack get the scar before he was turned?

I know I shouldn't have been shocked. I deal with vampires all the time. But the truth is vampires rarely manage to live past a century. They usually get hunted down long before then. Really old ones are uncommon, to say the least. The photo put Jack at close to two hundred years old.

Then my attention was caught by something else in the old sepia-toned photo. Around Jack's neck, on a thin chain, hung an amulet—the same amulet Darroch had shown me a picture of a few days before. The supposedly worthless one he claimed the sunwalker had stolen only recently. Yet here Jack was, wearing it in a photograph taken more than one hundred and fifty years ago.

A lot can happen in a hundred and fifty years, sure. He could have lost the amulet in a card game, sold it, anything. But I strongly doubted it with that same sixth sense that had saved my ass on more than one occasion. Darroch had claimed his family had owned the amulet for generations. Still, it didn't pay to be too hasty.

"Nice pic." I handed it back to him. "Ever hear of Photoshop?"

He smiled. "I thought you might say that." He handed me another photo. It was a Polaroid. An old one. Circa the 1970s. Jack was lounging against the side of a hippie van wearing a pair of bell-bottoms and a ridiculous vest thing covered in beadwork. Around his neck was the amulet from the previous photo.

I glanced up at Jack. As far as I know, Polaroids can't be faked.

Something about the sunwalker, Jack, made me believe him. Trust him. I knew it was crazy and probably *really* stupid, but part of me honestly believed he was telling the truth. The other part wondered if my anti-vamp mojo was on the fritz and I'd finally fallen for some weird vampire glamour that nobody knew about.

"Listen, I want to believe you. I do, but…" I put on my stern Kabita voice.

"But what?" His voice was getting dangerously loud, and this time he ran his hands through his dark hair so vigorously I was afraid he would pull it right out. Instead, it just ended up spiking out in every direction as though he'd had a run-in with a light socket. And dammit, it made him even sexier. I groaned.

"But I just met you. Up until a little while ago, I wasn't even sure sunwalkers existed. I don't know who you are or what you are, and for all I know, you could be putting some kind of glamour on me or something." It sounded ridiculous, but I wasn't about to back down.

"What can I do to make you believe me?" The frustration in his voice was clear. Sometimes I have that effect on people. "What do you want to know?"

"First of all…um…when were you…um…?" I trailed off. I had no idea how old he was, and it seemed somewhat indelicate to ask.

"Turned?" he offered with some irritation.

"Sure, yeah, turned."

He smiled a little. I seemed to amuse him an awful lot. "Not long before the Second Crusade."

I blinked. "Second Crusade? As in, the Christian Crusades?" He gave me a "duh" look.

Good grief. That made him over nine hundred years old.

"The Crusades. Right. I thought sunwalkers were a myth."

"Do I look like a myth?" he snarled.

"Then why don't we hunters know about you?"

He sneered. "Ever heard of a thing called misinformation?"

He had me there. "Fine. Let's say I believe you. That still doesn't prove the amulet is yours or that Darroch stole it."

He looked about ready to throttle me, which was fine. He was causing me a great deal of discomfort. I figured he deserved a bit of the same.

"My word is my bond."

I crossed my arms over my chest. "That may have worked during the Crusades, but this is the twenty-first century, pal. Your word means very little. I need proof."

Jack leaned up so his face was inches from mine. "Ask Darroch."

"Don't worry. I will." I really didn't want him to know his pheromones or whatever were getting to me. "Listen. Forget it, OK? I'm really tired and I want to go home." And I needed to think about this whole weird plot twist. I also needed to confront Darroch.

Jack was still inches away, staring straight into my eyes, and I could feel his breath warm on my face. "Fine," he said. "Call me after you talk to Darroch."

"OK, sure. I'll get back to you on that."

He gave me a look, and I knew defying him would be a really bad idea. "See that you do." He spun on his heel and strode for the door.

"Um…Excuse me!" I called after him.

"What?" he snapped. His ocean eyes were fierce. I had no doubt that this man, this sunwalker, was still every bit the warrior he'd been nine hundred years ago.

"Exactly how do you propose I contact you? It's not like you're listed in the phone book under 'sunwalker.'"

He stalked back to the table and slapped a business card down before spinning and stalking back to the door. I glanced at the card. My eyes widened a little. "You're kidding, right?" I called after him.

He stopped and half turned.

"You teach piano lessons?" I was pretty sure he blushed before he slammed out, the bell above the door jangling crazily behind him.

I twirled his business card through my fingers and grinned happily to myself. Beautiful. Suddenly, I was feeling incredibly perky. That big, tough, macho ex-Crusader turned sunwalker taught piano to little kids for a living. Beyond brilliant. Sometimes life is just way too bizarre for words.

Chapter Seven

Sometimes life so totally sucks. I mean, big-time.

My plan made sense at the time. Barge in. Demand the truth. Blah, blah.

Unfortunately, things don't always turn out quite the way I picture them in my head. This was definitely one of those times.

After a good night's sleep (or rather, morning's sleep), I headed over to Brent Darroch's house the next afternoon. I knocked on the door—really, I did. Nice and loud too. Rang the doorbell, even. No answer. So I tromped around the house peeking in windows and trying doors. Just in case. I mean, he could be lying wounded or something.

All the doors were locked, the windows mostly curtained. And then I found it, a small window high up in what appeared to be the laundry room. It was open just a crack, and there weren't any alarm sensors. Probably a small enough window some cheapskate had decided it wasn't worth wiring. I honestly didn't think I'd fit. Kabita would have, but me, I have hips. Hips that are not designed to squeeze through tiny pantry windows. So imagine my surprise when I was actually able to wiggle through with only a couple of minor hiccups.

I hauled myself up onto the sill and swung my legs through the open window. I don't know why I sucked my stomach in. My stomach wasn't the problem. As I suspected, my hips were just a tad too wide to fit through the window horizontally. I wriggled myself around to the right a bit so my body was slanted and my hips slipped right through.

Unfortunately, my ribs got a bit of a banging as my side scraped along the window frame on the way in. It left a lovely little welt from waist to armpit. That was going to sting.

I hit the laundry room floor with a rather audible thud and managed to stagger to my feet without crashing into anything. The room was dim; the only light came from the afternoon sun filtering in through the small window I'd just crawled through.

I knew I was breaking every rule in the book and Kabita would no doubt kill me. You just don't go breaking into your own client's house searching for clues. It's rude. But I had to do it. Darroch had given me the creeps from the start, and I was determined to find the truth one way or another.

I edged the laundry door open and stuck my eye to the crack. Darroch's kitchen was truly impressive, with dark granite countertops, rich wood cabinets, and enough stainless steel to build a skyscraper. It was also empty. I slid out of the pantry and into the kitchen, keeping my eyes peeled for Darroch or one of his goons—ah, bodyguards. He'd had plenty of them around on my last visit.

There were several doors leading off the kitchen. The first one led into a large family room with a glass door leading to the patio. It was empty like the rest of the house. Another door led straight out into the backyard. And behind door number three? I found a short hallway with a staircase leading up.

I'd gotten the distinct impression on my last visit that the downstairs office was just for show. You know, the sort of place you jam full of expensive furniture and fancy doodahs and only clean when you have someone you want to intimidate. I mean impress. The real important stuff is somewhere else, and that amulet was nothing if not extremely important to Darroch, so I headed up the staircase.

In my experience, most people keep personal stuff as close to their personal space as possible. And there is nothing quite as personal as one's bedroom.

I'd just found what had to be Darroch's bedroom, a single man's room if ever I saw one. There wasn't a feminine touch anywhere. No perfume bottles, pretty pictures, or fancy throw pillows. The furnishings were sparse and heavy, the sheets were black satin, and the room smelled heavily of men's cologne.

I'd just started poking around when I heard a car pull into the drive. I froze as I heard the car door slam; then I tiptoed to the bedroom door, debating whether or not to head back down to the pantry, before I realized there was no time. Whoever it was already had a key in the front door, and the front stairs and most of the upper hallway, unfortunately, could be clearly seen by anyone entering the house from the front. I could head for the back stairs, but I wasn't sure I had time. I stepped back out of the line of sight.

The front door opened and I heard the unmistakable voice of my client. Even worse, he was headed up the stairs toward the bedroom.

Not good. Oh, so very not good. Not only would Darroch probably have me arrested, but Kabita would be extremely pissed off. Darroch gives me the heebie-jeebies, but I've seen Kabita angry before and she scares me to death. Kabita is not the type of person to get all mad and stomp around issuing threats. She is the type of person to go completely cold and still, and then murder you in your sleep. She believes actions speak louder than words.

A quick glance around the room gave me two options: the closet or under the bed. I opted for under the bed. I shimmied under just in time for Darroch to walk through the bedroom door.

"I don't pay you to make excuses. I pay you to do what I tell you." There was only one set of feet in shiny black shoes, so I figured he was on his cell phone. "What I told you was to have her followed, Kaldan, not have your idiot flunky attack her."

Kaldan! The only Kaldan I know about is the head of one of the local vampire clans, Terrance's master. Had Kaldan sent

Terrance after me on Darroch's orders? And why on earth would Kaldan be answering to Darroch in the first place?

Whatever Kaldan said really pissed Darroch off, because he started screaming. "Listen, you idiot, I don't care if he was starving to death! Her blood is not to be taken! He was to follow, not attack…I don't fucking care…You know what, Kaldan? Deal with the problem, or I will!"

Darroch slammed down the phone, then sank down on the bed to take off his shoes. I winced as the springs sank toward my head. I tried to think. Why would my client have me followed? If I believed Jack—and I was beginning to think I did—Darroch already had the amulet, so it couldn't be that.

Did Darroch want me to lead him to the sunwalker? The sunwalker he'd hired me to kill?

Either he didn't trust me—which was understandable, since I was currently lying under his bed and therefore not exactly trustworthy—or there was a lot more going on here than I knew. I was voting for the latter.

Now, how to get out of here? Preferably without getting caught.

Unfortunately for me, Darroch had apparently decided he needed a nap. One by one, articles of clothing hit the floor, inches from my face. Then, with a sigh and a slight creak of bedsprings, he stretched out fully on the bed.

Freaking fantastic.

I lay there for what seemed like hours, dust bunnies tickling my nose. Finally, I heard a faint snore come from above me. It was now or never.

I rolled out from under the bed and scurried for the door. A quick peek into the hall showed all clear, so I hurried down the stairs.

I'd almost reached the bottom when the knob on the front door began to turn and I heard voices coming from the other side. It sounded like some of the human guard dogs—Darroch obviously wasn't alone, after all. I had seconds before someone walked through that door and found me standing like an idiot in the middle of the hall.

I darted toward the door on the right side of the hallway and twisted the knob. Locked. *Shit. Now what?* There wasn't time for me to find anywhere else to hide.

My eyes scanned the hall. Seconds now and they'd find me. Next to the front door was a hall table with a small black vase filled with orange roses. It didn't provide much cover, but it was all I had.

I hurried over and tucked myself into the space next to the table on the side away from the door. I could only hope they wouldn't glance this way.

The front door swung all the way open and three men walked in yammering about the latest Yankees game. Apparently, it had been a really good game, because none of them looked my way.

Before I could move from my spot, one of the goons hesitated. He started to turn back toward the front door. *Shit.* Had he seen me, after all? I could stay where I was or make a run for it. Either way, I was going to get caught.

Before he could turn all the way around, one of the others asked a question, snagging his attention. I let out a silent sigh of relief.

The goons headed toward the kitchen, still deep in discussion. The minute they were out of sight, I slipped out of my hiding spot, headed straight to the front door, and walked right outside, bold as brass.

One of Darroch's neighbors was taking his garbage out. The guy was about eighty and peered at me suspiciously through the thick lenses of his glasses. I nodded, smiled, and gave him a little wave. He smiled back and gave me a salute. When in doubt, act like you belong.

I decided to skip a run-in with Kabita and headed home. I really needed some sleep, and I didn't want to spend the next hour arguing. Besides, I needed to figure out why Darroch would be giving orders to the most powerful vampire in the city. And even more important, why Kaldan would be taking them. And what any of it had to do with me.

∽

White-knuckled hands gripped the smooth railing as I gazed out over the sparkling city below. The spire of the Great Library, the tallest building in the world, glowed red and gold in the afternoon sun. The Dome of Enlightenment sparkled in blues and silvers below, beckoning those who saw it to enter and partake of its serenity.

This city stood for millennia, first on our home world and then here on this beautiful new planet when our own sun died. It had been a beacon of enlightenment in an uncivilized universe, but now…This was the end of it, then. The end of all things, for both the city and for the people of Atlantis.

I whirled from the railing, stalking back into the temple, the marble floor cold beneath my thin silken shoes, robes swirling around my ankles. Something must be done. Something would be done. Saving the treasure of my people for a future generation was paramount. Surely there was some way to ensure survival? A way to stop the madness?

I paced wildly, clenching my hands together, willing my shattered mind to pray. How could we have known that a tiny little infection would turn the most peaceful race on the planet into mindless, bloodthirsty beasts? Raveners impossible to cure or to kill? We would destroy all of humankind if I didn't do something. A paradise planet turned to a wasteland.

It was only a matter of time before the sickness reached the temple and the priests and priestesses succumbed, the royal family along with them. As the high priest of Atlantis, I would be the last to fall. I was, after all, the strongest, chosen as a conduit for the gods. The energy that flowed through me, as it flowed through the city of Atlantis, would protect me. For a time.

I scrubbed a weary hand across my face. What to do? How to save all the good that was Atlantis? How to save a remnant of the Atlantean people, the last of our kind in existence?

A thought came to me. There was, perhaps, a chance. I strode across the room, purpose flooding my veins.

"Send me Varan." The young acolyte bowed and hurried out of the room. Our only chance for success lay in the half-breed children Atlantis had borne. They alone were immune to the sickness, both the ravening disease that struck only pure-blooded Atlanteans, and the nightwalker sickness that struck pure-blooded humans. Even our greatest physicians did not know where the disease had come from or the reason for the immunity of the half-human children, but it might prove our salvation and that of the human race. There was only one member of the royal bloodline who possessed both Atlantean and human blood.

My thoughts were distracted by the chinking of armor and the scent of well-oiled leather. The man who entered was a warrior through and through, every inch of his armor polished and gleaming, eyes constantly alert, ready for anything. Even at so young an age, Varan was already the first warrior of all the warrior priests of Atlantis. A son to make a father proud. And proud I was, indeed. He was the only one to whom I would dream of entrusting the royal bloodline and the hope of our people.

"Ah, Varan." I gave the young warrior a strained smile. "I have need of you and your men."

Varan bowed, crossing his right arm over his chest, fist pressing against his heart. "As my lord wishes, so shall it be." His right hand dropped to clench the hilt of a bloodstained sword.

I jerked awake to a room flooded with sunlight. Not another crazy dream. They were getting all too frequent. First, some guy digging in the dirt, and now this.

I frowned. The guy digging in the dirt felt familiar. Not just because in my dream I'd been the guy, though that was strange enough on its own. No, it felt like I knew him, as though I'd met him before. Except, I hadn't. Had I?

I slid out of bed and went to the bathroom for a glass of water, thinking about my dream. Nightwalkers obviously meant vampires. I wasn't sure what raveners were supposed to be, but they seemed to be even worse. A knight digging in the dirt. A priest worried about some kind of plague. I'd been the knight, and I'd been the priest, at least within the dreams. They seemed connected somehow, only I couldn't figure out how.

I shook my head. They'd felt real, but surely they were just dreams. They had to be just dreams.

I sighed and ran my fingers through my hair, pushing aside thoughts of the dreams. I had other things to deal with. It was past time to pay the piper. I'd have to tell Kabita about my meeting with the sunwalker—Jack—and my nighttime foray into Darroch's house.

I decided to take the coward's way out and call her. She answered on the third ring.

"Uh…morning, Kabita." I winced. I sounded guilty. "Thought I'd catch you up on the Darroch case."

"Great, he's been asking for an update."

I closed my eyes, took a deep breath. "You're not going to like this."

ॐ

I was right. She didn't like it. Not one bit. In fact, she was seriously pissed, and not in the English way. In the very American way. Though, it being Kabita, there wasn't a lot of yelling, just a lot of deadly silence and very pointed "ohs" and "ums," which was worse. A lot worse.

"I don't even know why you took this guy on." I paced back and forth, flailing my free arm wildly. "There's just something off about him. Then there's the whole amulet thing. I'm not sure he told us the truth about that."

"And you're going to take the word of this…sunwalker…that our client is lying?"

"Oh, come on, Kabita. There was the picture! Plus, Darroch has given me the creeps since the minute I met him, long before I met Jack Keel. Did you meet him in person? Darroch, I mean." The pause on the other end of the line was just a little too long. "You didn't! I knew it!" I was practically jumping up and down in sheer delight. Then a thought occurred to me. "Why didn't you?"

Kabita always, always meets with the clients in person. She's very careful about the sort of jobs we take on and the people we work for. The government requires us to take on certain tasks for them, but the rest of the jobs and clients are up to us.

She let out a long sigh. "He came recommended. Highly recommended."

My eyes narrowed. Normally, that isn't enough. Recommended or not, Kabita always checks out the clients in-depth. The recommendation must have been very high, indeed. "Who recommended him?"

"My government contact." Which essentially meant her handler and therefore, by extension, my handler. The whole idea of having a "handler" has always rubbed me the wrong way. It just isn't right.

"Are you telling me the *government* wants Jack dead?" Not the sunwalker—Jack. He was becoming real to me now, a person, like Inigo or Kabita or Cordelia. So not good.

"No," she snapped. "I'm telling you that Brent Darroch has friends in high places. Very high places. He called in a favor."

Great. That meant we were that favor. It also meant Kabita hadn't asked any questions. When the government is involved, asking questions isn't particularly good for the health. It also meant that Darroch was a lot better connected than I'd thought. This could get a bit hairy.

"Listen, Morgan. Just do your job, OK? Dust this sunwalker, get the amulet, and everybody goes home happy."

Except for the sunwalker. I doubt he'd be thrilled with the plan. And me. I wasn't happy with the whole thing anymore, either. Something felt so off about it all, but Kabita wasn't in a listening mood. This government contact obviously had her between the proverbial rock and hard place. Just what that rock and hard place involved was a question for another time, but you'd better believe I planned to find out.

Maybe I could throw her off for a while. Give myself some time to figure things out. "I don't think it's going to be as easy to dust this guy as we thought."

Her voice was diamond hard. "Are you telling me you can't do your job?"

"I'm just saying it's not going to be your routine hunt. This isn't like killing a vampire. It may take some time to figure out his...vulnerabilities. Not to mention finding out where he's stashed the amulet."

"Just get it done," she said and slammed down the phone. It was so rare for Kabita to lose her temper over something like this. I was the short-tempered, emotional one. Kabita was the calm, coolheaded one. The sane one. Whoever was pulling her strings must really have had something over her.

But I'd worry about that later. For now, I had bigger fish to fry. I needed to hunt down Terrance and dust him before he attacked me again. It might also be a good idea to find out *why* Darroch wanted me followed, which probably meant trying to track down Kaldan. Then there was the little matter of the amulet.

I rubbed my forehead. I had an almighty headache coming on. I don't do well on lack of sleep, and the crazy dreams I'd been having were wreaking havoc with my sleep patterns.

Going back to bed wasn't an option. I doubted I'd be able to relax anyway. I decided a very large cup of coffee was in order. When all else fails, I drink coffee, preferably by the gallon.

I staggered into the kitchen, only to find Inigo sitting at my table. I frowned at him, then at my back door. It's one of those sliding-glass patio doors with the little screws at the bottom, the kind that can't be opened from the outside short of breaking the glass. The door was still firmly closed, the screws still tightly in place.

I turned and walked down the hall to my front door. Still locked with the safety latch in place. Not impervious to break-ing and entering, but certainly unlikely, what with the safety latch and all.

I did a complete circuit of the house, checking every window in the place. All of them were closed and locked up tight. I walked back into the kitchen, still frowning.

"I give up. How'd you do it?"

He gave me an impish grin, his blue eyes sparkling merrily. "I'll never tell." He leaned back in his chair, crossing his arms over his chest, which drew my attention to his very well-formed pecto-ral region. Maybe I needed a cold shower instead of coffee.

"Honestly, Inigo, you've really got to stop breaking into my house."

"And spoil all the fun?"

I ignored him and got to work on the coffee. I dumped some of my favorite Italian-roast beans into the coffee grinder and whizzed them before adding them to the French press. It is my humble opinion that coffee from a French press just tastes nicer than drip coffee. Plus, there is that whole Zen thing that comes from the ceremony of making coffee. I dumped sugar and creamer into my mug (yum!) and left Inigo's pure.

I set the mug in front of him and tried really hard not to drool over the muscles his T-shirt didn't quite hide. I cleared my throat. "So, to what do I owe this…uh…pleasure?"

He flashed a devilish grin. Cheeky. "I heard you broke into Darroch's house last night."

"How'd you hear that?" I'd only just gotten off the phone with Kabita.

He shrugged. "I've got my sources. I also heard you finally met your sunwalker."

"Geez, the grapevine works fast. Yeah, I did. And he's not *my* sunwalker." I scowled at him over my coffee mug. The steam brought a slight flush to my cheeks. Honest, it was just the steam. Nothing else.

He raised a single brow. He'd either been spending too much time around Kabita or this was some weird family trait.

"Did you also hear I was attacked by a vampire after my date with the loser?"

He laughed. "Yeah, Kabita mentioned something."

"It was Terrance, the one I've been hunting. Apparently Darroch hired Kaldan to have me followed, and Kaldan sent Terrance. Except Terrance has impulse-control issues and decided to attack."

He frowned and took a sip of his coffee. "Kabita didn't mention that."

"I just told her this morning. She was in a mood. She *really* wants me to kill this sunwalker. I've never seen her quite so… insistent." I tasted my coffee, then dumped in another spoonful of raw sugar. Better.

He leaned forward, his brow furrowed. "What's going on I don't know about?"

I shrugged. "Depends on what you know. Did you know Darroch is connected? As in government connected?" He shook his head, so I quickly ran down my conversation with Kabita for him. By the end, his blue eyes were like twin shards of ice, so coldly angry. This was beyond furious. "OK, Inigo, now what do *you* know that I don't know?"

"Nothing," he insisted. "At least not now. Listen, I've got a major IT job, Morgan. I might be gone for a while. Do you think you can handle everything while I'm gone? Hunt down Terrance, keep the sunwalker under control and alive?"

"Uh...sure, no problem." Well, the hunting part would be no problem, but controlling the sunwalker was another matter entirely. I wasn't about to get into it with Inigo, though, especially not before I'd finished my coffee. "Why alive? I mean, I know why I don't want to kill him, but you never met the guy."

A strange look crossed over Inigo's face. "I'm not sure. I just know keeping him alive is important."

Bring on the mysteriousness.

Chapter Eight

After Inigo left for his job, I hopped in the shower. Nothing like coffee and a hot shower to get a girl revved up for hunting vamps. I lathered up with my favorite Champneys rose body wash. So I have one girlie indulgence. Sue me.

I slapped on a little makeup, blew my hair dry, squidged in a bit of hair gunk so I had the whole spiky windswept thing going on, and considered it good enough for hunting. I learned long ago that full war paint on a hunt is completely pointless. Vampires don't much care whether you wear eyeliner, and you usually ended up looking like a raccoon within the first fifteen minutes of a hunt. Better to go minimalist than end up looking like Tammy Faye Bakker after a crying jag.

A few minutes later, I was dressed in my standard outfit of jeans and a black T-shirt and standing in front of my closet contemplating footwear. I sort of have a thing for boots. Most girls get all gooey for a pair of spiky-heeled Manolos or strappy Jimmy Choos. Not me. With me, it's all about the boots. Preferably knee-high leather waffle stomper types with serious ass-kicking capabilities. Doc Martens are a particular favorite. And if you can hide a retractable blade in the toe, so much the better.

I decided on my favorite pair of hunting boots. They are like army boots gone bad. They lace up all the way to the knee, and the leather is supple enough to give me a good range of movement; plus they are a lot lighter than they look. I can not only kick bad-guy ass, but I can run like hell if I need to, which, frankly, I'd rather not. Running is so not my thing.

I turned to give myself a critical once-over in the mirror. Didn't want to go out with something hanging out that shouldn't.

Except, it wasn't my reflection staring back at me from the mirror.

He wore chain mail and a dirty white tabard with a dull red cross on the front. His long hair was tangled and coated in dust, so it looked nearly gray. Blood seeped through a cut on his stubbled chin, while his fist clutched a gory falchion sword. Screams of dying men abraded my ears; the stench of death stained my nostrils. I swallowed hard as eyes the color of a sun-drenched ocean glared back at me. I knew those eyes. They were the eyes of a sunwalker.

I closed my own eyes, took a deep breath, and looked again. This time my own moss-green eyes stared back. Just me. Only me. The warrior was gone, but deep in my gut, I knew he wasn't just the sunwalker. He was also the knight I'd been dreaming about. The one who'd been attacked in the cave by the ancient vampire, the one who'd felt so familiar. And now he was invading my waking life as well as my dreams. So not good.

I pushed the vision away and headed out the door. I'd face all this later. Much later. Right now, I had a vampire to find.

∽

I love my car, I really do. These days, with the whole energy crisis thing, it's not entirely PC to love your car, but I do.

Ever since I was a kid, I'd wanted a Mustang. Not just any Mustang, either, but a classic red one. So the minute I moved back to the US, I bought myself a beautiful 1965 Mustang in mint condition. Then I pulled an act so sacrilegious it'd probably get me hanged in some circles: I yanked out the gas-guzzling V-8 engine and put in an eco-friendly electric engine. It no longer had the throaty grumble of a classic muscle car, but it could go fast enough and it didn't spew crap into the air.

I had just pulled out of the drive when my mobile rang. I pulled over and let the car idle by the curb while I took the call. "Hey, Cordelia. What's up?"

"Are you OK?"

Now, that was a loaded question. "Um…Yeah, why wouldn't I be?"

She paused for rather longer than I thought necessary. "Something is awakening in you, Morgan," she said softly. "It has me worried. I'm not sure you're ready to handle it."

What on earth did that mean? "I'm fine, Cordelia, really. Just a bit tired." I rubbed the middle of my forehead where a headache was starting to form.

"You haven't been…seeing things?"

Crap. "Just…um…some crazy dreams, you know. But that's all they are. Just dreams."

"So, nothing in the waking world?"

How did she know I was seeing things? "I'm fine, Cordelia." It wasn't an answer, but I wasn't about to let her know I was seeing Crusaders in my bedroom mirror. That just sounded nuts. "I've just got a vampire to hunt, an amulet to find, and I've got to figure out how to save the life of a bloody sunwalker. I'm a little stressed." My voice was going a little high-pitched and whiny. I hate when it does that.

"So, you've discovered the sunwalker is more than he seems?" I could hear the smile in her voice. In fact, she sounded downright smug.

"I've gotta go. Vampire to hunt, remember?"

She laughed, and for a moment, my headache went away. "OK, Morgan. Go get your vampire. You might want to check the waterfront tonight."

"Sure. I'll do that. Thanks, Cordelia."

ᔎ

I like the waterfront. Much like the Park Blocks, Waterfront Park is one of those odd mixtures of peacefulness and energy. It slices its way through the heart of the city along the seawall right on the edge of the Willamette River. If Pioneer Courthouse Square is considered Portland's living room, the place where everyone gathers to relax and chat over a cup of coffee and a bento box, then Waterfront Park is its playground. All summer long, it plays host to a plethora of festivals, from the Blues Festival to the Bite of Portland. When it isn't acting as the site of a citywide party, it's the home away from home for skateboarders, a romantic spot for couples in love, and a fun place for kids and grownups alike to escape the heat in its giant fountain. And through it all, there is the river rushing on its way toward the ocean.

I parked the car a couple of blocks from the waterfront. Portland's World Trade Center buildings are nearby, and ever since 9/11, parking has been restricted due to security concerns. It's a pain, but what can you do?

I always carry a couple of weapons on me. Never know when they'll come in handy. I rarely weapon up fully, however, until I've actually found the vamp I am looking for. This time, though, Cordelia had given me the heads up, and I was starting to realize that when Cordelia gives you the heads up, you'd better listen, so I was going in fully loaded. In addition to my usual built-in boot knife and favorite bra stiletto knife, I slid a small sword into its sheath (which was slung at an angle across the back of my leather jacket), strapped a blade bracelet on each of my wrists, and slipped a couple of silver-tipped metal spikes into my belt.

In addition to my other weapons, I had a new toy I was itching to try out. I get all my weapons from Tessalah, because she is the best in the business.

Tessalah is a freelancer with an indeterminate and somewhat shady background. In fact, there are rumors she isn't from our world at all, but some parallel universe where the laws of physics are a bit more mutable. But if you need to kill a demon, slay a dragon, or dust a vampire, you go to Tessalah. If she doesn't have a weapon that can kill it, she'll invent one. And if she can't invent one, then you are pretty much out of luck.

My new toy looked something like an aspirator for babies. The bulb was glass that had been infused with "magic," so it was flexible like rubber. I don't know how to describe Tessalah's magic in scientific terms. It was a little beyond me, but it gave a faintly visible purple luminescence to the clear glass. The bulb was bracketed by thin bands of sterling silver, which in turn attached to the thin needle-like neck of the aspirator, also made of sterling silver over steel.

Instead of sucking baby boogers, this aspirator supposedly kills vamps. Theoretically, the silver neck stabs into the vampire and then the bulb squeezes, injecting saltwater straight into the vampire. Saltwater acts on vampires the same way holy water works on demons—like acid. Ejecting it straight into the body essentially melts it from the inside out. Tessalah has a way with magical weapons.

I'd yet to try it out. In fact, I was a little hesitant. I knew it would do the job, but it was a nasty way to kill someone, even a vampire. It was more a "when all else fails" sort of weapon.

The lights glinted off the water, turning the river into a Monet reflection of the city. I've seen numerous photographs and paintings try to recreate that image, yet not a single one does it justice.

I breathed in the night, reveling in the glory that is darkness. Sometimes I worry whether I am a little too much like the creatures I hunt, loving the night as I do. Other than right after my attack, the night has never been about fear, even as a child. Most nights, the darkness wraps itself around me like a well-worn blanket and asks me to stay a while. Tonight was no different.

As I strolled along the waterfront, I wrapped the night around me like a cloak, sending my essence, my spirit, wandering out into the darkness.

I stopped dead. OK, so maybe tonight *was* different. Sending my *essence* out? What the heck was that all about?

So I did what any sane person would do. I did it again. I let my senses go rushing out through the darkness, and I felt them, the lives, spirits, along the waterfront. A man, human, trying to sleep curled on a park bench. Three boys were smoking pot and talking smack over by the giant anchor. Two were human, but the other...He was something else, something other. Not evil, not vampire, just trying to be normal, human.

Farther down, there were two more, a man and a woman. I frowned. The human was a bright fire, hazed by overwhelming lust. She wanted sex, and she wanted it now. The man was dim and overwhelmed by...hunger. I felt his hunger burning in my veins as that slow, throbbing ache I sometimes sense around vamps began to build at the base of my skull. Hunger to rip and tear and drink. Hunger for flesh and blood. It wasn't my hunger; it was his, and I had to stop him before it was too late.

My senses snapped back into my body, and suddenly, I was running, drawing in the energy of the night to carry my feet faster and faster along the sidewalk. The river flashed by. The old man asleep on the bench didn't even stir. The boys started, one stiffening in fear. I could feel them relax as I flashed by, the nonhuman one letting out a sigh of relief. And finally, I reached the couple locked in a passionate and hungry embrace.

I grabbed her with my left hand, wrenching her away with more strength than I knew I had while catching the vampire by the arm with my right. She tumbled to the ground with a cry. Through vision gone strangely hazy, I saw her throat unblemished. Good, I'd gotten to her in time.

She gazed up at me with eyes full of terror. "Go," I snapped. Then I turned to the vampire, ignoring her while she scrambled to her feet and ran.

It was Terrance. I recognized him instantly. My lips drew back in a feral grin. He snarled back, flashing fang.

With a flick of the wrist, I unleashed my left blade from its bracelet and plunged it into Terrance's chest. Unfortunately, I wasn't quite as good with my left hand as with my right, and with the awkward angle, the knife glanced off his ribs.

Adding to my misfortune, whatever ability had let me cross eight blocks' worth of space in less than a minute had now deserted me. The shadows receded and the night was just the night again. I was just me. And Terrance was a hell of a lot stronger.

With a scream of rage, he wrenched the blade out of his chest and sent me flying across the park to land with a jarring thud next to the ship's anchor that stood in the middle of the park. Fortunately, I landed on the grass instead of the monument itself, but it still hurt like hell.

The boys gaped at me for a minute, then scattered into the night, the nonhuman one pausing for just a moment before following his friends. Smart boys.

I staggered to my feet, pretty sure nothing was broken, just badly banged up. Terrance was much, much stronger than I'd expected. I pulled my sword from the sheath across my back. Made of ultra-light steel and edged in silver, it goes through a vampire with hardly a hint of resistance. I was so not messing around with this guy.

His eyes flashed red in the darkness, and he tossed his blond hair back with a laugh. "Stupid hunter," Terrance jeered. "You think your little knife can hurt me? You are pathetic!"

"Oh, come on, Terry," I goaded him. "I don't know why you vampires always insist on taunting hunters. I mean, for gods' sake, it's like bad B movie dialogue. Bram Stoker would have been so embarrassed."

He hissed angrily. "Fine. Why don't I just kill you, then?" He stalked toward me. His eyes were very definitely red. Vampires' should be a normal human color, just a bit paler, like some of the color they had in life got leached out after death. Red is most definitely weird.

"What? You mean like you tried to the other night?" I circled to the right, keeping my sword up and myself just out of his reach. "Bet Kaldan was mad about that."

"Kaldan can kiss my ass," he snarled back.

"Do I sense dissension among the ranks?"

"You can sense whatever you want, Hunter. It won't do you any good after I've killed you."

I laughed. "Right, 'cause that's gonna happen."

He rushed me then, and even though I was ready, I barely missed getting taken down. He was faster than I, even with my more-than-human speed. I did manage to flick my sword fast enough to slice him open at the waist. He screamed—more in rage than in pain, I thought.

"Stupid bitch!"

"Oh, come now, Terry. That's not very creative. You can do better than that, surely." Taunting an enraged vampire is a dangerous business, but a girl's gotta do what a girl's gotta do. If I could get him mad enough, he'd make mistakes.

Terrance rushed me a second time, but I was more than ready. I danced out of the way, flicking the blade at him again, taking the cut a little deeper. Unfortunately, my reaction time was getting sluggish, and he caught me with a backhand that sent me sprawling. The whole world spun for a moment, and I realized I'd lost my sword somewhere in the grass.

Terrance was bleeding. Badly. Unfortunately, it wasn't nearly enough, and my strength was waning. I had to take him down—and fast—before I tired any more. I was also short on weapons, and he was far too strong. I had one option left—this time I rushed him.

I ran straight at him, my eyes never wavering from the red glow of his. I saw the triumph in those glowing eyes as he grabbed me by the throat and reared back to sink his teeth in. Then I watched the triumph turn to shock as I plunged the needle-sharp neck of my brand-new toy straight into his stomach, right through the cut I'd given him earlier. "I'll give Kaldan your regards," I told him and squeezed the bulb, flooding saltwater straight into his body.

I jerked the aspirator out and danced back out of his reach as his body froze in shock. The flesh around the wound began to bubble, then melt, and the bubbling and melting spread from the wound out over his entire body as he stood there and screamed and screamed and screamed. I finally had to cover my ears.

The stench was unbearable. Good thing most people can't smell the undead the way I do. This would have drawn a lot of attention.

With one last scream, it was like something let go and his body dissolved into a pile of steaming gunk that slowly melted away into the grass, just like demon spawn with holy water. I held the aspirator in the palm of my hand. I wanted to puke. The thing had saved my life, but the horror...Vampires might be bloodsucking vermin without conscience or soul, but nobody deserves to go out that way.

I turned to throw the weapon into the river, but hesitated. I hated myself for thinking it, but I might need it again someday. I tucked it into my pocket and went to hunt down my blades.

Chapter Nine

I was still revved from hunting on the drive home. Sure, I knew taking out Terrance would only delay things. After all, Kaldan was still out there, and if Darroch really were paying him to have his flunkies follow me, they'd just send someone else. Still, I finally felt like I was getting somewhere, or at the very least, taking control of things.

I tapped my fingers on the steering wheel. If Darroch thought I would be easy to manipulate, he had another thing coming. I am not so easy to distract, and even less easy to kill. The vamp attack that changed my life three years ago had proven that. They say what doesn't kill you makes you stronger. Seriously, they have *no* idea how true that is.

That thought led me right to another thought I was trying to avoid. What exactly had happened out there at the waterfront? I vaguely remembered the feel of the night all around gathering close to me, feeding me. I shuddered. The most worrying part of all is that while the first time was an accident, the second time I'd done it on purpose. *What the hell is going on with me?*

My cell rang. I knew it was Cordelia before I picked it up. She was starting to show a knack for knowing when an extra dose of weirdness was happening in my life.

I waited to answer until I'd pulled off the road. "Hi, Cordelia."

"Morgan, be straight with me. Are you all right?"

I sighed. I wasn't all right. Not really. But I wasn't ready to talk about it just yet. "I'll be fine for now, Cordelia. I just want to get home, get some sleep." Pale streaks of dawn painted the horizon. Bedtime for me. "Can I come by your house tomorrow?"

"Of course you can. Are you sure you're OK to wait until then?"

"Yeah, I'll be fine. Thanks." Apparently, she was bound and determined to become my Mother Confessor. I wasn't even Catholic.

I could picture her smile quirking at the corners of her mouth. "Anytime, Morgan. Bastet says hello." And with that, she hung up.

"I don't even want to know how she knows what the cat is thinking," I muttered to myself before I pulled back out into the street and headed for home.

∽

I could feel the tension drain from my body as I locked my front door behind me. Like the girl said, there's no place like home. Sometimes I wish home still meant London, but this is good too. The closets are certainly bigger. Plus, I was born in Portland and have spent most of my life here. It gets in your blood, this city.

I propped myself against the wall and yanked off my boots, letting them drop right there in the middle of the hall. The socks followed before I let out a sigh of blissful relief. I may be a boots kind of girl, but there is nothing in this world quite as delicious as bare feet.

I padded quietly down the hall toward the kitchen, not bothering with the lights. Like I said, the dark is a friend of mine. I shoved that thought aside. The dark was getting just a little too friendly lately.

I headed straight for the sink and a glass of icy water. Moonlight filtered softly through the window, filling the kitchen with oddly shifting shadows. Halfway through the glass, it finally registered: I wasn't alone. I slid my stiletto quietly out of my cleavage, keeping my hand hidden from view of whoever was behind me while cussing myself out mentally. I must have been more tired than I'd thought. How could I have been so bloody stupid?

I whirled, stiletto at the ready, only to be confronted by a familiar figure lounging at my fifties-inspired kitchen table. "Dammit, Inigo," I sputtered. "You nearly gave me a heart attack."

I couldn't see his expression in the darkness, but I sensed his amusement, nonetheless. "I take it your hunt was successful?"

I snorted. "Of course it was." I hesitated. I wasn't sure I wanted to discuss my current situation with Inigo, either.

He didn't say anything. He just waited.

I let out a groan and collapsed onto the kitchen chair opposite him. I knew he wouldn't give up, so I might as well spill it. I needed to talk to someone about it. "I just don't know. Something weird is going on with me. You know, weirder than usual."

"Weird? Weird how?"

I shrugged. I liked Inigo. More important, I trusted him. That's saying something for me. When it comes to men, I don't trust easily. I've worked with him for a long time, and he's proven himself more than once. He is my best friend's cousin, for crying out loud. Still, I wasn't sure I was ready to tell him I was losing my grip on reality. I wasn't sure I was ready to admit it to myself, because if I wasn't going crazy, then something much scarier than impending insanity was happening.

He got up slowly from the table, unfolding his long, lithe body from where he'd been lounging. I watched him walk over to me, desperately trying to hide the fact that my pulse was pounding hard enough that I was half-afraid I'd crack a rib.

I couldn't really see in the dark, but I was pretty sure I saw his lips quirk into something very like a smirk. Bastard.

He stepped behind me and I tensed up before I realized what he was planning. Then I felt his hands on my shoulders, sending a little electric thrill straight to my nether regions. Dear gods, I was in trouble. "Uh, Inigo…"

"Shh. You need to relax. You're too tense." His hands began kneading the muscles of my shoulders, which, until that moment, I'd had no idea were so beyond tense they closely resembled a rock.

I was pretty sure I let out a moan, but things were starting to go a little fuzzy around the edges. I could feel that odd tingling again, that pulling of the dark. It was rushing around me, swirling and tugging and surging into me, through me. In the dark, there were sparkles, like tiny stars, dancing and dancing on the edge of my vision. The night began to wrap itself around me, its energy driving deeper. I was a little worried I was beginning to lose my grip on reality.

"Morgan?" His voice was rough, full of desire and need. He pulled me out of the chair and turned me to face him.

His eyes had gone all funny. The icy blue was gone, and instead, they were glowing and kind of dark yellow. No. Gold. His eyes had gone gold and red. Not red like that vampire's eyes, but more an orange red, like the flames of a fire. His pupils were narrow slits of greenish black and the gold-and-orange flames danced around them.

I tried to say something, to ask him why his eyes had changed, but I couldn't get any words out. I just stared into his eyes while my brain went hazy and the darkness swirled and surged in my blood. I wanted him. I wanted him with a fever that was almost unbearable. I grabbed the front of his shirt and tried to pull him down to me.

He groaned again and I could tell he wanted me as much as I wanted him. I might not have been fighting it, but he was. "Morgan, no. Morgan, stop."

His hands were still on my shoulders, heavy and warm. I didn't know what it was he wanted me to stop, and I didn't care. I wasn't in the stopping mood. All I could feel was the rush of pure need, pure desire, surging through my veins like molten lava. I was hot and wet and so ready for him.

I finally found my voice, but it came out all funny. Sort of husky and breathy and not like me at all. I wanted to tell him it wasn't me, that I wasn't doing anything, but instead, I said in that strange, breathy, not-me voice, "Don't fight it, Inigo. Don't fight it."

He did for half a second before his mouth came crashing down on mine, his hard body pressed up against my softer one as he molded himself around me. Fire surged through me, chasing the darkness. Electricity tingled through my body, desire so strong I thought I'd die from it. Darkness, fire, the little sparkles grew brighter. There was only me and Inigo and our breaths, our mouths, our bodies.

I wrapped myself around him, burying my fingers in his silky hair. His skin nearly burned me with the heat of him. I gave myself over to his kiss, to the feel of him, losing all sense of time as I fell into the sensation of him. And then there was darkness.

In a cave under a plateau in a desert land, I sat, feverishly clutching a golden amulet. The blue stone in the middle glowed weakly, barely lighting the dank earthen walls around me. I'd spent nearly all my remaining energy painting the story of our dying race on the walls of this cave. One day a city would be built on this plateau, a city that would be the center of a thousand conflicts. I, however, would not live to see it.

I swiped at my forehead, my hand came away slick with sweat. The sickness ravaging my body was finally winning, taking over a little at a time. Soon, there would be nothing of me left at all.

The Heart was closing. I could feel the protection of its power slipping from me little by little. Soon it would be beyond my reach and the sickness would take over. The last high priest of Atlantis would be no more. Instead, there would be a ravening beast, hungry for blood and flesh and for violence.

I'd already witnessed so much violence. Shocking to a man who'd spent his entire life devoted to peace. I clutched the amulet tighter to my chest and felt myself slipping in and out of time. "I now become Death." I smiled weakly. I would not be the only one in history to utter such words. I could see this as I had seen so many other things in my lifetime.

And I had become death. I had done my duty as high priest all too well, and now Atlantis and all her people, the last of the full-blooded Atlanteans, lay buried beneath an ocean of rock and lava. I had stopped the disease in its tracks, but at such a cost. Now Varan and his warriors had only to find and destroy the few humans still carrying the disease, the nightwalkers. This world would be safe only when every last one lay dead.

I closed my eyes, breathing in the rich scent of earth, and sent a prayer winging to gods who refused to answer. It wouldn't be long now. Surely Varan would come soon with the news that the last of the royal bloodline was safe. Only then would my work be done and I could turn the Heart over to its new guardian, my only son, Varan, and end this existence with some shred of myself intact.

Please let it have worked. My fingers twitched against the dark blue of my robes, twisting and scrunching the rich fabric. It would take a miracle, but perhaps Varan could deliver that miracle. The most important thing of all was the bloodline. The royal bloodline must be saved. To save the future, to save all that was truly Atlantis, the bloodline must survive.

There was a scratching sound at the entrance and Varan entered, eyes wild, blood streaking his muscular body. "Quickly, my lord, we must leave. The hunters have tracked us!"

I hastened toward him, but it was too late. A rumble from outside told the story. A landslide. We were buried inside the cave, deep within the desert, where no one would ever find us. The half-blood *warriors and their human allies had done the job I'd set for them far too well.*

Varan swore. Anxiously, I gripped the younger man's arm. "Tell me, Varan, is it done? Did you succeed?"

"Yes, my Lord Danu. The bloodline is safely hidden, and the humans and my warriors hunt the last of the raveners and night-walkers, as you commanded. There is only the Heart."

A faint blue light pulsed in the absolute black of the cave. I clutched the amulet, fevered eyes drinking in the dying light. "I am sorry, Varan. So very sorry." He and his descendants should have been the guardians of the Heart until the time was right for it to be reunited with the bloodline. The last part of the plan had failed.

The only hope now lay with future generations. Perhaps there would be a distant son of Atlantis who would one day discover our tomb and become the Heart's guardian. That was how I had designed it, after all. But still, sorrow clutched at my soul, a soul already far too faded.

I felt Varan smile, if a bit sadly, and grip my hand in his. Softly, he whispered, "It is all right, Father. I forgive you." I wasn't sure I could forgive myself.

The faint blue light finally went out. The rich, metal tang of blood filled my mouth as the sickness at last took over my body.

There was no one to hear Varan's screams.

I sat bolt upright in bed, a scream ripping at my throat. Barely holding it back, I sat for a moment, gasping for breath and trying to collect myself. A dream. Just another stupid dream. I had been the priest again. I could still smell dirt, and the taste of blood lingered in my mouth.

I tried to recall some of the other details from the dream. I had a bad feeling the cave the priest and Varan had been trapped in was a little too familiar.

I closed my eyes and brought the details into focus: smooth floor, rough dirt walls, and an earthenware jar leaning against a low flat stone. A beautiful mural painted along the back wall. Yes, it was the same cave, the cave where the knight from my other dream had found the ancient bodies, where he'd been attacked by a corpse that should have been dead for thousands of years.

The attack, the ocean-colored eyes, the dusty tabard, the familiar face—it was all clear. I knew for sure now whom I'd been dreaming about, or at least who the knight was. I was also fairly certain that it was no dream.

I scrambled to the edge of my bed and yanked open the drawer of my nightstand. I dug around until I found the card I was looking for and pulled it out. Jack Keel. It made all too much sense. Jack had been a Templar Knight, a Templar who'd been transformed into something that was more than human, yet not quite vampire. Jack was the knight in my dream. He had to be. But who was the priest, and how did he fit in?

I needed to talk to Jack. I needed to find out for sure whether what I was dreaming was real and what it had to do with me. I yanked down the covers and that was when I saw I was still wearing my black T-shirt. The one I'd been wearing last night. The one I'd had on when Inigo kissed me.

I gaped at my bare legs. No jeans. I double-checked. Panties firmly in place, thank the gods. I was alone in my bed, no sign anyone else had been in it with me. Granted, it was hard to tell. I flop about in my sleep like a fish. My bed pretty much consistently looks like it's been hit by a hurricane.

I hesitantly reached out and felt the extra pillow. No heat, but that didn't exactly mean anything. I leaned over and took a deep whiff. Just the scent of my shampoo, nothing else.

What the hell had happened? I racked my brain, but came up totally blank. He'd been giving me a massage. I'd gotten all hot and bothered. I felt my cheeks heat. Yeah, definitely hot and bothered, and I wasn't the only one. He'd picked me up, held me against him. We'd both been very aroused, no doubt about that. We kissed and then...

Nothing. I couldn't remember a damn thing after that.

OK, yeah, I'd been hotter than a furnace and ready to go. *That* I most definitely remembered. In fact, I was getting a little overheated just remembering it. But that was all I remembered. I couldn't remember anything after that kiss. In fact, the kiss itself and everything leading up to it was a little fuzzy. The more I tried to remember the details, the fuzzier they got.

There was something about his eyes. What was it? I tried to call up the memory, but it refused to come, retreating deeper into my mind.

I shook my head. No use prolonging the truth of the matter. Something weirder than usual had happened. I just wasn't sure exactly what kind of something. I wasn't even sure how far we'd gone, though I distinctly remembered being ready to go just about as far as two people can go. I just wasn't sure if we'd gone there. In fact, I couldn't even remember taking my clothes off.

Shit. Kabita was going to kill me. And when she got done killing me, I was going to kill Inigo. After I made him tell me exactly what happened between us. I'm not stupid. Satisfy your curiosity *first*, then commit murder and mayhem.

But first, I had an appointment with Cordelia. After that, I had a date with a sunwalker.

He just didn't know it yet.

Chapter Ten

I didn't even have to wait for Cordelia to buzz me into the building. The minute I hit the door, I heard the latch release. I wondered vaguely if other normal people have weird friends, or if I am just unusually blessed, thanks to my line of work.

Apparently, I also was getting used to the precarious stacks of odd objects around her apartment. I probably wouldn't have noticed the addition of a rather large collection of books on ancient Egypt if not for the fact they were topped by an enormous amethyst geode. I've always wanted one of those.

"Cool amethyst."

She grinned happily. "Why, thank you. Bastet likes it."

Of course Bastet liked it. "Um…yeah. I'm sure." Probably, she liked to scratch her back on it or something. I can't imagine cats care one way or another about crystal geodes. I know Cordy thinks Bastet is sentient and all, but truthfully, I've never seen her do anything outside the range of a normal cat, so I have my doubts.

I held my hand out until my palm was about six inches away from the crystal. I could feel the heat radiating off it, as though it were a living thing.

I caught Cordelia giving me a funny look. "You feel it."

It wasn't a question, and I didn't pretend not to know what she was talking about. "Yeah, I can feel it." I rubbed my fingers together. They were tingling a bit. "When I'm near gemstones, I can feel…" I hesitated, unsure how to explain what I could feel. "I feel heat from them. Not quite like body heat. More like…energy.

It's sort of warm and tingly. Sometimes it's warm and fuzzy, and other times it feels almost…jagged? Discordant, I guess." That sounds all kinds of dorky, but I've always been that way. As a kid, I loved hanging out in the rock shop down the street from my house. I didn't realize at the time exactly what it was that drew me, but I've since realized it was the energies radiating from all those stones.

"Of course you do. We all have our natural affinities." Cordelia led me into the living room jammed with the usual assortment of oddities. "It's your nature to attract the energy in the things around you. Since gemstones in particular help focus and channel energies, you feel their energies most strongly. And amethyst is, after all, your birth stone."

She was right about that. Spooky, since I'd never told her when my birthday is.

Bastet had draped herself over the mound of pillows on the couch. She gave me a haughty glare as I dropped into the only free chair. Seriously, that cat has issues.

Cordelia did the usual shuffle with some stacks of papers and books and what looked like a star chart before dropping into the seat across from me. Neither of us spoke as she poured us both a cup of tea from the pot that was already waiting. Sometimes silence is comforting.

The first sip of hot tea liberally spiked with milk and sugar made me sigh happily. So, it wasn't coffee, but it would do. The spicy tang of ginger and lemon hit my nose, giving me the sudden urge to bake molasses cookies.

"You're not crazy, you know."

"Huh?" Her comment came totally out of left field.

She gave me a steady look. "You know what I mean. The dreams. You've been afraid to tell anyone for fear you'll sound crazy. But I've already seen them."

"You've seen them?"

"Parts of them. They're still lurking in your mind. I can see them shifting through the surface of your consciousness."

I didn't know what to say to that, but part of me was relieved that someone else knew. Someone who didn't think I was a lunatic.

"Tell me."

It was all I needed to hear. I told Cordelia about the dreams I'd been having, about the hunt at the waterfront and what had happened with the darkness. I told her about Inigo and about how I couldn't remember what happened between us.

"I think there was something about his eyes." I frowned down at my cup. "I just...I can't remember what it was."

"His eyes?" She tucked both legs into a lotus position and leaned forward eagerly. I noticed her toenails were painted electric blue.

I shrugged. "I think I wasn't supposed to see it, whatever it was. But I did. Only...Well, now I'm starting to think it was all a dream."

Bastet strolled over and hopped up onto Cordelia's lap. The cat stared at me with those great yellow eyes of hers, unblinking. It was incredibly unnerving. Cordelia sipped her tea, deep in thought as she stroked Bastet's fur. "No, it wasn't a dream. Bastet agrees. It was very real."

I stared at Bastet, trying to see whatever it was Cordy did, but all I saw was an ordinary cat. "Why can't I remember?" I leaned forward, a little embarrassed. "I can't even remember if we... um...you know, *slept* together. I should remember that. I mean, if we did it or not." God, I was acting like a sixteen-year-old. *Idiot.* "I'm pretty sure we didn't, but not absolutely sure."

Cordelia frowned. "Well, that I can't answer. Whether you and Inigo had sex or not is not clear to me. Or to Bastet. We don't think that's the important thing." Not important? Was she nuts? "We do think that there's a reason you can't remember what you saw. We believe *that* is the important thing, what you must focus on." I doubted Bastet cared one way or the other, but I guess you never know about these things.

"And that reason would be?"

Her fingers traced a light wave pattern in front of her as though her eyes could see things mine could not. "Part of it is Inigo's energies. They are…different." She frowned for a minute, her eyes taking on a distant look. Then she continued. "It's also what I told you before, Morgan." Her voice was soft, gentle like she was trying not to scare me. "You're…changing. Something in you is waking up."

I swallowed. Hard. I really didn't like the sound of that. "What does that mean? What's changing?" I couldn't be turning to full vampire. That isn't supposed to happen. Not after three years. You either change right away or you don't. I am supposed to be immune. Then again, the blood tests they'd run had shown nothing unusual. Nothing they could use to create any sort of vaccine. No way they could replicate my supposed immunity. Maybe the doctors were wrong. I really, really do not want to have to drink blood.

She reached over and squeezed my hand. "Don't worry, Morgan. Bastet seems to think that, whatever it is, it's a good thing."

I glanced at the cat still perched on Cordelia's lap, glaring at me for all the world like I'd pissed her off six ways to Sunday. Fantastic. I felt so much better.

"So my memory loss or whatever is part of this change? What about my dreams?"

"The memory loss, possibly, yes. Along with the oddness, the otherness, of Inigo's energy and the sudden increase in your own affinity with the dark." Her fingers skimmed Bastet's fur and the cat let out a tremendous purr. "It's the dreams that particularly convince us that it's not just the vampirism taking hold. It's something else. Something more."

Something stronger than vampirism? For a minute, Jack and his sunwalker status popped into my mind, but I brushed the thought aside.

She stared out the window a bit absently. I didn't interrupt. I wanted to, but something held me back. I was sort of a jump-in-with-both-feet kind of girl. Cordelia struck me as needing a bit more processing time. Must be a cat-person thing.

"Yes, it's definitely something more. Something that hasn't been seen in this world in a very long time." Her voice had turned all singsong on me. It was a bit eerie, and that damn cat just kept glaring at me. I felt the sudden need to leave. Quickly. I just didn't have it in me to face any more truths right then.

"Great. Thanks for the help, Cordelia. It was good to just talk about it, you know? Makes me feel a little less like a crazy person." Operative term being *little*, but I didn't mention that.

Her laugh tinkled out, light and bright, as I stood to leave. "Oh, Morgan, you are many things, including crazy, but you've yet to lose your sanity."

I couldn't help but laugh at that.

As I turned to leave, Bastet hopped off Cordelia's lap and, with the arrogant grace of a goddess, strolled over and rubbed herself against my legs. It was only once, but it was the oddest feeling, as if she'd given me her blessing, a benediction of sorts.

"See!" Cordelia chirped happily. "I told you she liked you."

I'm not sure what I'd expected from the house of a sunwalker. Maybe the Bat Cave? Jack's house is definitely not the Bat Cave. It is a well-kept white Cape Cod thing with a big front porch and shutters painted forest green in what is an older, more genteel neighborhood. Not wealthy, exactly, but comfortable. The front yard is immaculate, with a neatly trimmed lawn and masses of roses perfuming the air. It is so totally Mayberry it is almost nauseating.

It even comes with its own sound track. I winced as the budding pianist inside hit a very wrong note before continuing plodding his way through what I was pretty sure was Beethoven's Ninth. Classic. I remembered it well from my own piano lesson days. No doubt I'd played it just as badly once upon a time.

The porch had a couple of very nice deck chairs, so I made myself comfortable in one of them. No point in disturbing the lesson. I'd called ahead, so I figured I'd wait it out.

It was a great afternoon for just relaxing. I leaned my head back, closed my eyes, and focused on the low drone of a nearby lawn mower and the distant sound of kids screaming and laughing at a playground. The sun was out, the breeze was light; it nearly put me to sleep.

"To what do I owe this dubious pleasure?"

I started awake to find Jack looming over me, his face impassive but his intense expression sending shivers dancing up and down my spine. The breeze kicked up a little, stirring his dark hair and wafting his scent under my nose just enough to kick my hormones into overdrive. Like they needed help.

I tried really hard to avoid staring at his crotch, which was, unfortunately, right at eye level. Damn. Too late. What was wrong with me lately? My libido was getting way out of control.

I heaved myself somewhat less than gracefully out of the chair and cleared my throat. I wasn't nervous. Honest. Just, you know, a little unprepared.

"Uh...Hey, Jack. How's it going?"

He quirked a brow at me. Damn, but I hate when people do that. Mostly, I hate that I can't do that. No matter how hard I try, I cannot get one brow to go up like that. Maybe I am genetically flawed.

"Listen, I need to talk to you about something."

He shrugged. "Fine. My student just left, and I've half an hour until the next one. Come in." He turned on his heel and strode back through the front door, letting the screen door slam behind him. Apparently, being more than nine hundred years old gives one the license to be rude.

I managed to refrain from growling and followed him into his living room. Again, totally not what I'd expected. The interior was large and light and airy, like any Cape Cod. The floors were beautifully polished maple wood, and the walls were painted a creamy, pale buttery yellow. The entire place smelled of cinnamon.

He plopped down on the chocolate chenille couch, which matched the two chairs opposite it, and stretched his jean-clad legs out in front of him. He seemed oblivious to the girly throws and pillows in robin's egg blue, chocolate, and butter yellow. I wondered who'd designed the place for him. I just couldn't visualize an ancient Templar Knight mucking about with throw pillows and designer swatches. Then again, you never know about people.

The throws might have been girly, but he certainly was not. His muscular chest under his pale-blue T-shirt was giving me heart palpations. Honestly, did he pick out his T-shirts to match his decor? And did they have to be so bloody tight? He was worse than Inigo.

His jeans were well worn and hugged his thighs just right. Don't even get me started on the other places they were hugging.

I crossed over the Persian rug in the middle of the room that was breathtaking in its beauty. It was all creams and blues with hints of reds and browns, and I had the sudden urge to take off my shoes so I could feel the fibers with my bare toes. Gorgeous, just gorgeous. And probably nearly as old as Jack himself. Not that I know anything about rugs, but it just looked way too yummy to be cheap polyester.

Add the expensive bookshelves crammed with books and the glossy grand piano in the corner, and it looked more like my rich aunt's house (if I had a rich aunt) than the lair of a Templar Knight. I mentally corrected myself. A *former* Templar Knight.

Then I saw the falchion sword hanging over the fireplace. It wasn't a replica. It was the real deal. Now, that had knight written all over it. Wonder how he explains that?

"I tell them it's a family heirloom." He'd caught me looking.

Well, if you don't want people staring at your sword, you shouldn't hang the thing over your mantelpiece.

"It's beautiful." It was. I know my swords.

His smile was a little grim. "It's deadly. You wanted to talk to me about something?"

How to broach the subject delicately? "I want to know how you were turned." When in doubt, go for the jugular. I've never been any good at subtlety.

"I was bitten." Apparently, neither was he. I gave a mental head shake.

"Yes, I figured that." My voice fairly dripped with sarcasm. "What I want to know is specifically what happened when you were turned. How exactly did it happen? And why didn't you turn vampire? Why sunwalker?"

He sighed in what sounded suspiciously like annoyance. He leaned back, crossed his arms, and started rattling it off like he was giving a report. "I don't know why sunwalker instead of vampire." He shrugged. "I was stationed in Jerusalem with my brother knights. We found evidence that there was something of value buried beneath our headquarters on the Temple Mount, so we excavated. And we found…" He hesitated.

"A cave," I prompted him, remembering the details from my dream as though I'd been there myself.

He frowned at me. "Yes, a cave."

"A cave with a smooth stone floor and dirt walls painted with some sort of mural. There was a flat stone, like a seat or an altar, in the middle of the cave and an earthenware jar next to the stone.

On the floor were two bodies, one a skeleton and the other perfectly preserved as though he'd only just fallen asleep." I stopped, my heart thudding in my chest, waiting for his response.

He made none, so I finished telling him what I'd seen. I told him everything, including the deaths of his comrades and his own attack by the priest turned ravener.

He sat there, expressionless. His voice was totally even, but I could feel the tension in him from where I sat. "How do you know?" he bit out the words.

I let out a long sigh. "So, it was real. That really happened."

"Yes. I repeat, how do you know?"

"I saw it. In a dream." In a way, it was a relief to know what I'd seen was real. In another way, it totally freaked me out. I was dreaming about people who had lived and events that had happened hundreds, even thousands, of years ago. That was not normal.

"A dream?" His voice was still completely flat, but the look in his eyes sent a shiver down my spine. It was not a very nice look.

I nodded. "I've been having dreams, seeing things, visions. I wasn't sure if I was going crazy, or if it was real. But since the dreams about you are real, maybe the other dreams are real too."

"Other dreams?" For the first time, there was an expression on his face. I just wasn't sure exactly what it meant. It was something between curiosity and expectation. I nodded slowly.

"Tell me." His voice was flinty. He leaned forward slightly, jaw tight, hands clenched. I couldn't even begin to describe the expression on his face.

I swallowed, suddenly very nervous. In front of me was the warrior who had survived countless centuries. Who had fought in battle with a bloody sword and nerves of steel, the sunwalker who quite possibly drank the blood of hunters like me. He was more than a little bit scary.

I slipped one hand under my jacket to grip the hilt of my knife, just in case. Then I told him about my dreams.

Chapter Eleven

Once I finished, I waited for Jack to comment. He didn't. He just sat there, a muscle ticking in his jaw. Mr. Silent and Deadly.

"Uh…Earth to Jack. These dreams I'm having about the priest, are they real too?" I wrapped my arms around myself, trying to ward off the chill I felt deep inside me. "Because if they are, I am so not happy about it."

His voice was low when he finally spoke. "They are."

"They are what?" I needed to hear him say it.

"They are real. Your dreams are real."

Damn. It's like trying to squeeze water out of a stone with him. "And?" I prompted.

He raked his fingers through his hair. Something I wouldn't mind doing myself. Then he got up off the couch and started pacing. I felt like I was watching a freaking tennis match, what with all the back and forth.

"Come on, Jack. Talk to me. You can't just tell me my dreams are real and then leave it." Though I was really enjoying the current view of his backside.

Whoa. Down, girl.

He finally stopped pacing and faced me. It was pretty obvious he'd caught me staring at his ass. For just a moment, amusement colored his features; then his expression turned grim. "All I can tell you is that your dreams of me are real. I was that knight in that cave. It's how I was turned. I know nothing of the priest, so I can't help you with those. I only assume if the dreams of me are real, the other ones must be too."

I was getting irritated. Hopping off the chair, I strode over and got all up in his face.

"Listen, Jack." I poked him in his chest. His incredibly broad, warm, muscled chest. Gods, I'd have loved to rip his T-shirt off and stroke that chest until...

I shook my head. *Focus, Morgan.* "Listen, I think I have a right to know." I gave him another poke for good measure.

His expression didn't change as he gently removed my finger but didn't immediately let go of my hand. Instead, his thumb traced circles over the tender skin of my inner wrist. A little thrill ran through me from the contact. Geez. What was I? Twelve?

"What do you think you need to know?"

The condescension made me want to smack him. I yanked my hand away from his. "How about raveners, for starters? Why haven't I seen any of them running around?"

"They no longer exist. Only full-blooded Atlanteans became raveners, and since there are no more full-blooded Atlanteans..."

There are no more raveners. Made sense. "OK, how about the difference between a vampire and a sunwalker? That might be useful." Yeah, I was full of snark.

He shrugged his shoulders. "The obvious. I can stand the sunlight; they can't. I eat solid food; they drink blood. I breathe air and have a heartbeat; they don't. Their driving force is feeding to the exclusion of all else. They don't feel love or hate, and they're not interested in sex, while I am interested in all those things."

I swallowed. Was it just me or had there been a slight emphasis on the word *all*? "And the similarities?"

"We're both stronger and faster than humans. We both live longer to the point of being nearly immortal, though sunwalkers usually live a great deal longer than vampires, since we can recharge from the sun and vampires need blood—blood that this day and age is too often polluted. Some of us are slightly...psychic, for lack of a better term."

"And that's it?" My voice was full of disbelief.

"I don't know anything else." Again with the deadpan expression. Liar, liar, pants on fire.

"Fine." I'd let it pass. For now. "How about telling me more about your turning? Or your life as a sunwalker?"

For a moment, I thought he'd answer me, but then he shook his head. "You need to go, Morgan. I have another student in five minutes."

If looks could kill, Jackson Keel would have been a dead man.

He shook his head slightly, and then before I could blink an eye, he swooped down and planted one on me. It started as just a little peck of a kiss, but it sent a heat wave billowing through me the likes of which I'd never experienced. Then it turned into something more.

Jack wrapped his arms around me pulling me tight against his hard body. His lips, soft and sweet, devoured mine. There was a hunger to his kiss, a need that matched my own.

My hands slid up his neck and into his hair, tangling with the silky strands. I moaned a little breathily into his mouth, and he answered with a slight growl, deepening the kiss even more. My whole body was on fire.

Then the doorbell rang.

"Dammit," Jack snarled. "You really have to leave now."

I felt a little shell-shocked. "Um…OK."

"But, Morgan…"

"Yeah?" I gazed a little dopily into his ocean-blue eyes, watching the gold flecks sparkle.

He leaned forward and gave me another hard kiss. "This isn't finished."

I frowned in confusion as I made my way back to my car. I might have been just a tad bit wobbly.

∽

My hands gripped the steering wheel until my knuckles turned white. This was all a bit surreal for me. The dreams were bad enough on their own. The fact they weren't dreams at all, but something much more like memories, only made it worse.

"Shit!" I smacked the wheel with my palms, causing the old lady in the car next to me to give me a startled look and make a sudden left turn the minute the light turned green. I almost laughed. Almost.

I had a feeling Jack was hiding something from me, something important. He knew something more than he was telling me, I was sure of it. He just wasn't admitting it.

I scowled out my windshield. It pisses me off when people hide stuff from me, especially important stuff that might help me do my job. This felt important. I had a strong feeling the priest was the key to everything; I just didn't know why.

My thoughts turned toward the kiss. Granted, it had been quite a kiss, but still, my reaction had been off the charts. It was ridiculous. How long have I been crushing on Inigo? And then this guy I barely know comes along and blows everything to hell.

Shit. Inigo.

I rubbed my forehead. Thinking about my confusion over the Jack/Inigo situation was not improving my mood, so I popped in a CD, cranked the sound system, and rolled down the window. Tom Petty's "I Won't Back Down" flowed from the speakers. I like Tom Petty. It's driving kind of music.

The wind teased at my hair, sending violet-red strands dancing around my cheeks. I love the wind. It reminds me of the night down by the river, how I gathered the night…

My brain stopped. I still hadn't figured out what I'd done that night, and I didn't want to think about it yet. I turned Tom up a little louder to drown out my thoughts.

Avoidance issues? Me?

Sometimes thinking is good. Other times, thinking makes it too hard to face reality, because frankly, sometimes reality is a just a little too bizarre for comfort. For the last three years, my reality has been one freak show after another, and overthinking things only makes my job, and my life, harder than it needs to be.

I forced my brain to refocus. Darroch. I needed to talk to Darroch. I needed to figure out why he was pretending he didn't have the amulet and why he wanted Jack dead. He was hiding something, I was sure of it, and I needed to find out what.

I needed to know why our government contact was insisting we do this job, no questions asked, because whether Kabita would admit it or not, our government liaison had something to do with all this. Yeah, there were lots of things I needed to know. Lots of people were keeping secrets these days. Brent Darroch was as good a place as any to start. Besides, it was time to give my client an update.

I smelled charcoal and cooking meat as I pulled up in front of Darroch's house. I love a good barbecue, but I was pretty sure Darroch was not going to invite me to stay. Not once I'd told him why I was there. I didn't fancy hanging out with him anyway, barbecue or no barbecue. Just thinking about him made my skin crawl.

Darroch's neighbor was out watering his lawn again. Did this guy ever do anything else? He lowered his eyebrows at me, so I smiled and gave him a cheery wave. He hitched up his saggy pants, gave me a brief nod, and went back to drowning his flowers. I was pretty sure he recognized me. Hard to miss the red hair. I was just hoping he hadn't mentioned my earlier visit to Darroch. Guess I'd find out soon enough.

I didn't bother going to the front door, just cut around to the back. Sure enough, there were Darroch and a couple of his goons surrounded by half a dozen swizzle sticks in bikinis. There were also a couple of other unsavory types puffing on cigars and swilling down imported beer by the pool. Didn't they know smoking was bad for the environment? They must not have gotten the memo.

I strode forward like I belonged there, until one of Darroch's goons caught sight of me and stepped into my path. He crossed his ridiculously muscled arms over an equally ridiculously massive chest and stood there glaring at me. His overdeveloped neck and shoulder muscles gave him an uncanny resemblance to a triceratops. It nearly made me laugh, but I figured that laughing would be bad for my health. Instead, I crossed my own arms over my chest in an equally impressive manner. It wasn't because of my muscles, obviously, but the sisters are definitely one of my best assets, and I am not above using them to my advantage. He didn't even blink. Dammit. Well, it had been worth a try.

The gods alone knew how long we'd have stood there glaring at each other if Darroch hadn't noticed. "Clive, let the pretty girl in to play. It's not nice to keep her standing there."

I couldn't help myself. "Clive? Seriously? Your name is Clive?"

Clive didn't answer. He just glared for a moment longer before slowly stepping to the side and letting me pass.

I had enough hardware on me; I could have taken him. Probably. Another look at his impassive face and rippling muscles had me second-guessing my assessment. In my experience, Clives are usually scrawny, pasty white guys, not big-ass African-American guys with enough muscle to rip a vampire's head clean off without breaking a sweat. I so did not want to get on Clive's bad side, which might be difficult, seeing as how I was about to piss off his boss.

As I moved in Darroch's direction, I glanced at his other... well, whatever he was. I wouldn't call him muscle, certainly. This one concerned me a hell of a lot more than Clive did. He was the one who should have been called Clive. Pasty white? Check. Scrawny? Check. Not to mention he was short. Really short. At least a good three or four inches shorter than my own five foot five. Not exactly goon material, but there was something about the way he held himself, the look in his eyes, that told me differently.

That's why, of the two, I knew he was the dangerous one. Clive might have been big and scary, which was good for show, but this one was no doubt completely lethal. You don't go hiring muscle unless it looks like muscle. That's the point. The only reason you'd hire a goon who doesn't look big and scary is because he is in reality the scariest one of all.

It's horribly clichéd, but I'd bet the farm the guy was an expert in several martial arts and probably had a few blades stashed about his person. I was so not looking forward to pissing Darroch off, but I really didn't see that I had a choice.

"Ms. Bailey, so nice to see you again," Darroch said as he turned one of the steaks over and the scent of sizzling meat hit my nose. Damn, I was hungry. I hoped no one could hear my stomach growl.

He was wearing a pair of baggy cargo shorts that showed off his tanning bed–fried legs and a flowery Hawaiian shirt. All he needed was a lei and a camera and he'd look like a tourist. He waved at me with the hand holding a beer bottle. "Come on over. Pull up a chair. There's plenty to go around."

I stepped a little closer. The steaks smelled like heaven, but for whatever reason, my sixth sense was going haywire. There was no way I could sit down for a meal with this man. My stomach was in knots just standing next to him.

I flipped a glance at Darroch's guests. They were studiously ignoring us, intent on their cigars and one of the swizzle sticks who'd suddenly decided taking her bikini top off was a good idea. "Listen, Mr. Darroch, I need to talk to you."

He gave me a smile just this side of smarmy. "Of course, Ms. Bailey. Shall we take it inside?"

"Sure."

"Clive, take over the steaks." He ushered me into the house while the expressionless Clive manned the grill.

The pool was just off what appeared to be the same large family room I'd spotted during my clandestine visit. I doubted it got much use as a family room. There hadn't been any sign of a wife or kids either on my first legitimate visit or later when I'd broken in. The enormous TV screen along one wall and the autographed football on the mantelpiece hinted that it had probably seen quite a few Super Bowl parties. Odd. Darroch hadn't struck me as the Super Bowl–party type. Then again, I'd never pictured him as the manning-the-barbecue-in-a-Hawaiian-flowery-shirt type, either.

"To what do I owe the pleasure, Ms. Bailey?" He was still playing jovial host with just a touch of smarm as he settled onto the black suede sectional. In case I haven't mentioned it before, I hate smarmy and I loathe fake jovial. I decided to get straight to the point.

"Listen, Darroch, I need to know why you want me to kill the sunwalker and why you lied to me about the amulet."

He didn't even flinch. Kudos to him.

"I'm afraid the reason I want the sunwalker killed is none of your business, Ms. Bailey. He's a monster, and your job is to find and kill monsters. End of story. As for accusing me of lying, well, I find that to be extremely rude." He crossed one leg over the other, took a sip of his beer, and gave me a look that was just a tad too smug for my liking.

Rude, my ass. I noticed that he'd avoided the question of the amulet.

I leaned forward. "I don't need to find the amulet, Darroch. I know you already have it. In fact, you've had it for the last twenty years. Why the charade?" I actually had no idea whether Jack had been telling the truth about that, but I decided to bluff and see where it got me.

Was it my imagination or had he actually frozen for just a second? He took another sip of beer and then carefully placed the bottle on the side table next to the couch. He leaned forward, eyes boring into mine. I resisted the urge to squirm in my seat like a kid in the principal's office. Barely.

"Ms. Bailey," he bit the words off one at a time, "I will say it once more. Your job is to find my amulet. If you can't find the amulet, then killing the sunwalker will have to suffice."

"And if I refuse?"

He leaned back and, for the first time, gave me a genuine smile. Frankly, it was a little disturbing.

"You would not like the results. Trust me on this, Ms. Bailey."

"Why? You have contacts, am I right? You can just get another agency to handle it."

The expression in his eyes was beyond cold. "Possibly, though good hunters aren't exactly easy to come by. But that is not the point."

I got it. I doubted there were many people who crossed Darroch without paying a very steep price.

"Let me get this straight. You want me to find an amulet that you already have in your possession—and which, by the way, doesn't belong to you—and you want me to kill a man who, so far as I can see, is completely harmless. You want me to murder an apparently innocent person and pretend he's just another monster. Another vampire who snacks on humans." I didn't actually know Jack wasn't a monster, not for sure. Not yet. But my gut instinct said he wasn't.

Darroch's smile grew even broader as he flashed a perfect set of pearly whites. "I am so glad you are finally grasping the situation. I was beginning to think you were a little slow."

"You do realize this is illegal. Not to mention morally unethical. My purview allows for the extermination of vampires and demons, not murdering supernaturals willy-nilly."

He shrugged. "And yet, you have no choice. You have been ordered by your own SRA to kill the sunwalker and return the amulet to me. It's part of your contract, both with the government and with me."

"The amulet you already have. Does the government know that sunwalkers are not monsters?"

He laughed. "Semantics, my dear. The government can hardly be expected to catalog every breed of creature in existence, and you can't prove he's harmless any more than you can prove that the amulet is in my possession. If the sunwalker gets killed while you are trying to find my property"—he shrugged—"then what is one to do? Just another monster dead at the hand of a talented hunter."

"You are an ass."

"Oh, no doubt."

This was going nowhere. Darroch wasn't going to hurt me. Not yet, anyway. He wanted me to do his dirty work, and he didn't want to go to the trouble of finding another hunter. Though, why he insisted on pretending I needed to find that damn amulet was beyond me.

I stood up and strode toward the front door. No way did I want to walk past Clive again. I turned and gave Darroch a measuring look. "If I say I won't do it?"

His laugh made my skin crawl. "Oh, but you will, my dear. You will kill the sunwalker or else you and your friends will suffer the consequences. Believe me, it won't be pretty."

I turned my back on him and strode down the hall and out the front door into the fresh air, taking a deep, cleansing breath. Then I froze. The priest from my dream was standing in the neighbor's yard holding a garden hose.

I closed my eyes, pinched the bridge of my nose, and counted to ten. When I looked back, the priest was gone. It was just the neighbor giving me a very odd look. I was losing my frigging mind.

I stomped down the front walk to my car. On the way to the office, I nearly blew my speakers out I cranked Tom Petty up so loud. Sometimes a girl just needs a little rock 'n' roll.

∾

"We need to talk."

Kabita just gave me a look. "Hello to you too."

I dropped into my usual chair across from her desk. It gave a slight creak in protest of my abuse. "I'm serious. This thing with Darroch is way out of line."

She narrowed her eyes at me and folded her hands neatly on the desk in front of her. "I told you. Darroch's connected. We don't have a choice."

"There are always choices." I had no idea where that piece of wisdom came from. Next I'd be channeling Yoda.

Kabita just smirked at me.

"Listen, Kabita, I know you've been ordered to take this job. No, let me get this right. *We've* been ordered to take this job, but come on. There is something really hinky about all this."

"Hinky?"

"Yes, hinky," I said stubbornly. "I talked to Darroch today."

She rolled her eyes and gave a very exasperated sigh. I have that effect on people for some odd reason. "For goodness' sake, Morgan."

"Well, somebody had to do it."

"What did he tell you?" She sounded resigned as she leaned back in her chair, folding one slender leg over the other.

"Not much," I admitted. "I told him I know he already has the amulet and that I know Jack isn't one of the monsters. He just kept insisting I find the amulet and kill Jack. He finally as much as admitted he already has the amulet in his possession and that he knows sunwalkers aren't evil, but he still insists I kill Jack. I mean, he's obsessed."

Kabita just sat there staring at me. It was her stare that told me she knew there was more and was just waiting for me to spill.

I sighed. "Then he threatened me."

"Threatened you how?"

"Well, us really. He didn't exactly give specifics, and I wasn't asking, but the phrase 'or else' did cross his lips."

"Jesus, Morgan. You've gone and done it this time." She groaned, shaking her head wearily.

"So, what do we do? Jack's no monster. I know it. He shouldn't die just because of his"—I flung my hands about searching for a word that made sense—"race. OK, OK, I know we do that with demons and vampires, but that's different. If we let them run amok, they'd exterminate the entire human race in a week. The government has never before asked us to kill a creature unless it's a danger to humans. So far, Jack hasn't proven he's a danger. And that whole amulet business? Now, that is just messed up. I simply don't understand why Darroch won't give it up. He knows that I know he has the amulet in his possession, so why this stupid charade?" I jumped up and started pacing her office.

"Why does the government care about any of it?" I wondered aloud. "OK, I get it; Darroch's got friends in high places, but still. This is obviously a personal vendetta. Not to mention I don't think Darroch wants anyone to know he's got Jack's amulet. That's it!" I stopped dead in my tracks and whirled to face a rather startled Kabita. "I've got it! It's the amulet."

She looked understandably confused. "What about the amulet?"

"It's so obvious! I can't believe I didn't see it before."

"See what?" She was starting to lose her patience, so I plopped back into the chair and leaned forward. I couldn't believe I hadn't figured it out sooner.

"Listen. Darroch has the amulet, right? There's no reason at all for him to pretend otherwise if it's really his. So, why would he lie? Because it's not his, and he doesn't want anyone to know he has it. What he does want is Jack dead. I'm not sure why, but he does."

"You're sure Jack's not a monster?" She sounded like she didn't quite believe me.

"I'm sure."

"How?"

"I feel it. I don't know why or how, I just do."

She nodded. That's the thing about Kabita. She is willing to take it on faith just because I believe it. "OK, with you so far."

"Right, so he wants Jack dead, but he doesn't want anyone to know he's already got the amulet. Maybe he doesn't want anyone *ever* knowing he has the amulet. So he's using it as an excuse to have Jack murdered without implicating himself.

"He hires us to find the amulet with the express instructions to kill the sunwalker, since he's supposedly a monster and that's our job. So, while I am innocently doing my job, trying to find my client's stolen property, I kill the apparent bad guy. Then, with Jack dead, there's no one to say who has the amulet. Darroch assures us it's all right, not our fault. We did the best we could. The government covers everything up as usual, and the amulet conveniently 'disappears,' nobody knows where. Darroch never has to worry about anyone coming to claim it or knowing he's had it all along."

Kabita thought for a moment. "All right, that makes sense, in a really twisted way. Just one question, though. Why does Darroch care whether anyone but Jack knows about the amulet?

He could have just hired us to hunt down the sunwalker and left it at that. He's certainly got the contacts to pull it off, even if sunwalkers aren't technically monsters. Money talks."

"Yeah, that's the weird thing," I admitted. "According to Jack, Darroch's had the amulet for a while, twenty years or so. Since Jack didn't exactly go to the police about it, there's no proof it was stolen, or that it ever belonged to Jack in the first place, and no real reason Darroch couldn't admit, at least to me, that he has it. What is with this amulet, anyway?"

"Maybe you should ask Jack." Kabita leaned forward and propped her chin on her hand. The chunky gold bracelets on her wrist made a slight clanking sound. The symbols I'd seen on the amulet were strangely similar to the magical symbols etched on her bracelets in ancient Sumerian. Interesting. "If anyone other than Darroch knows the answer, I'd think he would be the one."

She had a point. Problem was that Jack liked to order people around a lot, but he sure didn't like to share information very much. What the hell. It was worth a try. "I'll have to catch him later. It's a full moon tonight, and this little huntress is going to be busy."

"Need any help?"

This time it was my eyebrow that went up, or actually, both eyebrows, since I'm incapable of raising only one. "You're offering to help me with vampires?"

"Heck, no, I've got things to do. Inigo can help."

"He's got that big IT job."

She appeared unmoved. "He needs to earn his keep. Lately, he's been spending way too much time on IT and psychic plane investigations and not enough time getting his hands dirty." She busied herself shuffling stacks of papers on her desk.

I gave Kabita a thoughtful look. I might as well ask. "Is Inigo human?"

Her expression was perfectly blank. She didn't show even the slightest hint of surprise at the question. "What do you mean?" Her voice was as bland as her expression, which meant she knew exactly what I was talking about.

"Exactly what I said. Is Inigo human?"

"He's my cousin. Of course he's human."

"He doesn't have any, I don't know, fae blood or anything?"

She snagged a file off her desk and flipped it open. "He's an ordinary human who happens to have a talent for the clairvoyant. That's all. Why on earth would you ask a question like that?" I know her far too well to fall for her innocent act, but she obviously wasn't ready to share whatever it was she was hiding.

I sighed. "I don't know. It's just…Some very strange things have been happening lately when I'm around him and I thought… Well, I don't know what I thought."

Her other eyebrow went up. "What sort of strange things?"

"Nothing. Never mind." I shook my head and started for the door before a thought struck me. "Kabita, what color are Inigo's eyes?"

She gave me a look that I'm pretty sure you reserve for a crazy person. "They're blue. Why?"

"Just checking." I left before she could call the men in white coats.

Chapter Twelve

Sometimes when things are going to shit and life just gets too darn confusing, the only thing left to do is pummel the heck out some unsuspecting monster. And while I wouldn't have minded pummeling our SRA contact, whoever he was, I didn't really fancy getting arrested for assaulting a government official. Fortunately, Kabita was the one who had to deal with him, not me.

The century-old Pittock Mansion sits a thousand feet above the city up in the West Hills. The breathtaking views and its secluded location among forty-six acres of wooded land make it a popular place for teenage make-out sessions at night, when the museum is closed and all the younger schoolkids are home snug in their beds. That means it also makes a very popular dining spot among those who like to munch on unsuspecting couples. It's a great place to hunt.

You'd think the stories of kids gone missing over the years would deter the couples, but no. The edge of danger only seems to encourage them. Hormones apparently overrule common sense. Teenagers.

When I don't have a specific job or I just need to burn off some energy, I like to head up there and pose as one of those unsuspecting couples and dust a few vampires. I usually use Inigo for that kind of work. He's great at playing the fake boyfriend, but after what happened between us, whatever it was, I was sort of avoiding him. Making out with him for the sake of hunting vampires was so not on the agenda. I supposed I could call my date from the other night. He'd sure gotten all hot and bothered over the whole vampire hunter thing, but seriously, I'd rather make out with Brent Darroch.

Ew. Now I needed to go wash my brain out with soap.

I could call Jack. The thought of making out with him sent my hormones into happy-dance overload. Problem was that making out with him would be so very distracting. I'd probably end up getting sucked on by a vampire, and not in a good way.

Only one thing to do: hit the hill on my own. I could hide in the bushes like some creepy stalker and pounce the minute a vamp showed up. I really needed to blow off some steam.

And so I ended up lurking in the shrubbery around Pittock Mansion just before midnight, with the old gothic building looming like a ghostly sentinel behind me. I can't even imagine what it must have been like living here one hundred years ago when the place was first built. It had been outside the city limits then, and the roads up the hill must have been an absolute nightmare. Talk about living in the middle of nowhere.

I was feeling a bit edgy, trying to ignore the moans and rather more intimate noises coming from the couple writhing on a picnic blanket just a few feet away. Gods, I felt like such a pervert, but they'd thank me once I prevented a hungry vamp from sucking them dry. Well, probably they'd thank me, if they didn't turn me in to the cops first. That'd be fun to try to explain to Portland's finest. Then again, sex on the front lawn of a national historic site isn't exactly legal.

It didn't take long. It never does. Vampires are drawn to sex as much as they're drawn to blood, though not for the usual reasons. It's something about all the adrenaline and pheromones and whatnot. Apparently, it makes blood taste better, advertising how delicious you are. Kind of icky, if you ask me.

There were two of them, a male and a female. Not that it makes any difference once they've turned, since vamps aren't interested in sex. The only passions that remain in undeath are killing and drinking blood, and sometimes power.

They were both gaunt, as though they hadn't drunk in quite a while, and their skin was nearly translucent with age. Even their hair was scraggy and bleached almost white, which happens only when a vamp is not only very old, but dangerously malnourished. Unlike in the stories, vampires do age, just in a different way from humans. It's more like they fade, growing paler and more colorless with time.

I could feel the vamps, the pressure building at the back of my skull. Their age pressed down on me so hard I lost my balance, hitting the ground with one knee. Really old, then, more than four hundred years at least, maybe even twice that. Once they get that old, it's kind of hard to tell, but if I weren't expecting the energy spike that came with a really old vampire, it could knock me a bit off-kilter. There were two of them, which made it worse.

The male lifted his head and sniffed the air, scenting like a bloodhound. He couldn't smell me, of course. It was all part of my "gift" inherited from the virus that should have turned me but didn't. Vampires can't seem to scent me like they can normal humans.

I closed my eyes and forced back the overwhelming pressure as I slid my blade carefully from the sheath across my back. I prefer my gun, but the UV light doesn't work very well from a distance, and while swords may not be faster than bullets, they are more accurate than UV guns, and just as effective. Especially since my little baby has a blade edged in silver and anointed with a holy blessing. Not that the holy blessing does much to the vampires, but it makes me feel better. Plus, there are an extra couple of magic spells added by Kabita for strength and accuracy of the blade. Overkill? Me? Naw.

I stepped out of my hiding place just as the female vamp made her move. The moment she lunged for the couple on the ground,

I swung my sword. I was too far away to do serious damage, but the edge of the blade sliced across her midriff, spilling dark blood down her front. Not fatal for a vamp, but it would seriously hurt. She shrieked like a banshee and lunged again.

This time she went for me instead of the couple. I caught a brief glimpse of their horrified faces as they lay frozen in terror on the blanket before she was on me. I looked into her face and saw nothing but madness there. All instinct, pure rage, she jumped on me, knocking me to the ground. My breath went out of me in a whoosh, and I was pretty sure I saw stars.

Damn, she was strong. I hadn't expected that with how malnourished they were. Her eyes were that same eerie red Blondie's had been. Her bony fingers curved into claws as she went for my eyes.

"No, you fucking don't," I yelled at her. I swung my right fist up to punch her in the side of the head. She reared back with another shriek, this time more of anger than pain, and swiped fingernails along my cheek while I twisted my hips under her, trying without much success to buck her off.

A sword is pretty useless in close quarters, so I dropped it and scrabbled for my UV gun with my right hand while trying to hold her off with my left. She was strong. Really strong. Even nearly starved as she was, there was no way I could hold her off for long, and while I was focused on her, I had no idea what the male was doing.

I managed to twist my head around enough to catch a glimpse of him out of the corner of my eye. He was headed straight for the two kids. I needed to at least slow him down.

I managed to leverage myself up just enough to send my elbow straight into the female's face. She made a gurgling sound as she grabbed at her broken nose. It gave me just enough time to send one of my throwing knives hurtling across the lawn, where it lodged itself in the male vamp's thigh.

He stumbled a bit, but I didn't see whether he went down, and I didn't have time to worry about it. The female screamed and lunged at me again, her foul breath strafing my cheek, making me gag. Her fangs glistened in the moonlight as she reared back. I so did not need another set of fang marks on my throat.

The only option I had was to put her down fast so I could deal with the male—hopefully before he did too much damage to the kids. It would have been better if they'd attacked me at once. It might have been harder to fight them both, but at least I'd have known the kids were safe.

My fingers finally found my gun just as she struck. I turned my head and twisted my upper body at the same time. Her fangs hit my collarbone instead of my throat, sending sharp pain shooting down my body. I was pretty sure I screamed loud enough to wake the dead, but her bite didn't scare me. It hurt, and it pissed me off. My right hand closed around the gun and jerked it out of its holster while I grabbed her throat with my left hand and squeezed as hard as I could.

She screamed, this time a strangled, choking scream, her face filled with fury. She really didn't like me much. She surged for my throat again, and I prayed to the entire Pantheon that I could hold her off long enough.

I finally got my gun up and wedged it between our bodies, the barrel pointed against her chest as close to the heart as I could get, and pulled the trigger. She froze, her eyes going wide, suddenly realizing through the rage and bloodlust that something was very, very wrong. She stared down at my gun barrel pressed against her breast and the black mark slowly spreading its way across her body. She threw her head back and shrieked at the moon. This time, there was an edge of fear to it.

Then she burst into a cloud of ash and smoke.

I think I might have been shaking a little as I slid the gun back into its holster and wiped the ash from my face. The UV had done its work. She'd been relatively easy, as old and weak as she was, but I still had the male vamp to deal with, and he was another matter.

While I'd been fighting off the female vamp, the male had grabbed the couple. The girl was on her knees, sobbing, with the vampire's fangs sunk into her throat, blood dripping down her pale skin. One move and he could snap her neck. If he didn't drain her first.

The vamp had the boy by the hair, the kid's neck twisted at an odd angle so he couldn't move very well. The poor kid was terrified, but he was still doing his damnedest to struggle against the vamp. Not that it mattered. The boy wasn't even close to strong enough.

The vamp smiled at me as he lifted his face from the girl's throat. He gave the boy a little shake. Their whimpers brought a twisted smile to his eyes. *Shit.* He was some kind of sadistic psycho. That was why the vamps hadn't attacked me together, and why he hadn't killed the kids while I was busy with the other vamp. He wanted me to watch while he killed them. Worse, despite his age and malnutrition, he was strong enough to control two people at once. This was going to get ugly.

The vamp tossed the girl to the ground. She hit with a thump and didn't move. I had no idea whether she was dead or not, but things weren't looking good. By now the boy was sobbing uncontrollably.

I snatched up my sword and staggered to my feet. There was no way I would make it in time. The vamp used the boy's hair to yank his head back, baring his throat. I was running by the time he reared for the strike. Too late, too late, too late.

I rushed toward them as the vamp's fangs sank into the boy's throat, praying for a miracle to every god I could think of and a few I was pretty sure weren't even gods. I raised my sword, but before I could bring down the blade, he moved. He was so fast my eyes couldn't track him, but I sure felt the punch to my stomach.

With a grunt, I went tumbling backward, sword spinning off into the bushes somewhere.

I lay in the grass staring up at the stars, mouth gasping for air. Finally, the breath came wheezing back into my lungs, but before I could move, the vamp was on me.

He grabbed me by the hair and hoisted me off the ground so fast it made me light-headed. Pain shot through my scalp as he gave me a good hard jerk. I kicked out, connecting with something solid. He staggered but didn't go down.

Dark blood dripped from the corners of his mouth, ringed his lips, and soaked his clothing. I glanced over his shoulder to the boy now lying still on the blanket next to his date. *Shit.*

I gave another good hard kick with one foot while trying to pry his fingers out of my hair. Instead of dislodging him, I pissed him off. This time when he tossed me, though, I landed in some azaleas. The little bushes were crushed under my weight. The gardener was going to be pissed.

Before I could stagger to my feet, the vamp was on me again. Twigs snapped underneath me. I was lucky it wasn't my bones. Yet.

He jerked my head back, baring my throat. I struggled, but he had me held so tightly I couldn't move an inch.

My mother always says I am a stubborn one, and she isn't wrong. With a little flick of the wrist, the knife in my left wrist sheath slid smoothly into my hand. There wasn't much of the vamp I could reach, but the knife was extremely sharp and the femoral artery was just a hairsbreadth from my hand.

I plunged the knife in deep. Warm, sticky blood flowed over my hand, soaking my sleeve. The vamp's grip loosened enough so I could break his hold.

And then the vamp was flying through the air. I stumbled to a halt, my mind whirling. *What the...?* I blinked and Jack was standing over me. My brain finally caught up with what my eyes had seen: Jack appearing out of nowhere, ripping the vampire away from me, and literally throwing him across the lawn.

The vamp staggered to his feet, shook his head, and let out a primal scream. Damn, but he was pissed. He flew at Jack, but Jack didn't even bat an eyelash. He just stepped in front of me and waited. But despite having just had my ass handed to me, I staggered to my feet and pulled out a second blade: my handy little silver-edged dagger. This was my kill, dammit.

The vamp leaped into the air, but this time I was there first.

The darkness swirled inside me as I moved in a blur, stepping in front of Jack as the vamp flew through the air toward us and plunging my dagger right up through the vampire's heart. He had only a second to realize what had happened before he too burst into ash. Gotta love the twin wonders of gravity and momentum. Physics is a beautiful thing.

I stood there for a moment, just trying to catch my breath. I touched my throat and met smooth skin. The vamp hadn't had a chance to bite me. I turned to face Jack and froze at the look on his face.

Hunger. Pure, unadulterated hunger. Not bloodlust. I'd seen that on way too many faces to mistake what I was seeing for simple bloodlust. Jack wanted me. Wanted me badly. Not my blood, but my body. I sucked in a breath as my heart started hammering in my throat.

Jack moved to the young couple, who lay still on their picnic blanket. He knelt down, feeling for their pulses. "They're alive."

"How alive?"

"The boy is fine. He's got a nasty bite, but he didn't lose much blood. He'll make it. The girl…Her pulse is a little thready, but she'll survive with proper medical treatment." Which meant they wouldn't turn.

"Good. Let me give Kabita a call." She would arrange for medical attention for the physical injuries and a little special attention for their memories. Theoretically speaking, quantum energy manipulation won't affect memory, but there are other ways involving hypnosis and neurolinguistic programming. All the kids would know is that wild animals or gang members or something had attacked them. No doubt they'd never use Pittock Mansion as a make-out spot again.

After sticking bandages from my hunting kit on the kids' wounds, Jack stood up. "There's nothing more we can do for them. They'll be fine until help arrives." His voice was deep and rough and made things down low tighten with arousal.

Well, wasn't this just a nice turn of events?

I glanced down at their pale faces. So impossibly young. I was glad they'd be OK and that they'd wake up with no memory of what had really happened. They didn't need to remember this.

Jack never even looked in their direction. He stalked toward me, slowly, a predator hypnotizing his prey. Except this prey wasn't scared, and she wasn't even close to hypnotized. OK, maybe a little hypnotized.

I stood my ground and looked him full in the eye. Probably stupid, but what can I say? My libido was running out of control, and I no longer cared what sort of weird magic mojo sunwalker powers he had.

"Jack." My voice was embarrassingly breathy. "Why are you here?"

He flashed me a smile. "I heard you." His voice was rough and oh so sexy.

"Heard me? What do you mean, heard me?"

"In my head. You were in trouble. You called me. I came."

He was closer now. Close enough to touch. "I didn't call you." I'd barely had time to think. There certainly hadn't been time to pull out my cell phone and have a chat with my friendly neighborhood sunwalker. "Wait, what did you say? You heard me in your head?"

"On the psychic plane."

"But I'm not psychic. I couldn't have—"

"Enough talk," he snapped, his ocean eyes swimming with hunger and deeper, darker things. He grabbed me around the waist and hauled me up against him so tight I could feel the hard length of him pressing against my belly.

So I stopped talking and did what any sensible woman would do in my situation: I kissed him.

It was like falling into a deep, warm well. He tasted like chocolate, and sunshine, and sex, and his lips and tongue were soft as velvet. Somebody made a little moaning sound, and I wasn't sure whether it was him or me.

I wrapped my arms around his neck and buried my hands in his silky hair. His hands were on my backside, pulling me in tight against him so I could feel every solid bit of him. He was happy. Oh, man, was he happy. I rubbed myself right up against him and couldn't help but grin a little at Jack's growl.

He dipped his head and started kissing my collarbone, then nibbling the tender skin up along the side of my neck and behind my ear. It was unbelievably erotic, and I swear I'd have purred if it were humanly possible. I was completely lost in the sensation of his mouth and his tongue and his touch.

And then, all of a sudden, Jack went still. He froze; then he lifted his head, and as our eyes met, I realized the hunger was gone. Instead, he wore a look of horror. "Jack? Jack, what's wrong?" His hands dropped limply from my backside, and he slid through my arms to the ground.

That was when I saw the dagger sticking out of the left side of his back, angled toward his heart, and Kabita standing behind him, a look of determination on her face.

"What the fuck did you do?" I meant to yell, but it came out a lot quieter than that. Shock must have paralyzed my vocal cords or something.

This couldn't be happening. Jack couldn't be dead. I dropped to my knees, my hands on his face, at his throat. Does a sunwalker have a pulse? I couldn't feel a pulse. Shit, I couldn't feel a pulse.

"Morgan," Kabita's voice snapped me out of the haze, "we were *hired* to execute him. He was about to kill you."

"He wasn't killing me; he was *kissing* me, you idiot." A sob caught at the back of my throat, but I stuffed it down. I grabbed the hilt of the knife. You're not supposed to pull out objects when people get impaled, but Jack wasn't human. Jack was…something else.

I yanked the dagger out of his back. Nothing. "Jack? Jack?" Nothing.

His blood pooled beneath him, shimmering black in the moonlight. The thick, coppery scent hit my nose and sent my stomach heaving. I tried to stop the bleeding, but there was too much of it.

I didn't care that we'd been hired to kill him. Killing him had long since ceased to be an option. Apparently, Kabita hadn't gotten the message. And I was evidently in a lot more shock than I realized.

I felt Kabita tug at me, trying to pull me away from his body, but I didn't budge. I just held on tighter to the shell that had once been Jack. He'd lived for more than nine hundred years, and tonight, I'd gotten him killed.

Chapter Thirteen

I wasn't sure how long I sat there with Jack's blood seeping into my shirt from where I'd cradled him, but after a while, I started noticing things. Kabita was talking quietly to someone on the phone, her voice a low murmur against the other night noises that had finally returned. My butt ached from the cold ground, but my chest was warm, almost hot, from the blood. Jack's blood.

I pressed my cheek against the top of his head, feeling the silk of his hair tickle my chin. I honestly didn't know what to feel. One minute we'd been kissing and the next he was dead. I'm used to death. Heck, I'm usually the one dealing it, but this was just a little too much. Jack wasn't a monster; he was…he was alive and he was good. Well, maybe he wasn't good, but I'd never know for sure, because now he was dead. Gone just like that. I couldn't wrap my head around the fact of someone I cared about being dead in my arms.

Kabita put a tentative hand on my shoulder. "Morgan?"

"How could you do it?" My voice felt stuck in my chest. I sounded broken, not angry. "How could you kill him? You knew he wasn't one of the monsters. I told you. He wasn't hurting me."

She sighed. "I'm sorry, but he was biting your neck. What was I supposed to think?"

I shook my head a little. "He wasn't biting me. One of the vamps we dusted bit me. He was just…we were just…necking." It sounded so ridiculous.

"You barely knew him." My vision was kind of watery, but I was pretty sure she looked exasperated. Frankly, I didn't give a damn if she thought I was an idiot. Probably, in my saner moments, I'd think I was an idiot too. Sanity seemed a rare commodity lately, especially where Jack was concerned.

I brushed a lock of hair back from Jack's eyes. Pupils dilated and fixed. They are always saying that on those crime scene shows. I used to love those shows before my life changed three years ago. Now they seemed rather trite. People killing each other over stupid shit like money and revenge when there are real monsters out there.

Definitely dead. I struggled to hold back what felt suspiciously like a sob as I pressed my lips against his forehead; then I laid him gently back on the ground before closing his eyes.

They used to say the soul escapes to heaven through the eyes when a person dies. I wondered whether Jack had a soul to escape. I couldn't imagine him sitting around strumming a harp on a cloud somewhere, but I hoped his soul was at peace anyway. I just didn't know what I was going to do now that he was gone. I couldn't believe he was really and truly dead. There were still too many questions left unanswered.

Something niggled at the back of my mind. Something not quite right.

"Kabita, Jack didn't dust."

She shrugged. "Probably has something to do with the whole sunwalker thing. Maybe they don't dust like normal vamps. Don't worry about it. I called Inigo. He'll help."

With the body. She didn't say it, but I knew she meant he'd help us get rid of the body. Couldn't very well have the cops around asking questions. They aren't exactly in on the whole supernatural secret, and the feds like it that way. Having to explain why my best friend had just stabbed someone was not something any of us wanted to do.

I was still a bit stunned. I couldn't quite wrap my head around what had just happened. My mind was also going off on tangents, which meant I was probably going to cry myself to sleep later and then not eat for days on end. That's what I'd done when my ex dumped me. That's how I deal with grief, which is kind of weird, because I barely knew Jack.

Kabita was pulling me away from Jack's body, whispering words that weren't quite making sense. Either I was in worse shape than I thought or it was a spell.

"Don't you pull that voodoo shit with me," I snapped at her. Anger surged up to take the place of whatever fugue state I'd entered for those few minutes.

"It's not voodoo, and you know it," she snapped right back. "It's just a spell to make you feel better."

"I don't care what it is; I don't *want* to feel better." Gods, I was being such a child. I knew very well the difference between vodun and witchcraft; I just wanted to piss Kabita off. Nothing pisses off a witch more than calling her spells voodoo. I was actually OK with pissing Kabita off right then.

She sighed, and there was a lot of sadness behind it. "I'm sorry, Morgan. I'm really sorry. I honestly thought he was going to kill you. If I'd realized…I'm sorry." Moonlight turned her into shadow, but I felt her sorrow just the same. Sorrow for me, not for Jack.

I closed my eyes. Woulda, shoulda, coulda. "Yeah, I know." I pulled my arm out of her grasp and knelt back down on the grass next to Jack's body. The moonlight shimmered on his skin and turned his hair black. I ran my fingers through the heavy silkiness of it, cool in the night air. I leaned down to press my lips against his one last time, and his eyes flew open.

I nearly had a heart attack.

His mouth moved like he was trying to talk, and then his body arched off the ground as he drew in a gasping breath, lungs heaving. Coughs racked his body.

"Jack? Jack!" It was like his body was relearning to breathe. I grabbed him and rolled him on his side in the recovery position. Hooray for first aid training.

He'd been dead. I'd seen him die. I'd bloody well held him in my arms while he died. Kabita had driven a dagger through his heart, for fuck's sake. Nobody comes back from that, not even a vampire. Hell, they'd have dusted.

I used one hand to keep him still in the recovery position while I pulled out one of my knives and sliced open his shirt so I could see his back. Where there should have been a gaping hole was smooth, flawless skin marred only by a rough coat of dried blood. He grunted a little as I ran my fingers over the warm silk of his back. He was perfect. Not even a scar to show where the stake had gone in. We were both still covered in blood; there'd been a lot of it, but no marks.

As his breathing eased, I helped him sit up, using my body to brace him. Kabita was staring at both of us with her mouth hanging open. I couldn't blame her.

I brushed his hair out of his face and stared into his eyes. He stared back. Neither of us said a word, but I knew he was back. He'd been dead a minute ago, his soul, spirit, whatever, gone. I didn't doubt that for a second.

"Jack, what the hell just happened?" My voice was a little husky.

"I died."

"No shit. But you are very much alive now."

"Yes."

I glared at him. Honestly, the man needed a good smack upside the head. "Now would be a really good time to explain."

He sighed and winced a little.

I frowned. "Do you still hurt?"

"A little. It will pass." He gave me one of those brave smiles that men give you when they're badly hurt but trying to be all macho. Men are so weird. They get a paper cut and act like they're dying, but a true injury and they try to play the hero.

"Uh-huh. I'm sure. I still want an explanation." I almost didn't care, I was so glad he was alive, but the hunter in me needed to know.

"My fate is tied to the amulet. I am its keeper, its guardian, and I will remain so until the true owner of the amulet is found."

I am used to the mystical and the strange in my life, but this was a whole new level of weird. "This has to do with that stupid amulet? What do you mean, 'true owner'?"

"It's a long story." He shook his head. He pulled out of my arms and staggered to his feet. He swayed a moment, then gathered himself together. He stretched a little, testing his skin and muscles as though to make sure they still held.

I sighed. He obviously wasn't ready to share, but I was beyond tired of secrets and half-truths. Eventually, I was going to find away to make him tell me everything. "I'll take you home."

He shook his head. "I'm fine. I'll see you later, Morgan." He started down the hill, but he was moving pretty slowly compared to earlier. Before he'd taken more than half a dozen steps, he collapsed.

I started to move toward him, but he managed to haul himself to his feet and continue across the grass. It wasn't long before he was on his ass again. Jack wasn't going anywhere without help.

I strode across the lawn and leaned over to help him up. "Yeah, Mr. Badass, it's obvious you're fine. I'm giving you a ride home and that's the end of it."

He muttered something that was clearly a rude word and allowed me to help him to his feet. "All right," he acceded. "But that doesn't mean I'm going to let you grill me."

I smiled. "Wanna bet?"

ᔕ

If Inigo was disappointed that he had no body to clean up, he didn't show it. Though I did get the distinct feeling he didn't like Jack much. Oh, sure, he did his usual jovial thing, but there was a dark look in his eyes that I couldn't quite put my finger on.

Jack didn't have a car despite Pittock Mansion being several miles from his house. I imagined the speed with which he'd gotten there had something to do with his sunwalker skill set.

I helped Jack into my car, against his rather loud protestations he could do it himself. Probably, he could, but the last thing I wanted was for him to give himself a concussion getting into the Mustang. There were some things I really wanted to get straight with old Jack. Of course, I would have also liked very much to go home to a hot shower and a change of clothes, but that could wait.

I gave Jack a sidelong look. His face had an eerie greenish glow from the dashboard lights. I figured I'd ease into things. "So…" I prodded. He didn't respond. "So, you can't die, huh?"

"No."

"At all?"

He threw me a look. "I am the guardian of the Heart. I am truly immortal. Unlike a vampire, I cannot die, even if you take my head. As long as the amulet exists, so do I."

"So, what, if I chop your head off, I'll just have this talking head to stick on my shelf?"

He shrugged. "More like my old body would die and my head would grow itself a new one."

"Seriously? Like a worm?"

"Pretty much."

I wasn't sure if that was gross or cool. Maybe a little of both. "Has it happened to you before?" I was trying to imagine his decapitated head growing a new body. The image was icking me out just a little.

"No." He didn't elaborate.

"OK, then how do you know that's what'll happen?"

"The Heart showed me," he said.

"Heart?"

He sat in stubborn silence. It was like pulling teeth.

"Listen, Jack, there is some major shit happening here, and I think I deserve to know about it. In case you forgot, I've been hired to kill you, so I'd kinda like to know what exactly I'm supposed to tell my client."

"Tell Brent Darroch to go to hell," he said mildly.

I glared at him a second before turning my eyes back to the dark road in front of me. "Yeah, right. That would go down real well. 'Excuse me, Mr. Darroch, but I just found that Jack the sunwalker can't really die. Not as long as the amulet you stole from him exists. So would you please fuck off?'"

I was pretty sure I saw his lips twitch. I didn't think it was an actual smile, but it was close. "Not quite what I had in mind, but it works."

I smacked myself in the forehead, which was kind of hard to do while driving. "You're an idiot."

"I've been called worse."

"Anyway, I already told him I know he's got the amulet."

"What did you do that for?" He sounded irritated.

I shrugged. "It seemed like the thing to do at the time."

He shot me a look.

"Fine, I misjudged him. I thought if I got a bit confrontational, told him I knew the truth, he'd—"

"What? Confess?"

"Something like that, yeah."

I am no lady, but Jack's language made even me blush. He eventually ran out of English cuss words and switched to what sounded like French.

I pulled up in front of his house. Thank goodness it was still dark. I wouldn't want to frighten Jack's upper-middle-class neighbors with my less-than-stellar appearance. "There you are.

Front-door service, sir." My voice sounded a little overbright, even to me.

"Do you mind helping me in? I still feel a bit...delicate."

Delicate? Jack? "Uh...sure."

I hopped out and ran around the side to help him out of the car. He was right. He was definitely a bit wobbly still and nearly brought me down right there on the pavement. Even with my extra strength, I could barely hold him up. "Sheesh, Jack," I said, panting, "you weigh a ton."

"Sorry." He didn't sound particularly sorry.

Between us, we managed to stagger to his front door and get him inside the house. He sagged down on the sofa. He needed a shower; heck, I needed a shower, but there was no way in hell I was going to get him up the stairs.

"Don't worry, there's a shower in the downstairs bathroom."

"What? You're reading my mind now?"

This time he did grin. "You're thinking too hard."

I scowled at him. "There is no way in hell I'm getting naked with you, Jack."

His grin widened. "Well, now, that's a pity. But I think I can manage to shower on my own."

Yeah, right. The guy could barely stand, let alone do anything as strenuous as taking a shower. I fiddled with my key ring. "We still need to talk."

He hesitated. "You won't let this go, will you?"

He wasn't wrong about that. "No. I won't." I glanced down at my filthy clothes. "I'd like a shower myself. Not to mention I think these clothes need to be burned."

"Just wash them with some hydrogen peroxide. The blood will come out."

I stared at him. *Who is he? Jackie Homemaker?* "Sure. I'll get right on that."

"You can use the upstairs shower. It's in my bedroom. You'll find some sweats and T-shirts in the closet, and there are some garbage bags under the sink in the kitchen for the bloody clothes."

I nodded. There was no way I was leaving his house until I had answers.

So, after I helped Jack into the bathroom for his shower and grabbed a plastic bag from under the sink, I headed upstairs to Jack's room. His bedroom was what you'd expect from a guy. An enormous California king graced the middle of the room with matching nightstands on either side. The bedside lamps were sleek chrome things. It was all very modern and minimalist and masculine. Not my taste, but it sort of suited him. More so than the living room.

His closet, however, was pretty much a girl's wet dream. Calling it a walk-in doesn't do it justice. It was huge, nearly as large as my entire bedroom. There were cubbyholes and shelves and hanging racks on every wall, crammed with more suits and shoes and ties and whatnot than I'd seen outside a clothing store.

There were four sets of bureaus standing back-to-back in the middle of the room. I pulled open one of the drawers. Socks. All black. Who in the world has an entire drawer of nothing but black socks?

The next drawer had white socks. Below that, boxer briefs in an assortment of colors. Now, *that* is what I like to see in a man's drawers. No pun intended.

A few more drawers and I found T-shirts and sweatpants. I picked out a pair of black sweats and a green T-shirt with a peace sign on the front. Jack hadn't struck me as a peace sign kind of guy. I guess you just never know about people.

The bathroom was even better than the closet, if that were possible. It looked like he'd knocked a couple of smaller bedrooms together and converted them into something even the ancient

Romans would have drooled over. I was pretty sure you could have fit an entire football team in the bathtub alone.

I'd have loved to try out that bathtub, but a shower would have to do. Not that his shower was anything to sneeze at. It was enormous and tiled in what looked like Italian marble or something equally expensive and a pain in the ass to clean. There were knobs and jets and things everywhere. I swear it took me twenty minutes just to figure out how to turn the thing on.

The therapeutic effects of a hot shower are highly underrated. The clothes left a lot to be desired, but at least they were clean. Jack's sweats required several rolls so as to avoid breaking a leg, and his T-shirt made me look like a five-year-old dressing up in Dad's clothes. Even worse, I was sans makeup and Jack didn't appear to own a hair dryer, so my hair was all wet and slicked back. Not an attractive look.

I was pretty sure Jack didn't mind. If I hadn't caught the look in his eye when I rejoined him in the living room, I wouldn't have thought he noticed. It was the barest flicker of heat, but it was there. Then he did the blank thing again.

Of course, it might have been because I was braless. But only because mine had been ruined and it wasn't something Jack had hanging around in his closet.

His eyes flicked to my chest as I curled up in the arm-chair across from him. Yeah, it was definitely the braless thing. There is no way on earth a woman with D cups can possibly go around braless without someone noticing. Particularly a male someone.

"OK, Jack. Let's talk."

He gave me a long look. "What do you want to know?" His tone told me that just because I asked didn't mean he was going to tell.

"Tell me about the amulet."

He leaned back, wincing a little as his newly healed muscles contracted. "Your dreams, the ones you've been having about the priest? I'm familiar with them."

I nodded, urging him to continue. "You've had them too?"

"It's the amulet's way of communicating with its guardian. It sends me dreams, mostly. And the ones about the priest are the first ones I had." He paused for a moment. "You can't tell anyone about my connection to the amulet."

"Why? Why would anyone care?"

"Trust me, there are people who would care. Powerful people. People like Brent Darroch." His voice was cold and hard. There was definitely some history there.

"All right, fine. I won't tell. Continue the story." I'd promise just about anything if he'd tell me the truth.

"The details are sketchy, but it appears that there really was a city of Atlantis that was destroyed thousands of years ago. From what I've seen in the visions, there was a sickness they brought with them from"—he frowned before continuing—"their homeland. I'm not sure exactly where this homeland was, but the sickness was part of what drove them out. They left in order to escape it. They thought they'd cured it, but there was a new outbreak. It made them crazy, bloodthirsty."

I nodded. I'd known that much. I even suspected where, or what, this homeland was. I decided to see how much he knew. "It's pretty clear from my dream that the homeland had actually been another planet."

"Yes," Jack admitted. "I saw that as well."

"And it wasn't just the sickness that drove them out, but a dying sun." An ancient race from a dying world? It was the stuff of legends. "But they weren't vampires?"

He shook his head. "No. They weren't human, I don't think, but they weren't vampires, either. Or sunwalkers. I think the sickness had a similar effect to vampirism, but not entirely. Believe it or not, these raveners, as they called them, were far more vicious than any vampire. It seems that, when they attacked humans, the disease mutated and the human survivors became the first vampires, or nightwalkers, as they were called back then."

"Shit." My dream was starting to make a lot of sense now.

He smiled a little at that. "Before all this happened, humans and the people of Atlantis had already begun intermarrying. There were many people who were of mixed blood, and they alone were immune."

"How is that possible?"

"No idea. But something about the mix of human and Atlantean genetics was resistant to the disease. The last high priest discovered this and decided to use it to his advantage to save what he called the Treasure of Atlantis. So he created the Heart."

"The amulet," I said.

"Yes. His original plan was to entrust the Heart to his son, who was half human and a trained warrior, and therefore immune to both vampirism and the ravening disease. Unfortunately..."

"They got trapped in the cave and he ate his son for lunch. Figuratively speaking, of course," I finished for him.

Jack just gave me a dirty look. Can I help it if I have a sick sense of humor?

"Something like that, yes. From what I can tell, though, he had a backup plan. Anyone bearing the genetic code of one of his son Varan's elite squad of half-human warriors who came into contact with the Heart would become its next guardian. I was that person."

"So why not Varan? Why didn't he rise as a sunwalker and become the guardian?"

Jack shrugged. "I'm not entirely sure, but from what I can tell in my dreams, his injuries were too severe. Maybe if he hadn't been trapped with the ravener priest, he might have survived. I don't know. Also, I'm not sure he would have turned sunwalker anyway. That seems to have been something that happened later in history."

"You are a descendant of one of Varan's warriors?"

"So it seems."

"But how did you manage not to turn into a vampire when the priest attacked you? Or were you immune?" Good thing I was starting to get used to being confused.

"The priest carried the original strain of the ravener disease, not the mutated human form. The human form is vampirism, but the original strain is something else. That's part of it, I imagine, but the biggest part is that humans who carry Atlantean DNA are still partially immune to the disease that creates vampires. If we are bitten, we don't turn into vampires. We become sunwalkers."

I blinked. So he did know why he hadn't turned vampire. I really hate when people hide stuff from me. "It doesn't make sense. I'm getting the dreams too. How is that possible?"

"That's most likely because you also carry Atlantean DNA. The Heart recognizes you as one of its own. You could even be a descendant of one of Varan's original warriors, just as I am."

I was starting to get a really funny feeling about all this. "Jack, I was attacked three years ago by a vampire. I actually died, but they brought me back. I certainly didn't become a vampire." My heart thudded in my chest so hard it hurt. "I just got stronger, faster. And...um...I can sense vampires when they're near. Their age, that sort of thing." Damn, I sounded like a freak.

"That's because, Morgan Bailey, I believe you became a sunwalker."

Chapter Fourteen

"That's just crazy." *There is no way I am a sunwalker.* "I'd have known by now if I was one. Wouldn't I?"

Jack laughed. "What do you think sunwalkers are, Morgan?"

"Well, I don't know. You won't bloody tell me anything!" I winced at the distinct whine in my voice.

That really set him off. By the time he was finished laughing he was holding his side in obvious pain. Good. He deserved a little pain. I glowered at him.

"Oh, Morgan, you are such a miracle."

I didn't know what on earth he meant by that, so I just glared at him some more. Honestly, the man was getting on my very last nerve.

He managed to pull himself together. "Let's see, the signs of being a sunwalker: faster, stronger, quick healer, almost immortal. Getting warm?"

"I'm not immortal. I'm not even almost immortal."

"How do you know?"

He had me there. "Well, I have no interest in drinking blood."

"I told you, we don't drink blood, Morgan."

"Then what are the fangs for?"

He ran his tongue over his canines. "These aren't fangs. I was born this way."

"What?" I wasn't sure it was possible to be more confused, but I was.

"Morgan, some people are just born with longer canine teeth. It's genetics. Like yours."

"Mine aren't long!"

"Nope, but they're sharp." His smile was just a little too smug, but he had a point.

"So, no blood drinking? Then why were you nibbling on my neck?" I still didn't believe I was a sunwalker, but I felt some relief at knowing that if I were, I wouldn't be slurping down the red stuff anytime soon.

"Because you're tasty, that's why." His voice held just that edge of a growl that told me he had *really* liked sucking on my neck. Oh, boy. I licked my lips.

"Come here." His voice was rough around the edges.

"Why?" I was pretty sure I knew why, but I wasn't going to make it that easy for him.

"Come here." Rougher now.

I got up. Jack's body radiated heat as I curled up next to him. He wrapped a solid arm around me and pulled me in for a kiss. Hot and wet and completely erotic. It was a good thing I was sitting down.

Fortunately for my sanity, my phone rang right then.

"Leave it," Jack ordered.

I ignored him. "It's probably Kabita. I need to take this." I really needed to get my head together. Kabita checking up on me was just the opportunity I needed. By the time I got off the phone, I pretty much had my hormones under control, but I figured a quick subject change wouldn't hurt.

"The blood thing?" I prodded, scooting away from him just a little. I needed some space.

"We don't need to drink blood to survive," Jack continued, though there was an edge of what sounded like frustration in his voice. "We get our energy from the sun, not from blood. I need so much sunlight every day or I grow weak. The sun is as necessary to me as it is dangerous to vampires. That's why we're called sunwalkers."

"So you moved to Portland? How's that working out for you?" Portland isn't exactly known for being the land of eternal sun.

He grinned as he reached over and tangled his fingers in my hair. "These days, I use a sun lamp when there's not enough natural sunlight. Makes my life a lot easier."

"If I really am a sunwalker, does that mean I'll need more sun?" I wasn't exactly a sun worshipper, so the thought didn't thrill me.

"I would assume so, yes. Though you appear to be doing fine."

That was a relief. "OK, so no blood, but you need sunlight. What else?"

He cuddled me a bit tighter against his side. I didn't want to admit it, but it felt good. Really good. "As you noticed, I'm faster and stronger than any human and most vampires."

Yeah, I got that. "But I'm not that strong. I'm stronger than humans, sure, but not as strong as a vampire." Not strictly true. I was as strong as a new vampire and even many older ones, but not nearly as strong or fast as a truly ancient one, and definitely not like Jack. It was my extra senses and being able to keep a reasonably cool head that gave me the advantage in a fight against an old one. Being able to sense vamps before they can sense you can give a girl a real edge.

"Of course not. Just like with humans and vampires, male sunwalkers are generally stronger than females. Besides which, I was a Templar Knight, a trained warrior, not to mention a few years older than you," Jack pointed out.

I snorted at that. "But you're also immortal. That's tied to the amulet. You said so yourself."

He shrugged. "That's sort of true. I am immortal because of the amulet, but sunwalkers, while not truly immortal, are very long-lived. We don't age like humans, and we heal very fast, even from most mortal wounds."

I heal fast. Very fast. "I'm not immortal," I whispered.

"You're not listening, Morgan. Sunwalkers aren't immortal; they just live a long time."

"How long?"

"The oldest I know of personally lived to be over two thousand years old." He acted like we were talking about the weather.

Shit. Shit, shit, shit, I am not a sunwalker. I can't be! "I am not going to live to be thousands of years old. Am I?"

Jack shook his head. "I don't know, Morgan. I wish I did, but you aren't like any other sunwalker I've ever met. You're different somehow. I've never seen a sunwalker who draws power from darkness. I've never met one who can sense vampires. I honestly don't know if you will live a long time or not. None of us do. There were some of us who lived only a little longer than a normal life span and even some who died young, murdered or killed in battle. We've no idea how long we have any more than anyone else does."

Well, that's something, anyway. I could still be a normal human when it comes to living. Or dying, as the case may be. Odd that the idea of living such a long time freaks me out.

I shifted against him, settling more comfortably, and bit my lower lip as I mulled things over. I knew I couldn't ignore this whole sunwalker thing, but I needed some time to myself to really consider the ramifications.

"So," I asked, "what happened to the rest of them? The sunwalkers? You made it sound like there used to be a lot of you."

He was quiet for a moment, the expression on his face one of deep sorrow. "Remember the tales of how the Templar Knights found something hidden under the Temple Mount? How what they found made them suddenly the most powerful force on the earth, more powerful than kings or even the Church?"

I nodded as he got up off the couch and started doing the pacing thing. "Sure. Some have said they found proof that Jesus was married and had kids, or that the Church lied about some of its doctrines or something." I can't count the number of books that have been written on the subject.

"It wasn't any of that." He smiled grimly, a faraway look in his eyes. "The only things we found under the Temple Mount were an undead priest and the amulet."

"So how did that give the Templars such power?"

"The amulet provides its guardian not only with the knowledge needed to survive and protect the amulet but also the ability to thrive. I don't know how they did it. Some kind of technology that is able to record and interpret what's going on in the world. I don't know. But when I changed, the amulet provided me the information I needed to become rich and powerful enough to protect it. Where to find ancient lost riches, whom to trust, where to invest. I passed that knowledge to my brother knights."

A lightbulb went on. "Knowledge you used to further the power and wealth of the Templars."

He nodded. "Yes. Sometimes the amulet even led me to other descendants of Varan's original warriors so that, when they were mortally injured in battle, I could turn them, with their permission, of course. You can imagine how powerful a fighting force a few dozen sunwalkers would have been during the Crusades."

"Uh, yeah, no kidding." The Templar Knights had used sunwalkers to establish a massive power base. The thought was mindboggling. No wonder they had practically brought the Church to its knees. Back then, sunwalkers probably would have been viewed as demons or angels or something. It must have terrified both the Church and every government in Europe.

"So the massacre on Friday the thirteenth, the one that ended the Templar reign, wiped out the sunwalkers, didn't it?" It was becoming clear. Those in power always destroy what they fear, what they can't control. The Templars and their sunwalker allies would have definitely been something to fear.

"Yes." Infinite sadness filled his voice as he sank back down beside me. "Every last one of my brothers who was in France that day was slain. Only I escaped with the Heart. The others stayed behind to cover my escape."

"So what happened to the other sunwalker? The one that you said lived two thousand years?"

"She died."

A female sunwalker who'd lived longer than anyone I'd ever heard of. Interesting. "But not with the rest of the Templars?"

He shook his head. "No, women were not allowed to serve with the rest of us. Not even if they were sunwalkers. She was an ally of the Templars, and she gave me a place to hide when I escaped."

"Is she the one who got you out of France?"

"Yes."

It was clear he was reluctant to talk about this woman, so I tucked the information away for later. "Where did you go?"

"Scotland. The country had been excommunicated from the Church, so it was safe until such a time as I could reunite with those of my brothers who survived the purge."

I can't imagine how terrifying it must have been to be hunted like some kind of animal. "Obviously you got to Scotland OK."

"Yes, we arrived safely and met up with others of my brothers who had escaped. Nearly all of them were human."

"The sunwalkers?" I had a bad feeling I knew where this story was going.

"Phillip killed the sunwalkers first." It wasn't a question. Killing the sunwalkers would have weakened the Templars enough to bring them down entirely.

"Yes. Eventually, I realized I had to leave my brother knights, if only to keep them safe. So we hid out deep in the Highlands until memories faded and it was safe to live elsewhere."

By *we*, I had no doubt he was referring to himself and the mysterious female sunwalker. "And after you left the Highlands?"

"We arrived here in the New World in 1640. We nearly died of starvation that first year. We can't get human illnesses, and we can't carry them, either. We can't have children. We can't die of old age. But we can starve." He didn't give any more detail, and he didn't need to. I'd studied enough history to know just how many people had died from lack of food during the early colonization of North America. "Things got better after that, and we spent the next few centuries exploring this new world."

"What happened to her?"

"She was murdered. Twenty years ago." His voice was very cold.

Things started clicking in my brain. "Twenty years ago. The same time Darroch stole the amulet from you."

"Lydia was home alone with the amulet when Darroch's men came. She couldn't fight that many, so he killed her and took the Heart. Slit her throat from ear to ear, then cut out her heart to make sure she didn't heal."

His story made me feel physically ill. If he were right, Darroch was such a bastard. "You are sure it was Darroch?"

He got up abruptly, nearly toppling me off the couch. "I wasn't at the time, but I've been tracking the killer for two decades. I am sure."

So this wasn't solely about the amulet and Darroch's plans to rule the world or whatever. This was also about revenge. I needed to know more.

"How would he have known about the amulet to begin with, let alone that you had it?"

He stared out the window, jaw working. "I don't know, but he must have had help from someone. Someone with a lot more knowledge and connections than he has."

"You've waited twenty years to seek justice. Why?"

"Darroch is a very difficult man to track. He always seemed to know when I was coming, just in time to slip away, and then I'd have to start all over again. That's part of the reason I believe there may have been someone else involved, but I've no idea who."

"Why haven't you turned more sunwalkers?"

He shrugged. "There is no need. There are plenty of us. It wouldn't do to overpopulate."

"So then you aren't the last sunwalker? There are others?"

"No, I am not." He just smiled at me. My not including myself as a sunwalker didn't fool him one bit. "Who told you I was the last?"

"Darroch."

He snorted at that. "I wouldn't go around believing everything Darroch says. I'm simply the last of the Templar Knights."

I had to admit that, as bizarre as that might sound, it was really incredibly cool.

"But I don't understand what this all has to do with Darroch. I mean, OK, the Templars used the amulet to gain knowledge and power. You helped them do it. But what could Darroch possibly do with that amulet that makes it so bloody important? He doesn't have you. He's not the guardian."

He looked away from me, to the sword over the fireplace. He let out a deep sigh. "It doesn't matter. If he has even a fraction of Atlantean blood in his veins, he will be able to access at least some of the ancient knowledge the amulet contains. It would be enough to make what modern witches do look like child's play. With that information and just a little ambition, he could rule the world. Or destroy it."

ʃ

After Jack's revelation, it had been obvious he wasn't in the mood for company, which was fine with me. I had a lot to think about. So I made my excuses and headed home.

I sighed as I pulled my car up in front of my house. I was really tired of all this world-in-peril shit. An amulet that could either control or destroy the world if it got into the wrong hands? Honestly, it was so clichéd it was downright boring, except that Jack had seemed pretty serious about the whole thing, and while I hated to admit it, the Templars had already done it once before.

If I were honest, I was also feeling more than a little confused by the whole thing. Putting aside everything else Jack had told me, the possibility that I might be a nearly immortal sunwalker was more than a little overwhelming. Wasn't it enough that my life had drastically changed three years ago? That I'd gone from being a normal office drone with a moderate social life and a penchant for drinking caipirinhas to working for a semisecret government subcontractor chasing monsters around the city?

I sighed. I really needed to get my head on straight.

The porch light was out, so I fumbled around for a moment trying to get the damn key in the lock while cussing under my breath. OK, not exactly under my breath. It was more like a conversational tone, if the person on the other end of the conversation was halfway across the street.

That's when I felt it, that prickle that started somewhere at the back of my mind and spread until my spine was crawling with it. I closed my eyes, hands stilled, and breathed in the night, sending my senses out across my property. I couldn't tell the exact number, but several vampires were closing in from the left where my backyard lay in shadows, and another two or three were coming from the street.

I took another deep breath, darkness seeping into my soul. That should have scared the crap out of me. Darkness isn't supposed to creep up and take residence in a person's soul, even temporarily. Especially if I really were a sunwalker. Fortunately, I didn't really have time to think about it.

They came at me in a rush, all at once, surrounding me on every side. The first one to reach me got a silver-tipped blade in the heart for his troubles. He was newly turned and stupid enough to think he was the top of the food chain. I showed him just how wrong he was. Unfortunately, it kind of went downhill from there.

The next vamp was female and at least a century old. She was also a lot smarter and a lot more experienced. Instead of heading straight at me, she feinted and ducked to my other side. She was a lot faster than the baby vamp—smarter too. She grabbed me by the nape of the neck and swung me at the door. It probably would have broken my nose, but I managed to turn in time so my right shoulder took most of the force. I was so going to have a bruise in the morning.

She snarled at me, flashing fang, going for my face with her nails. I managed to grab her left wrist and keep her from ripping my eyes out, despite the fact that my arm had gone nearly numb.

One of the other vamps grabbed my knife hand before I had a chance to use it. The two of them had me pinned and the rest were scrambling to get a piece of me.

The vamp who'd grabbed my knife hand gave it a twist, sending pain shooting through my wrist and arm. Anger surged with it, and I kicked him right in the knee, driving his patella back through the joint. He let out a howl as I pushed him off me. I rammed my stiletto knife into the female's chest and she vaporized, but not before I noticed her eyes were the same eerie glowing red as the other vamps I'd been dusting lately. Something hinky was going on.

The darkness gathered into me faster and faster; the night took a sharper edge. I could feel them out there, all of them rushing at me. And I could feel him, Kaldan, the oldest one of all; his dim outline flickered on the edge of my vision, mimicking life.

He was out there, watching and waiting in the darkness. Except, tonight, the darkness was mine.

The rest of the vamps hit me like a ton of bricks and I went down. Hard. One of them dived for my throat, only I caught his first. I breathed in the darkness. Breathed out and tightened my fist until I felt his windpipe crush under my fingers. It wouldn't stop him—vampires don't need to breathe. It would put him down for a minute, though, and it'd hurt like hell. He fell back, scrabbling at his throat, latent human memories causing him to panic.

Another one went for my throat, but hit my arm instead as I blocked him. In some far-off part of my brain, I could feel the searing pain, but it didn't touch me. I was filled with the darkness, and darkness doesn't feel pain. Instead, I calmly slipped the silver-tipped knife between his ribs and closed my eyes while he turned to dust. Ashes to ashes and all that.

There was no time to gloat. In one smooth spring, I was on my feet with my sword in one hand and a dagger in the other. I'd drawn it so fast even I barely registered the movement. I desperately tried to ignore just how freaked out I was by the whole darkness thing. Too many vamps to kill, too little time.

They were on me, those strange red eyes filled with something very much like glee, ripping and tearing at my clothes and skin, trying to shred muscle and open veins. They wanted the good stuff, and damned if I was going to let them. I slashed out with my sword, followed quickly by the knife. Another vamp vaporized.

As yet another pair of fangs sank into my shoulder, the world went fuzzy around the edges, just like it had the night I'd dusted Blondie—the first night the darkness took me. Just like before, I didn't fight it. I welcomed it, that soft, warm darkness. Probably, I should've worried about that.

I didn't. I let the darkness take me, and it laughed with joy as it filled every corner. Things got a little hazy after that.

I did remember blood, a lot of blood. Not my blood, but vampire blood and pieces of...other things. I remembered flashes of silver light from my blades, the feel of steel slicing through flesh.

And there was fire. At some point, the fight was lit with the orange glow of a bonfire.

In the vague part of my brain that was still me, I found that a little odd. Vamps aren't terribly thrilled with fire—no idea why, but they aren't—so I couldn't imagine they had anything to do with it. Who exactly had started a bonfire in my backyard?

Sometime after the fire, I realized Inigo was there with me, fighting alongside me. The darkness must have known he was an ally, or I'd have probably tried to kill him. I wasn't exactly myself.

Instead, the darkness welcomed him like an old friend. A very old friend. For the first time, I felt the same buzzing tingle I felt when I was around vampires, especially really, really old vampires. In that split second, Inigo felt older than Kaldan. Older than anything I'd ever felt before.

He flashed me a fierce grin, his eyes gleaming gold in the firelight, and the feeling was gone. He was Inigo again. Just Inigo. Maybe I imagined the whole thing. The darkness in me grinned back and laughed with joy.

ဢ

I didn't dare open my eyes. I was pretty sure if I did, I would puke everywhere. Headache didn't even begin to describe the way my head felt. This was more like the mother of all migraines.

I rubbed the surface underneath me with my forefinger. Even that little movement hurt, but I realized I was lying on my own bed. The satin throw underneath me was one I'd brought with me from England. I could smell the faint lingering scent of roses from my Champneys body wash.

"How are you feeling?" Inigo's voice reverberated through my head, making my skull pound and my stomach roil in rebellion. I let out a groan that sounded more like a whimper.

"Like shit. Without the warmed-over part."

"Nice imagery." His voice was softer this time, and there was laughter in it. I felt him press something damp and cool to my forehead. I risked opening one eye, then wished I hadn't, as the daylight light filtering in around the edges of the curtains started my head pounding again. When it finally subsided, something occurred to me.

"Why are you wearing my robe?"

"My clothes are in the wash. They were kind of…gory. Your clothes are in the wash too. I didn't want to waste water. All about living green."

My oversensitive skin told me I was wearing a T-shirt and not much else. I didn't even want to know how I got out of my clothes and into that shirt. I risked another peek at Inigo. "But why that one?"

He looked down at himself and fingered the silky material of that robe I kept around "just in case."

"It was the only decent one you had. There's no way I'd be caught dead in that other thing."

I figured he meant my regular terry cloth robe. Inigo refused to wear anything even remotely comfortable. "It's from Victoria's Secret." I tried to sound haughty, but it came out pained.

"Sure. From their granny line."

I rolled my eyes, which set my head to pounding and my stomach to roiling again. I must have looked as bad as I felt, because Inigo pressed a glass of water and a couple of tablets in my hand with a sympathetic look. I swallowed them and laid my head gingerly back on the pillow. "Why is it that every time you stop by, we end up in my bedroom?"

He gave me a wolfish grin. I would have rolled my eyes again but thought better of it.

"What happened?" I asked instead.

Inigo shrugged and brushed his hair back from his face and then adjusted his glasses. "I don't know. One minute you were fighting like you were possessed, and the next minute you just... dropped. Right after you staked the last vampire."

I frowned at him. The geek-chic, bespectacled Inigo sitting on the edge of my bed was a far cry from the fierce warrior from earlier tonight or the smoldering seducer from a few days ago. Granted, my memory of that night was hazy, but not that hazy.

"Not the last vampire. I didn't get Kaldan." I knew that much. The darkness knew that much. It still wanted him.

"We'll get him later. For now, you need some rest. You thumped your head pretty good when you fell."

I struggled to recall just exactly what had happened. I didn't remember much except the fighting and the smoke. "There was fire..."

He frowned. "I think you hit your head harder than you thought. Get some rest, OK? I'll be in the kitchen. Just in case." Then he leaned over and pressed his mouth to mine. His lips were soft and warm and a little dry, and tasted faintly of autumn leaves, wood fires, and toasted marshmallows.

It was a chaste, almost brotherly kiss. Except that, underneath, there was heat that told me he definitely didn't think of me as his sister. He pulled back and tucked a strand of hair behind my ear, a tender expression on his face unlike anything I'd ever seen before. My heart gave a little jump.

He stood up, leaned over to wrap the duvet around me a little more snugly, and whispered, "Sleep, Morgan."

I frowned into the darkness long after he was gone. I hadn't imagined the fire, like I hadn't imagined his eyes turning gold. Just like I hadn't imagined that his lips against mine had been way too warm to belong to a human being. I wasn't sure which worried me more: the weird things I was finding out about Inigo or the weird things I was finding out about myself.

Despite the headache still throbbing at the base of my skull, I staggered to my dresser, where Inigo had left my bag. I fumbled inside until I found what I wanted. Pulling my duvet over my head to block out the light, I dialed the number on the card and listened to the other end ring.

"Hi," I said softly down the line. "This is Morgan Bailey. I need your help."

Chapter Fifteen

Majicks and Potions was exactly how I'd remembered it. The same bell danced its merry jangle as I pushed open the door that evening. My headache had finally subsided, thanks to a few hours of sleep and a handful of painkillers.

I wandered happily through the shop. The crystals and stones gave off the same glowing, tingling energy as I passed them on my way to the counter. The incense was a different blend, but it still made my nose tickle, and the slight musty smell of old books still lingered underneath.

The music was even the same jarring fusion. I wouldn't go as far as to say it was growing on me, but I was beginning to associate it with the eclectic madness that was Eddie Mulligan.

There was something so familiar and comforting about Eddie's shop. Unlike the stuffy, cramped little occult shops back in London, Eddie's had the dreamy coziness edged with old-world charm that one *expected* to find in London but never did. This was the type of shop you itched to explore. I could imagine happily losing hours in a place like this.

Just like before, the counter was empty, so I went around and stuck my head out back. "Hey, Eddie! You here?"

Eddie's cherubic face popped down from the ceiling, tufts of gray hair sticking up in all directions. Déjà vu all over again. He beamed at me. "Hello, Morgan Bailey. Come on up," and he disappeared back into the ceiling.

I gave the aluminum ladder a malevolent look. While I have no problem with heights, I'm not terribly fond of ladders. It's not that I am afraid of heights or anything. Falling is another matter. Ladders never feel very sturdy. But I wasn't about to let a ladder defeat me, so after mumbling a couple choice words, I started up the rickety thing. I had the rather alarming feeling I was ascending into Professor Trelawney's lair. Gods, I hoped there wasn't any more incense.

There wasn't. It was just an ordinary attic jam-packed with overflowing trunks and boxes and assorted odds and ends and smelling of must and old perfume. It was more like something you'd find in the attic of some old lady's house than at the top of a shop. Eddie's back half was covered in green plaid pants and sticking out of an especially large trunk, where he was a rustling about industriously. Little poufs of dust erupted and Eddie backed out of the trunk, sneezing rather violently.

"You OK, Eddie?"

"Of course, my dear. I was just going through some old inventory. Amazing what gets lost up here." He looked around somewhat vaguely and started patting himself down. "Even more amazing what gets found. Where on *earth* have I put my glasses?"

I grinned. Couldn't help it. "Top of your head, Eddie."

"Oh, right." He plucked them from their precarious perch and shoved them back on his nose. "Better. Have a seat." We both sat down, him on a rickety chair that looked about a hundred years old and me on the top of a closed trunk. It appeared safer than the chair, but only marginally. "So, dear Huntress, how may I be of assistance?"

I wasn't exactly sure why I had called Eddie, of all people. After all, I barely knew the man. But my gut told me Eddie and his sentient book could help. I just wasn't sure how, and I really hoped he didn't decide to call the cops, because what I had to tell him sounded all kinds of crazy.

I tucked my legs up and perched cross-legged on the trunk with a sigh. Might as well spill it. "There's been some really,

really…*weird* shit happening to me lately. I mean, my whole life's been crazy the last three years, but this is *über*-weird. I tried to talk to Cordelia about it, but she was kind of vague, and frankly, that cat…" I had no idea what to say about the cat.

Eddie chuckled. "Bastet is in a league all her own. She helps, or doesn't, as the whim takes her. Who can understand the inner workings of the cat mind?"

I lifted an eyebrow. "Sure. Good point." Even normal cats have minds of their own, and Bastet is clearly anything but a normal cat.

"As for Cordelia Nightwing, well"—he shrugged—"she's clairvoyant. Things are never very clear when one is communing with the Otherside. They're a bit strange over there. Granted, they used to be us, or we used to be them, but they can see everything in a way we can only dream of."

He had a point. Theoretically, the Otherside is more a between life than an afterlife. The place where our souls go while they wait to be reborn. A universal energy, if you will. Supposedly, we could see everything from the Otherside. Remember every past life, know every future. You'd have thought we'd be a little more communicative, but apparently not.

"It's all about impressions and pictures," Eddie continued. "Poor Cordy has to translate everything she sees into something that we can maybe comprehend. Just imagine"—he waved his hands in the air as if grasping for inspiration—"imagine you were shown a trailer for a pirate movie. Of course, you don't know it's a pirate movie because the sound is off and the picture's blurry and the screen jumps around a bit. Then imagine trying to describe not the trailer but the movie itself to someone who hasn't seen it. That's what being a clairvoyant is like."

I could imagine. They could make a whole TV game show out of something like that. "That's why I came to you. I need facts, not impressions or guesses or blurry images with no sound. I need to *know* what exactly is happening to me."

"Well," he said as a big smile stretched across his face, "you've come to the right place. Facts are what I deal in. Lots and lots of facts." He leaned back into his chair and gave me a wave. "Proceed."

I needed help, and I knew Eddie and his book might have the answers, so I told him about the darkness. I didn't tell him about Inigo or Jack or the amulet. And I certainly didn't tell him about the possibility that I was a sunwalker. I wasn't ready to believe it myself, let alone share it with anyone else. Half of me hoped Jack was wrong, and the other half was kind of excited by the prospect. I wasn't sure yet which half I wanted to win.

When I finished, Eddie studied the ceiling for long enough that I thought he wasn't going to say anything. Then he spoke. "Tell me about the day your life changed. How you became a hunter."

I blinked. Only Kabita and Inigo know the full story, though Cordy knows some of it. My mother certainly doesn't know. She thinks I was attacked by hoodlums, and I want to keep it that way. I'd only given Jack the quick overview. My experience isn't something I like to think about, let alone talk about. Eddie just sat there, gazing at me with complete and utter calm.

"I don't know…"

"Tell me only what you feel comfortable sharing." His voice was soothing. "It might be important."

So I told him about the night I died.

Chapter Sixteen

" **S**o you survived a vampire attack. And rather well, I might add." Eddie took out a handkerchief, polished his glasses, and popped them back in place. His brown eyes danced with excitement behind the thick lenses. I guess Eddie is a bit of a secondhand adventure junkie. I repressed a grin at the thought.

"Yeah, well, lucky for me the paramedics got to me in time. The guys were able to jump-start my heart, then rush me to the hospital. They didn't know it was a vampire attack, of course. Just thought I was another victim of gang violence."

The fact that they'd been able to revive me at all with so much blood loss was a major miracle. The reason for the miracle was starting to become obvious, no matter how much I wanted to deny it. Even without medical attention, I would have survived.

"Your injuries, how bad were they?"

I shrugged. "Bad enough. I had three broken ribs, my right ulna was snapped in three places, and I had a skull fracture and massive concussion. My kidneys were damaged, my spleen lacerated. Don't even get me started on the bruises and the teeth marks. He practically ripped my throat out." I didn't even want to think about how many stitches I'd had.

The British have become very adept at dealing with vampire attacks, as have most of the rest of Europe, since they've been aware of supernatural beings for centuries and have been fighting them just as long. Like the United States and the rest of the European Union, the British government doesn't officially acknowledge the existence of vampires and other creatures, but hunters are everywhere, and plenty of funding exists through MI8, the British Military Intelligence branch responsible for researching the "occult" and identifying threats of a supernatural nature. They aren't supposed to exist, but then, neither are vampires.

"When I reached the hospital in London, undercover MI-Eight operatives recognized the true nature of my injuries and immediately shut me away in a special ward and kept me under surveillance. Fortunately for me, British policy prevents killing the infected until they've fully turned, just in case." I'd been really glad of that policy when I finally woke up, though I was convinced the real reason was far less clear-cut.

I didn't mention that, though. Didn't want to sound like a conspiracy nut.

Eddie pulled at his lower lip. "Interesting policy, since 'just in case' has never been an issue."

He was right about that. "Nope. No one has ever survived being killed by a vampire and not turned. Not until me, and not since. That's what Kabita told me." I doubt the sunwalkers have made it into any official historic documents. They are too careful for that, and I wasn't about to mention the possibility that I might be one of them.

The transmission of vampirism, on the other hand, has been secretly studied by government scientists probably since the day the first vampire showed up. There are still a lot of unknown factors when it comes to turning into a vampire. Most people who get bitten don't turn.

Apparently, there has to be the perfect combination of dying from the attack combined with being susceptible to the virus. A lot of victims die from their wounds and never reanimate. Some don't die and recover without turning, their memories of the attack gone, whether from PTSD or some mechanism of the virus is unclear. Though, there are some victims who do succumb even from the simplest of bites. I suppose in the same way that some people are more prone to getting the flu than others. But an attack like mine, where the victim actually dies after being nearly drained, means turning is inevitable.

"I'm surprised they didn't stick you in a lab and study you."

I shrugged. "They might have if it hadn't been for Kabita. She's got some clout over there." A surprising amount, actually. Something to do with her family, though I've never understood exactly what. I know her mother was from India and had died many years earlier. Her father was British, though Kabita had been raised in Malaysia, and they'd had a serious falling out. I tried to talk to her about it once, but she'd gotten really upset. Sometimes being a friend means knowing when to back off. There are some wounds that just never heal.

"Still, I would have thought they'd want to use you to create a vaccine."

"Oh, they did," I admitted. "But when they drew my blood, they could find nothing in it to explain my immunity."

"So they agreed to let you go."

"They tried to keep me, but she made a phone call, and suddenly, they changed their minds." To this day, I have no idea whom Kabita called or why they let me go.

"And she got you into the hunting game." He folded his hands over his ivory-colored waistcoat-clad tummy.

"She changed my life. I owe her a lot."

How different my life might have been if it had been someone else who'd come to the hospital that day instead of Kabita. I'd probably still be locked up in a lab somewhere.

He gave me a shrewd look. "So I take it you healed faster than you should have?"

I grinned. "Yes, but that was probably the least weird thing that happened. After I got out of the hospital and started training as a hunter, I realized a few other new things about myself."

He pulled at his lip some more, frown lines creasing his brow. "So you inherited many of the nightwalker's characteristics, without actually turning into one. Interesting. This darkness thing is new, is it? You've never been able to do anything like it before?"

I shook my head. "Not even close. It's only happened in the last couple of weeks. Since the whole sunwalker thing started."

"To be perfectly honest, this is all new to me. I've never heard of anything quite like it." He frowned. "No, I take that back. I do recall…"

He jumped up without another word and headed for the hole in the floor and that damned aluminum ladder. "Come on. We need the book." With that, he disappeared down the ladder.

Oh, joy. More ladder climbing. I shook off disturbing memories of the past as well as worries about my future and headed down the ladder to join Eddie. He already had the sentient book out. The thick, creamy pages made a rustling sound as he flipped through.

"OK, hmm…yes. This is it." He poked his finger at a page in the book brightly rimmed with beautifully painted orange-and-gold flames. In the center of the page was a picture of a cloaked figure standing in the middle of a ring of fire. The fine brush-strokes made the fire almost leap off the page they looked so real. The figure's hands were cupped in front, a small flame dancing between them. The rest of the page was filled with bold, black writing in what appeared to be Latin.

Eddie quickly scanned the writing. "Yes, I thought so. These were the elemental mages."

"Say what?" Was it my imagination, or were the flames on the page actually dancing?

"Elemental mages. There aren't very many of them left anymore, and their powers are pretty much…Well, they don't really have any. Not anymore. Their powers have diminished through the years until there's nothing left." His finger traced the flame glowing between the mage's hands. "But a thousand years ago or so, elemental mages had the most incredible powers. More than any other magic practitioner ever recorded."

"I take it they were into the elements." My voice was probably a tad drier than necessary.

"As the name would imply, yes, they worshipped the four elements as living beings, as gods. Each mage chose an element to worship: earth, air, fire, or water. That element also became his, or her, element to call. They could quite literally channel that element through their bodies. They believed it was the gods giving them strength and power. They called it 'kissing'—kissing fire, kissing water, that sort of thing."

"What did they do with the element when they'd channeled it?"

"Oh, all sorts of things." He was on a roll now, becoming more and more animated, hands waving about to emphasize his story. "Water mages could channel water to create rain for crops or into troughs for livestock during drought. They could even hold back rivers during flood season. Fire mages could keep fires burning for days without fuel so their people wouldn't freeze during winter. Air mages could speed ships on their course or lighten the impact of hurricanes, and earth mages could carve out roads or even encourage plants to grow. Amazing."

"Were these mages human? Or Atlantean?"

He smiled. "Good question. The mages were human, but it's my belief Atlanteans were the ones who taught them how to channel the energy. Sort of a quantum mechanics thing. We were once very good at it, but over time, people got lazy and the knowledge was lost. Even among the mages. It's a shame, because they could do so much with their power."

"But?" I knew there was a "but." People are people, after all, and there is something to the old saying that power corrupts.

There was a hint of sadness and anger in his voice. "But there was a use for their powers that was very dark, indeed. Much like your darkness, they could also channel their elements while in battle and use them as weapons. It made them stronger, faster, more deadly, and nearly impossible to kill."

I could tell from the hard look in his eyes that there was more, and it scared me just a little. "Isn't it good? Being hard to kill? Especially in my case, since I'm fighting vampires."

"It would be," he agreed. "Except that the elemental mages became addicted to the power, and it was not meant for humans to wield, even those with natural channeling abilities. Eventually, it drove them insane, as the craving for power overtook everything else. They nearly destroyed themselves, not to mention the people they were supposed to protect. They eventually had to be hunted down and killed."

So I was quite possibly teetering on the edge of crazy, thanks to some ancient magical ability. Fabulous. That explained a lot. "So my darkness thing, it's the same as what the elementals could do?"

Eddie pulled at his lower lip again before readjusting his glasses. "I'm not entirely sure. You see, the elemental mages worked and studied for *years* before they were able to channel even a small amount of their element. Some of them were more naturally gifted at focusing and channeling. Only the most powerful of them could channel power the way I described, perhaps one in every thousand. Even then, it took many more years of practice to control the power to the point where it could be used as a weapon."

"But this just happened to me. I didn't try or practice or anything. One minute everything was fine and then…" I shrugged.

"And you say that now you can control it?" He peered at me over the rim of his glasses.

"Well, sort of. I seem to be able to call it up now, at least when I'm fighting. I've done it a couple of times. The first time I actually called it on purpose it was just kind of, I don't know, mild. It was there, but it didn't really help much. Then again, I only sort of half tried."

I pulled out a stool from behind the counter and plopped my butt on it. "Last night, though, that was something else." I frowned a little, trying to remember what exactly had happened. "To tell you the truth, I don't think I really thought about it either time. It was just…there. At Pittock Mansion, I didn't really need it. There were only two of them. Last night, I definitely did."

His fingers traced the flame along the edge of the page. "And it came when you called it."

"Oh, yeah, in a big way. I can't even remember a lot of what happened. But I'm not sure how much that had to do with me channeling the darkness and how much was a result of…" I stopped. There was no way I was going into the whole Inigo thing with Eddie.

"So, no actual control, but it comes when you need it?"

I thought about it. "Yeah, sounds right. I mean, I haven't really *tried* to make it come during the day or when I'm not in a fight, so I don't know if it works when it's not nighttime or when I'm not, you know, in mortal danger."

"Probably best you don't." A little puff of dust danced in the air as he shut the book. "At least until we have a better idea what it is we're dealing with. Or rather, what it is *you* are dealing with. If it's anything like the elemental magic, then the more you use it, the more dangerous it becomes. Only…" He hesitated, obviously wanting to say more, but not sure how.

"Only?"

He sighed. "There is no record of elemental mages attempting to channel any other power beyond the four physical elements. That doesn't mean anything, of course. I suppose if one could channel air, one could also channel light, but there is no mention of anyone trying."

He shook his head and started pacing back and forth and muttering to himself, the change in his pocket making a chinking sound as he walked. "But darkness isn't light. Light is *something*. Darkness is not. It is the *absence* of light, not a thing in itself. How could one channel such a thing? Surely not. No, it can't be elemental magic—something similar, maybe?"

"Earth to Eddie!" I waved a hand in front of his face. "Still here."

"My apologies, Morgan." He stopped pacing and tapped a finger on the cover of the book. "I have no idea what's going on. I'm sorry. I wish I could be more helpful, but this is so far beyond anything I've read about that I just don't know."

"No biggie." I shrugged, hopping off the stool. My turn to pace. "We'll figure it out somehow, right?"

His smile was a bit wobbly. He didn't seem entirely convinced. "Of course. Of course. I will keep researching. Perhaps you should question the sunwalker. Maybe it has something to do with him? Or possibly the amulet you mentioned. Though, I don't see how..." He trailed off for a moment, lost in thought again, then shook himself. "I wish I could have been of more help."

I reached out and squeezed his arm. "Eddie, you *have* helped. More than you know. At least I have a direction to look, rather than just worrying I'm crazy." I flashed a grin.

He laughed at that. "Well, we have some idea about your darkness, if nothing else. Speak to your sunwalker. Who knows? He has, after all, been around for a few years."

I smiled. I already knew Jack couldn't help, and I had a feeling there was a lot more to this whole thing than either of us could imagine. Stranger things in heaven and earth and all that. Maybe Jack had heard of the elemental mages. That was something new, at least. "I'm off, Eddie. Take care, yeah?"

He squeezed my hand and went back to muttering over the book while I headed for the front door. "Hey, Eddie," I turned back, remembering something. "One thing before I go."

"Yes, my dear?" He glanced up from the book.

"Lately, I've been noticing something odd about the vampires I've been fighting."

He frowned. "Odd?"

"Yeah, their eyes. All the vampires I've seen over the last few days have had these red, glowing eyes. I'd expect to see that on a demon, but a vampire?"

"How odd, indeed." Eddie frowned even harder, if that were possible. "I only know of one way to make fundamental changes to vampire physiology and that is to change the power that controls them."

Vampire clans are usually controlled by one of two things: either by the one who turned them or by the most powerful vampire in their clan, if their maker isn't strong enough to hold them. Since both types of masters control using vampiric powers—a little like an alpha wolf holds a pack, but magnified—the physiology of the vampire being controlled won't change.

"What sort of change would have to happen to turn their eyes red? Would a demon do it?" The only time I've ever heard of any creature controlling a vamp other than another, more powerful vamp is the occasional demon who comes in and kicks the master's ass. Once the other vamps willingly share their blood, the demon is boss.

"I suppose it might, depending on the type of demonic power used to control the vampires. But I've never heard of anything like it." Eddie seemed unsure, but it was as good a theory as any.

"OK, thanks, Eddie. I really appreciate your help."

I headed out to my car, my mind in a whirl. I was starting to feel a bit like Alice, complete with rabbit hole.

Curiouser and curiouser.

Chapter Seventeen

The sun was setting as I exited Eddie's shop, leaving the bell above the door jangling merrily behind me. I gave Kabita a quick call. I could use a chat with a friend, even if I couldn't tell her about Inigo and me. Unfortunately, it went straight to voice mail, which meant she was either meeting with a client or on a hunt, so I decided to swing by Cordelia's. I thought for a moment about calling ahead, then figured it was pointless; I apparently had some kind of psychic Bat Signal where she was concerned.

Either that or Bastet told her. Gods know that cat is a piece of weird. Cordelia had probably already put the teakettle on.

The traffic was unusually light for rush hour, and I made it across town in record time, the Who blaring loud enough to wake the dead. Even more amazing was finding a parking space just around the corner from Cordelia's building. How lucky. I frowned as I locked the car door. Somehow I didn't think luck had anything to do with it. Call me skeptical, but finding a parking space anywhere near the Park Blocks during rush hour pretty much takes an act of nature or a miracle of the gods. I wondered if Cordy and her otherworldly connections had anything to do with it.

"Hello, precious girl!" I was engulfed in a flurry of jade silk and floral perfume the moment I came through the door. I managed to extricate myself from Cordelia's embrace before I completely suffocated. "Listen, I know you're having a challenging time right now," she said, patting me on the back, "but let's have some tea and a chat. That always helps."

She disappeared down the hall, her bright-green robe billowing behind her. Force of nature, indeed. Who on earth wears a silk robe over blue jeans and a turtleneck sweater? Especially one with a Chinese dragon embroidered on the back? It was pretty, though.

"Come on in. Bastet's really been looking forward to seeing you again." Sure the cat wanted to see me. Rolling my eyes, I stepped into the living room.

"We saw that." There was laughter in her voice. "I know I sound like a crazy cat woman, but trust me, she's talked about nothing else all week."

I blinked. "Of course not. What else would she talk about?" Catnip? Seafood-flavor versus chicken-flavor kitty treats? Honestly, what do sentient cats talk about?

As usual, there was a steaming pot of tea and two teacups perched precariously on the coffee table. Cordelia draped herself dramatically across an overstuffed chair, so I was left to shovel cushions around until I could find a spot on the couch large enough for my backside. Bastet glared at me from where she lounged on a particularly plush pillow dead in the center of the couch. Yep, she looked happy to see me, all right.

"So, tell me what's been happening. I want all the gossip!" Her rings sparkled in the late-afternoon sunlight streaming through the windows.

"Um…I thought you already knew everything. You know, psychic and all that." I leaned forward to take the cup of tea she held out to me.

"Oh, I don't know *everything*." She laughed lightly. "Just mostly everything. Bastet, now, *she* knows everything." She winked at the cat.

Bastet just glowered and twitched her tail. I was sort of glad I wasn't the only one she gave attitude to.

"So, come on, Morgan. I want all the juicy details."

I caught her up on the madness that had become my life, up to and including the stuff that was going on with Inigo and the trouble both he and Jack gave my hormones. And my nearly sleeping with Inigo, my making out with Jack, and the confusion I felt about the whole thing. It was a relief to have someone to talk to about Inigo. It wasn't like I could sit down and chat with Kabita about her own cousin.

I also told Cordy a little about the darkness and what Eddie had said, though, again, I avoided the sunwalker scenario. It was just too much for me to deal with right at the moment. Plus, I figured that she might very well already know. If she didn't, I wasn't telling. Not yet.

Cordelia nodded sagely and delicately sipped at her tea. "Catnip."

"What?" I blinked at her. Had she been listening in on my snarky thoughts about Bastet? Or maybe Bastet had tattled on me. With that cat, anything is possible.

"Have you ever seen a cat on catnip? They go completely crazy and rub themselves all over everyone and everything like they want to soak up every bit of pleasure they can. Jack's your catnip. Maybe Inigo too. Oh, how nice! Two catnips!" She looked entirely too pleased about the prospect as she clapped her hands gleefully.

"No. No, no, no! There is no catnip." I shook my head most emphatically. "I do *not* rub myself all over them. Well, maybe a little. But that's not my fault. There is no catnip!"

Cordelia just looked smug, and her eyes twinkled with laughter. "Methinks the lady doth protest too much."

I groaned in frustration. "Forget about catnip, OK? I just want to know what is going on with me. And what happened with Inigo."

"And Jack?" She smiled. "All right." She thrust her hand out. "Teacup."

184

I slurped the last of my tea, tipped the cup upside down on the saucer, and handed it to her.

"Let's see," she said, tipping the cup this way and that, trying to catch the dying light as if she were seeing something more than just brown, gunky tea leaves. "This darkness business. All I can say is that it's a part of you. Just like your green eyes and your bad driving."

"Hey!"

She smirked at me, then peered back into the depths of the cup. "It's a power. An ability. It's new, but it's not new." She frowned a little, as though struggling to explain something she understood but had no real words for, and I remembered Eddie's description of her abilities. "I mean, it's always been in you, part of you, but it's new. Something...something woke it up." Her frown grew deeper.

"What do you mean, 'something woke it up'?"

She shook her head. "I'm not sure. Something that was far but now is close. Something...ugh. This is all a little..."

"Hinky?"

Her laugh tinkled. "Yeah. Hinky. Has anyone ever told you that you've an interesting grasp of the English language?"

"It has been noted," I said dryly.

She smiled a little at that. "Well, this ability of yours to draw on the power of the dark, it's only the beginning. There is more to come. Much more." She frowned into the cup, obviously perturbed by what she saw.

"Shit, what does that mean?" As if some bizarre new channeling power and possible immortality weren't bad enough. What more could there be?

Note to self: Don't ask such stupid questions. The universe will be sure to answer them. Usually in a way you don't like.

She frowned some more, tipping the teacup back and forth and muttering a little under her breath. "I'm not really sure. All I can see is that there is more to come for you, both with this ability and with others, much more. There is someone who will show you the way, someone who knows the truth. Unfortunately, that someone isn't me, though I will be here to help you."

She placed the cup down and leaned back in her chair. "But this gift is definitely part of what I told you was coming, the changes. I'm sorry I can't be any clearer than that, but I can only work with what I'm given. Unfortunately, I'm not being given much." She threw an annoyed look in the general vicinity of heaven. I'd hate to be on the receiving end of that look.

I sighed. "Thanks for looking."

"Anytime. Now, about your Inigo…"

"He's not *my* Inigo. And I swear to all the gods, there's something weird going on with him."

"I'll ask." She folded her hands over her stomach and closed her eyes.

I glanced over at Bastet, who gave me a baleful look, then turned her head haughtily. Bloody arrogant cat.

"Well, I never!" Cordelia sat up abruptly. "How rude."

"What is it?"

"Do you know what they told me?" She spluttered. "They told me to mind my own business. Oh, they're happy enough to boss me around when it suits them, but the minute they don't want to answer my questions…irritating little trolls."

I could only assume that "they" meant the beings of the Otherside—angels, spirit guides, ghosts, or whatever you want to call our incorporeal forms after death. I wondered what they thought about being called trolls. "They couldn't tell you anything about Inigo, I take it?"

"More like they *wouldn't* tell me anything. I swear, some days." She drew in a deep breath and made fluttery motions with her hands as though splashing something on herself. "Positive thoughts. Positive energy." She gave me a beatific smile. "There. I feel much better now."

"Why wouldn't they tell you anything? What is going on?"

She shook her head, her expression pensive. "I honestly don't know, Morgan. But I think maybe it's something you shouldn't mess with. They were quite specific that Inigo was not something I should be getting involved with."

She frowned a little, and her eyes got a faraway look in them as if she were remembering something. "Sometimes there's a reason things are kept secret."

"Yeah, you could be right."

There was no way I was giving up on figuring out the whole Inigo thing, but I had other stuff to worry about at the moment. I had a clan of vampires trying to kill me, a magic amulet to find, the death of a sunwalker to prevent, and my lovely new ability to deal with, not to mention the very real possibility that I might no longer be human at all. Someday soon, though, I was going to figure out what was going on with Inigo, whether the Powers That Be liked it or not.

∽

It was dark out, with a slight chill in the air, when I left Cordelia's. A gentle breeze teased my hair, sending a few strands of red dancing across my face. It was a bit early in the year, but sometimes I felt things that weren't really there in the physical world. Like cold fronts in the middle of summer. I shoved my hands into my pockets and strolled slowly toward the car, my mind in a whirl over the things Cordelia had told me.

The phone ringing jarred me out of my thoughts. "Hello?"

"Morgan, it's Jack. Are you all right?"

"Of course I'm all right. Why?"

There was a slight hesitation. "Last night I got this strange feeling you might be in trouble. I tried to hone in on you, but I couldn't. Something was blocking me." His voice held an edge of frustration. "I called, but Inigo answered. Said you'd gone to bed with a headache."

Shit. Oh, shit. "Um...yeah. I'm fine, Jack. Like Inigo said, it was just a headache. I get them sometimes. Inigo brought me some herbs that help." I'm going to hell for lying. Or I would be if I believed in hell. Unless you count the parallel world where the demons come from. By all accounts, that is pretty hellish. No doubt why the portals between our worlds are called hellholes.

"Uh-huh." He didn't sound like he believed me.

"Listen, Jack, I appreciate your calling but...ah...I gotta go. Talk later?"

"Sure, OK." He cleared his throat. "Be careful."

"Sure. Bye, Jack." Awkward. Why did everything have to be so damn complicated?

I was nearly back to the car when I felt the tingling grip at the back of my skull. I quickly scanned both sides of the street, and then I saw him. The vampire was striding down the sidewalk on the other side of the Park Blocks, completely ignoring everything around him. He didn't even see me. And if he was in this area of town, he had to be one of Kaldan's. Vamps are very territorial.

It was beyond brilliant. I couldn't have planned it better myself.

Of course, it *could* be a trap; in fact, it probably was, but faintness of heart never kicked evil vampire ass. I could follow the vamp back to Kaldan's lair and wipe out the entire nest once and for all. When opportunity knocks, who am I to question it? So I yanked out my cell phone and hit speed dial.

"This had better be good. I haven't had my dinner yet." Kabita's tone was just about sharp enough to draw blood.

"Yeah, yeah, cranky. Listen. I just spotted one of Kaldan's flunkies over near the Park Blocks. I'm going after him." I think the sound she made was something between a shriek and a squeak, but it was hard to tell. It certainly wasn't a "yay, go you" kind of sound. It was much closer to a "you crazy lunatic" kind of sound, but I was used to that from Kabita.

"Not by yourself. Do you hear me, Morgan Bailey? Not by yourself, you bloody idiot!" Kabita's voice had gone high enough to make dogs deaf.

"I'm only going to follow him. Track him back to wherever Kaldan is hiding. I'll ring you when I'm there." I disconnected before she could start screaming at me again. I knew that, after she finished cussing me out six ways to Sunday, she'd round up Inigo and head my way. At any rate, I'd have a posse at my back before I hit Kaldan's. I wasn't stupid. Well, not often, anyway.

I followed the flunky as he hurried through the Park Blocks to Burnside Street and then up the street toward my old stomping grounds. I'd lived in an adorable little studio apartment just off southwest Burnside with a big claw-foot bathtub and a bed that slid into the wall under a set of built-in bookshelves before fate, and that ill-fated relationship with Alex, had sent me to London.

There are a lot of places vampires can hide in that area, not to mention its close proximity to Pittock Mansion's rich feeding grounds. Plus, the Shanghai Tunnels run under the area—a system of brick tunnels and archways built under the city in the 1800s to connect the basements of many of the shops above to the Willamette River to allow merchants to move their goods without having to deal with street traffic. The tunnels would make a perfect way to move about during the day without turning into a pile of ash.

Ten minutes later, the vamp stopped on a corner at the edge of the Pearl District, and I had to duck behind a parked car while he did a quick check to make sure no one was following him. Either he was really, really dumb or this was a definite setup.

He hurried down a narrow side street and disappeared through a steel door into the shadows beyond. The door clanged shut behind him. The building looked like another one of the many ordinary old brick warehouses in the Pearl District, but looks can be deceiving. Over the past ten years or so, most of the warehouses in this part of town had been remodeled and turned into everything from trendy art studios to snazzy high-security loft apartments. It's more common to see pretentious yuppies than blue-collar workers down here these days. I was betting whatever this particular warehouse had been turned into, the security would make Fort Knox look like a playground. Unless it was a trap, of course; then I'd be able to walk right in.

My pocket started vibrating.

"Where are you?" Kabita sounded pissed. OK, so I couldn't exactly blame her, but what did she expect? That I'd just let the thing get away? As if.

"Eleventh, just a couple blocks off Burnside. He's gone into one of the old warehouses in the Pearl District." I rattled off the building number to her. It wasn't far from her condo.

"Sit tight. We'll be there in five minutes. Do you hear me? Do not go in. Morgan? Morgan? Dammit!"

I disconnected and shoved the phone back into my pocket. Going in alone was really, really stupid. I knew that. Five minutes was a long time, though. Kaldan and his vampires could be doing anything in there.

I yanked the phone back out of my pocket to check the time. Four minutes to go. *Shit*. I paced back and forth on my side of the street. No windows, one door.

I wanted Kaldan badly. Taking out his nest meant destroying one of the largest groups of vampires in the city. Until now, I'd never been able to find the nest.

Three minutes. "Hurry up, Kabita," I muttered under my breath. I could only hope the waiting was making Kaldan as antsy as it was making me, because I'd bet anything he knew I was out here. Antsy vamps are dangerous, but just like humans, they are also more likely to make mistakes. Vamps who make mistakes are easier for me to kill.

Two minutes. I closed my eyes and inhaled deeply. Every molecule of my body was screaming at me to get inside, but I knew that was a good way to get myself killed. Something was wrong; I could feel it.

One minute. If Kabita didn't show in the next sixty seconds, I was going in alone, stupid idea or not.

I paced some more, checked my phone again. Thirty seconds. Before I could continue pacing, a scream shattered the still night. It was a scream that chilled me to the bone, the scream of someone in mortal terror.

Forget Kabita. Forget the danger of going in alone. I ran for the door.

Chapter Eighteen

Just before I hit the door, headlights flashed down the block. I slid my sword out of its sheath across my back and waited in the shadows as two figures got out of the car. Kabita and Inigo. I breathed a sigh of relief. Without waiting for them to catch up, I hit the door to the warehouse. I could hear Kabita cursing up a storm behind me.

The warehouse door led to a short, dark entry with a set of narrow metal stairs. It was pitch black, the only light streaming in from the streetlights outside the open door. Kabita clicked on a flashlight and shone it low on the steps. I'd have gone up without the light, but then, my night vision seemed to be getting better these days. My mind shied away from thoughts of just why that was happening. No time for that; we had vamps to kill.

Our rubber-soled shoes made barely a sound on the metal treads. "Which way?" Kabita pointed the flashlight beam up and then right. We'd hit a landing. Another flight of narrow stairs led up into the darkness. To the right was an equally narrow doorway.

I focused on that tight tingling at the back of my skull. Now that we were inside the building, I could feel it again. They were close, but not close enough. "Up." I pointed up the stairs, holding back a sneeze as a little cloud of dust trickled down from between the floorboards above our heads.

Kabita raised an eyebrow, but Inigo nodded in agreement. He doesn't have quite the same sense for vampires I do, but he still has a way of feeling things out that goes way beyond that of a normal person.

With a shrug, Kabita led the way, shining the light in front of her. This was going to get interesting if we had to fight in the dark. Although I do it frequently, I rarely have backup, so I'm not used to looking out for other people. Not an easy thing to do in the dark.

The stairs opened onto a narrow landing in front of an open door. This was it. I could feel them all around us now, hovering in the dark. I placed my left hand on Kabita's shoulder and squeezed gently, letting her know without a sound that we'd reached the right place. She halted, Inigo and I behind her.

Kabita pointed her light through the open door. It played over a figure sprawled out on the floor of the cavernous room, blood oozing from dozens of vicious tears in the flesh. For just a moment, I thought they'd killed someone while I'd been waiting outside. Then the body moved and I realized it was a vamp. They'd tortured one of their own to try to force my hand, hence the screams. Sick bastards.

Inigo kept his voice low. "How many?"

"A lot. A dozen at least. Maybe more." All I knew was there were far too many for me to get an accurate count. The minute we stepped through that door all hell was going to break loose.

I shifted my weight, a floorboard creaking under my feet. Not that it mattered. The vamps already knew we were there. They were just waiting for us to come through the door.

Eddie had warned me against using the whole darkness thing, but right now I needed it. I closed my eyes, took a deep breath, and focused on all that darkness around me. I imagined it as a thick, black cloud. I focused on drawing it into me. Nothing. I tried again, this time visualizing the darkness as inky ocean waves. No good. *Shit.*

"Let's go," Kabita said.

Between one breath and the next we were inside the room. I felt a rush of wind against my face and leaned back just in time to avoid getting my throat ripped out. I heard the flashlight hit the floor, and circles of light danced crazily against the walls as it spun out of control. For one panicked moment, I thought something had happened to Kabita, before I realized she'd dropped the light so she had both hands free for weapons.

I felt another rush of wind, and this time I hacked out with my sword, the silver-edged sharpness slicing through muscle and sinew and bone with a dull, wet sound. Blood rushed out of the vampire's neck and flowed down my left hand, making it slip on the grip of the sword. Human blood is warm and fluid when freed from the vein. Vamp blood is cold—unless they've recently fed— and viscous and slightly sticky. Frankly, it's kind of gross.

I quickly swiped my hand against my pant leg, then stepped in to follow up, the short blade in my right hand thrusting between the ribs, slicing through the intercostals and straight into the heart. The vamp exploded into dust and ash.

That was when it came.

One moment everything was normal—at least, as normal as it ever gets for me. The next moment I could feel it rushing and billowing toward me—the darkness crashing over me, inside me like a living creature, until I felt like I might burst from it. I realized I could see, and not just in a really good night-vision way. The dark all around me had become bright as day. A sort of purple-tinged day, but day nonetheless.

The monsters were good at hiding; there were at least twice as many as we'd guessed. To my whacked-out vision, they appeared as dim blue shapes tinged with dark bloodred. I turned toward Kabita, who was a glowing ruby red outlined in hot orange and pale yellow. Ingo was a living flame of oranges and golds with a touch of turquoise. Bizarre.

I didn't have any more time to think after that. Two vamps rushed toward me, saliva dripping off their fangs, eyes the same strange glowing red as those of the vamp that had attacked me outside the restaurant—the one I'd dusted later at the waterfront. The same red eyes I'd seen on all the vamps lately. I filed that little jewel away for later inspection.

Fierce elation that was mine and not quite mine surged through my veins, and I threw my head back and laughed. Even to my ears, I sounded like a crazy person. Then, with a snarl that rivaled that of any vampire, I hurled myself toward the oncoming vamps.

I don't remember much after that. There was a lot of blood and dust and the flashing of blades, a few screams, and an odd glow like something on fire. I was totally in the moment, yet standing outside myself at the same time as I slashed and hacked and stabbed.

I could feel my blades ripping through flesh, shattering bone, the copper tang of blood filling my nostrils. Every cut and hack and spray of blood sent bubbles of delight shooting through me until I wanted to scream for the pure joy of it.

And then I was kneeling over Kaldan himself, my blade against his throat, my knee pressing into his chest. His laughter held an edge of insanity.

"Stupid child," he hissed at me, ignoring the blood that slid down his neck from the shallow cut of my blade. "You think I'm it? You think I'm the one?" His laugh was harsh in the sudden quiet of the darkened warehouse. "You think I have the power to control the vampires of this city? You fool. You can't even see what is right in front of your face." His own face twisted somewhere between pain and victory.

I'd known Kaldan wasn't the master anymore. I just didn't know who was. Nor did I care. It didn't matter.

Did it?

"I don't give a shit, Kaldan. The only thing I care about is freeing this city of vampires. Killing you goes a long way toward that."

"You can kill me, Morgan Bailey, but it won't do you a damned bit of good. He will still destroy you in the end. You and all your kind." His eyes flashed with the same eerie reddish glow as the others.

I struggled to speak past the darkness that screamed at me to end his miserable existence. I needed to know what he meant. "What are you talking about? My kind? What does that mean? Do you mean hunters?"

A thought struck me. I didn't want to ask, but I had to. I dropped my voice to whisper, "Do you mean sunwalkers?"

He just snarled back, so I shook him. Hard. "Tell me! Is this some kind of conspiracy? Who controls the vampires?" I had no idea what it meant for me, for the city.

He laughed at me. "You already know the answers to your questions. You are just too stupid to figure it out. You pathetic, useless humans. One day soon, you will all serve us as we serve him."

"Yeah? Well, you won't be around to see it." My blade sliced through his throat, and blood gushed across the floor in a thick, syrupy mess as his head toppled from his body. As he turned to dust under me, my mind whirled furiously. Kaldan had admitted he wasn't controlling the vampires. Someone else was. Someone I know. Right in front of my face, he'd said. And he wanted to turn us humans into what, slaves?

Could it be Darroch? I didn't know how that could be possible. He isn't a vampire, and I've never heard of a human being able to control vampires.

The amulet. Could that have anything to do with it? But how? Why?

Dammit, but the darkness made it hard to think. The darkness didn't care about finding out who controlled the vampires or why that person wanted to subjugate the human race. The darkness just wanted to kill. I wanted to kill. But there was no one left except Kabita and Inigo, who were both staring at me like they'd just seen a whole lot of crazy and weren't quite sure it was over with. I guess they sort of had a point.

I took a deep breath in and closed my eyes. I willed the darkness to leave. For a moment, I didn't think it would, but then it slowly withdrew, like a wave pulling back from the sand, rejoining the night and the shadows all around me. When it went, it left behind exhaustion so deep, for a moment, I thought I'd pass out. I sank down into a heap, unable to so much as lift my head. No fainting this time, thank goodness. I must have been getting better at controlling this thing.

Inigo scooped me up off the grimy floor and held me against his oh so solid chest. I let my head fall against him, my nose pressed into that sweet spot where shoulder met throat. He smelled of sweat and man and, oddly enough, smoke. Wood smoke. Like from a campfire.

He was warm too, far warmer than even someone who'd just fought a bunch of vampires should be. It struck me as odd, but I was too tired to try to figure it out. All I wanted was to go to bed and sleep for a hundred years, preferably curled up against all that heat.

"Morgan." Kabita's face swam into view. She looked worried. More worried than I'd seen her in a long time. "Are you...are you OK?"

"M'fine. Jus' need sleep." I sounded like a drunk.

"OK, we'll get you home. Don't worry."

Just before I passed out, a single thought flashed through my overworked brain: I needed to confront Brent Darroch. I needed to find out whether he really was controlling the vampires and why. Or how, for that matter.

I started to struggle in Inigo's arms. I had to get to Darroch. I had to stop him. I had to...

Inigo whispered a single word in my ear: "Sleep."

I did.

The cold night air made my cheeks sting and my eyes water. I wanted to be home in my soft bed with the plump pillows and silken coverlets, but the big warrior had made me promise not to speak. Not to make a sound. A princess keeps her promises.

The warrior held me tightly, almost too tightly, curled up against his warm chest. Usually a member of the warrior line would never have been allowed to touch me, but the warrior Varan was also descended from a priest. That made him very special, and Nana had promised me I would be safe with him. Nana always kept her promises too.

He'd come in the dead of night to our secret hiding place, whispering to Nana in that tone grown-ups use when something terrible has happened. I knew that tone of voice. The high priest himself once visited Nana and whispered in that same voice. That was the night my father, the prince, died. The night the high priest moved Nana and me into a secret part of the palace. Before he left, he'd leaned down and said, "You will be safe here. Just remember: never leave this part of the palace until I send for you." He'd turned away, then hesitated and leaned back down. "It's a secret."

Then he was gone. From that day on, I never left the three rooms or the tiny garden that became my world. Until tonight.

"There it is." It was the first time the warrior had spoken in what felt to my child's mind like days and days, though it was still the same night. "The Temple of the Moon Goddess." The temple glowed softly in the moonlight like something out of one of Nana's magic stories. I could feel its soft light pulsing inside my own soul, whispering to me of adventures yet to come.

He set me on my feet before the great doors of the temple and raised his fist. The door swung open before he could knock and a woman nearly as tall as he stood before us. She was scary in a way even the warrior couldn't dare to be. The warrior was strong and brave and noble, like all warriors of the priest line. But this woman was something else. She wore the robes of a priestess, but her eyes were fierce beyond belief and her entire bearing spoke of power and magic. I tried not to quiver. A princess is always brave.

"Thank you, Warrior," she spoke softly, but there was authority in her voice that made even my warrior stiffen. "You may return to your duty. You must protect the Heart at all costs. She will find you when the time is right."

The warrior clasped his right hand over his heart in salute and bowed his head. "Yes, my lady." He turned and bowed to me. "Your Highness, it has been my great honor to protect and serve you, but now I must go. I bid you farewell."

Then he was gone into the night, blending into the darkness until he was one with the shadows. I knew I would dream of him for many nights to come. I felt a tear slip down my cheek and roughly scrubbed it away. A princess never cries.

I turned back to the priestess, feeling scared for the first time that night. I missed Nana. I missed my home. I even missed my warrior, though I'd only known him a short time. The priestess bent down and brushed her finger across my cheek. It was coarse, like a warrior's hand, yet gentle like Nana's. When she smiled, there was kindness and love in her eyes and I could see the light glowing brightly in her soul.

"Don't be afraid, little one. I am Artemisa, high priestess of the goddess. You will be safe here. This I swear on my life." She took my hand and led me through the gates of the Temple of the Moon.

သ

My eyes flew open and I found myself sprawled out in my own bed, staring at the cracks in my ceiling.

I rolled over and winced as my head gave a vicious throb. Great, it was going to be one of *those* headaches.

I sniffed the air. Cinnamon. I sniffed again. Vanilla. Maybe some cardamom. I love cardamom, but why did my house smell like it? No doubt Inigo had broken into my house yet again.

My bedroom door swung open, light slicing across my eyes and sending my head throbbing so badly I thought I'd have to make a run for the bathroom.

"Sorry." It was Jack.

"How…how…in here?" Fantastic. I was making no sense whatsoever. Not a good sign.

I felt Jack's smile more than saw it. "Kabita called me."

"Kabita?" Kabita called Jack? Had the world ended? I still wasn't entirely through being pissed at her for killing my sunwalker, and I was pretty sure she wasn't convinced he wasn't a monster.

Whoa. Wait. *My* sunwalker?

"Yeah, she was worried about you. She and Inigo had a client meeting, so she called and I came." Of course he did.

He set something on my bedside table. It was my favorite mug. The one that read, *I like cooking with wine. Sometimes I even put it in the food.* The scent wafting off it was the same spicy scent I'd smelled earlier.

"I brought you some tea." He sat down on the edge of my bed, dipping the mattress so I rolled toward him a bit. I didn't mind. His energy was really soothing. I'd never noticed that before. "It's my own blend. Something I picked up…well, a while back. It helps when I have headaches."

"You do this 'kissing the dark' thing too?" He is a sunwalker, after all. Maybe we have the same weird superpowers.

He shook his head. "No. That is something beyond my abilities, I'm afraid. I can channel some energy from the sun, as it is my nature, but dark is…dark is hard to channel without…"

"Without?" I took a sip of tea. It was sweet and spicy and tasted like heaven.

"Never mind, we'll talk about it later. Here, drink some more tea." He helped me sit up a bit so I could drink without spilling it down the front of myself. His arm behind me was hard and warm, and places in me went all tingly from his touch. This was so not the time to be getting all hot and bothered.

He took the mug from me and helped me lie back down. "Get some sleep. You need your rest to cure the headache." I nodded carefully and snuggled back down under the duvet.

His ocean-colored eyes caught mine for a moment, and his full lips quirked in a smile as he stroked my forehead. I felt myself drifting, sleep stealing closer and closer. Right before I drifted back to sleep, I felt him slide under the covers next to me and gather me in his arms.

Chapter Nineteen

"*Wake up, Princess. We must hurry!*" *I felt a hand on my shoulder, shaking me. For a moment, confusion befuddled my brain. In the ten years since the warrior had brought me to the temple, no one had called me by my title. For my own safety, Artemisa told me on that fateful night, no one could ever know my true identity.*

I was used to hiding what I was. As a bastard child of a royal prince and a human mother, I was anathema in the court with a death sentence over my head. At the temple, I was simply another acolyte of the moon goddess, nothing more.

I'd seen Artemisa rarely since that night, instead spending most of my time training with the other acolytes.

But now it was Artemisa herself standing over my bed, dressed not in the robes of her station but in full battle armor. "We must leave now. They've found us."

I had no need to ask who "they" were. I knew exactly who they were. The acrid stench of smoke burned my nostrils. They were burning the temple.

The ones who had destroyed my home and my family were hellbent on eradicating every sign that my people had ever called this planet home, and despite my human blood, they were particularly interested in killing me. Which was why the temple and my survival had been a closely guarded secret; we were the last bastion of our once thriving civilization. No one had known we existed.

Until now.

Artemisa wrenched open the door of my wardrobe and shoved aside the robes. After a moment of fumbling, she beckoned me forward. Instead of wood where the back of the wardrobe should be, there was utter blackness. My eyes must have been very wide, indeed, for Artemisa smiled just a little. "Did you think we would leave you without some way to escape, should the need arise?"

"I never thought about it," I admitted. "I just figured we'd fight our way out when the time came."

She shook her head, half in amusement, half in frustration. "Silly child. You are far too precious to risk in battle. Hurry now."

So I stepped into the darkness with Artemisa close behind me. She shuffled the robes back in place, then slid the panel shut behind us. It was so black I couldn't see my hand in front of my face. Not a ray of light seeped in from the other side of the panel.

I closed my eyes. I wasn't terribly fond of the dark. Silently, I wished for light, just enough to see. An orb appeared in front of me, floating about three feet off the ground, glowing with a soft bluish-white light.

"Very good. I see you've been practicing." Her voice held approval.

"Yes, my lady." She didn't need to know that I had needed no practice. The high priest and the warrior both had warned me to never show my true self to anyone. Not even the high priestess of the Temple of the Moon. No one was to know the true nature of my powers. It was my only real protection against those who sought my death as the last of the royal bloodline, bastard or no.

It was known that a full-blooded member of the royal line carried natural abilities and power beyond even that of the high priest himself. That was how the bloodline became the ruling class of Atlantis in the first place. It was either subjugate or be destroyed by those who feared such power. It was what made the royal line both incredibly powerful and frighteningly dangerous. It was only the gift of the gods, some said, that made the high priest more powerful than the bloodline once he'd been chosen, an unnatural power tied to Atlantis itself that kept the bloodline in check.

Half-breeds, however, did not possess such powers, even half-breeds of the royal line like me. They had some, much like any ordinary citizen of any of the common lines able to manipulate small amounts of energy, but nothing near what a pureblood had. Only purebloods could kiss the power of the universe and bend it to their will. And, strangely enough, pass their knowledge on to some humans.

For some reason, I was different. I was special. Even the high priest himself did not know why. All he ever told me was that he must protect me. That he'd seen I was to be the future of our race. I had no idea what that meant, but he'd given me the best advice I'd ever received: hide what you are at all costs. It had served me well for fifteen years.

The orb led us down a short hallway to a set of narrow, spiral stone steps that led into the bowels of the hill on which the temple had been built. Everything was thick with dust and cobwebs, and creatures with many legs skittered away from the light to hide in the shadows. Dust assaulted my nose and I itched to sneeze. Sneezing, however, would not be a good plan. We might be heard.

The staircase seemed to go on forever. My legs began to tremble and burn with every step. When we finally reached the bottom, several tunnels branched out from the main corridor. Each tunnel was marked with a carved symbol above the entrance. Artemisa led the way down the tunnel marked with the sign of the crescent moon, and my light darted ahead to illuminate the path.

The already low ceiling slanted lower and lower, forcing us to stoop. The passage became narrower and narrower, pressing in on us from every side. Water trickled down the walls and pooled on the floor, leaving streaks of green, slippery scum coating everything. I could feel panic rising, threatening to overwhelm me. I shoved it aside and focused on Artemisa and the glowing orb leading the way deeper into the hillside.

At last we came to a fork in the tunnel, the left branch marked with a crescent moon. The tunnel opened up and allowed us to stand for the first time in what seemed like hours.

"It's safe to speak now." Artemisa beckoned me to walk beside her. Once it would have been a great honor. In light of current events, it was meaningless. Without a temple, the office of high priestess meant less than nothing.

"Where are we going?" I wondered where on earth would be safe enough for us now.

"To the east of here, beyond Çatalhöyük," she said. "There are beautiful and wild lands, empty of humans. We will be safe there. I have been preparing for some time, sending warriors ahead with our most important treasures and scrolls."

I nodded. She'd known this day was coming, just as I had. The first dictate of the priestesses of the Temple of the Moon was to protect the royal bloodline. The second was to protect the knowledge of our people brought with us from our home world, what the humans called "magic." I was the last of that bloodline, half-breed or not. She would protect me with her life.

I hoped it didn't come to that.

We hurried down the left branch of the tunnel and, within minutes, found ourselves outside in the night air. Behind us was a hill on which the temple stood, and above it the sky glowed red. "They're burning the temple." There was infinite sadness in her voice. The last stronghold of the great city of Atlantis was gone forever.

"The other priestesses? The acolytes?"

She smiled at that. "Safe. I already sent them through the tunnels. We are the last."

Though I was sad to see the temple fall, I did not feel the same pain. The temple was not my home. My home had been destroyed ten years ago, when the citadel of Atlantis fell. Now the only thing that remained of my people were a few scattered conclaves hiding in plain sight, praying they would not be discovered, not daring to use their powers. I was used to hiding. I'd been hiding since the day I was born. First, my father had protected me; then, on his death, the high priest had taken over the task before sending me to Artemisa. Hiding did not bother me.

"If we should become separated, you must continue east for three cycles of the moon." Artemisa led the way down the slight incline and into a thicket of trees. "Look for a fortress of wood that sits on an island where three rivers meet. The locals will know it." She turned to me and gave me a fierce look. "You must get there, Princess. You must survive. You are our last hope. You know that."

I knew it. Any descendant of Atlantis could access the knowledge of the amulet to at least some degree, and with a special ritual known to all Atlanteans access some of its power as well, but only a member of the royal bloodline could access its complete knowledge and control its full power. And anything less than full access would lead to absolute power without the wisdom to temper such power with mercy.

To ensure this never happened, I was to be broodmare to the future, for that was part of the high priest's vision. It would be my line who would produce the key. It was a duty for which the high priest had prepared me since childhood. Until recently, I did not even question my fate.

Part of me hoped we'd get separated. A lifetime of being locked away had left me longing for adventure and freedom, to be an ordinary person just for once.

She cast a quick look back over her shoulder at the firelit sky, then turned toward the east, her face hard with resolve. "Remember what I told you."

Before I could say a word, loud voices erupted from the bushes. Pure instinct took over. Between one breath and the next, I wrapped the night around me, hiding myself from our attackers within the darkness. Three men burst into the open, shouting in a tongue I did not understand. They were covered in soot and armed with sharp spears.

Artemisa spoke to them in their own tongue. I did not understand her words, but her meaning was clear: Let us go. Or else.

The men laughed, their greedy eyes watching us in a way I did not like. Not at all.

"Artemisa…" I kept my voice low so as not to give away my presence.

"When they attack, you run."

"But…"

"Do not argue with me. The future of our people is at stake, remember that. Where do you go?" The men moved closer, weapons at the ready. "Answer me."

"East three cycles to the fortress where three rivers meet."

"Good. Now run." With a battle cry to put any warrior to shame, the last high priestess of the moon charged to her death. With tears streaming down my cheeks, I ran.

∽

I bolted upright in bed. "Jack! Jack!" Dammit, my feet were all tangled up in the duvet again.

Jack stirred next to me. So I hadn't imagined him crawling into bed. "What is it? Are you OK?"

"I know why Darroch took the amulet."

"What do you mean?" Jack tried to wrap an arm around me, but I pushed him out of the way impatiently. I needed to get up, get going, now.

I slid out of bed and probably would have continued sliding all the way to the floor if Jack hadn't grabbed me. My legs were jelly.

"Slow down, Morgan. You expended a lot of energy tonight. You are in no shape to go running around the city." He kept one arm around me, and I was suddenly very aware that not only was I not wearing a bra, but my left breast was squashed up against his very firm chest. I really hoped he couldn't feel how hard my heart was pounding.

"I have to. No choice. We have got to get that amulet back from Darroch before he uses it." I shrugged away from him and started scrambling about the bedroom. *Where are my pants? Where are my damn pants?* I finally found them folded neatly on the chair in the corner. Kabita's work, obviously. She's the neat freak, not me.

I jerked them on, nearly falling over in the process. "There's a reason Darroch has the amulet, Jack, and it's not because he wants you dead. I mean, he does, but that's not the main reason."

"I agree. He wants the knowledge the amulet contains. It will allow him to become even more rich and powerful than he already is. We already knew that."

I shook my head. "Wrong." I stuffed myself into a clean T-shirt. In the dark, I couldn't tell what color it was, but frankly, I didn't care. "He doesn't care about the amulet's knowledge; he wants its *power*. And I'm not talking about the power that comes with wealth; I'm talking about the ability to control people."

He didn't answer at first, but his brow wrinkled. I figured he was scanning through what he knew of the amulet and coming up blank. "Surely, that's not possible. Unless he's a member of the royal bloodline, which he obviously isn't, the power he can gain is very limited at best. Did you dream this?"

"Yeah, I did. I've been dreaming of it little by little, seeing bits and pieces of the puzzle, and tonight I finally got all the pieces, or at least enough to know why the amulet was created and how it can be accessed." *Shoes, shoes, shoes.* Why can you never find a matching pair of shoes when you need them?

I scrounged around on the bottom of my closet, tossing footwear left and right. I finally came up with a pair of black Chucks that matched.

"I know why it was created. It holds the knowledge of Atlantis." He folded his arms and watched me hop around, trying to get my shoes on.

"True." I flashed him a grin. "But it holds a lot more than that. It holds the *power* of Atlantis."

He frowned as he handed me my jacket. "What do you mean?"

"Well, you know this kissing business? Kissing the dark and so on with the elements? It turns out it was something only the most powerful Atlanteans could do. The priests, the royal bloodline. And apparently they were able to teach some of the humans how to do it as well. The Atlanteans were the ones who taught the elemental mages. That's how the mages got their power—until they got too greedy and eventually lost control."

He nodded. "Yes, OK, that makes sense. Though, all Atlanteans had at least some abilities far beyond that of humans, at least from what I've seen in my dreams."

"Exactly. With time and intermarrying with humans, the descendants of those few of Atlantean blood who survived the massacres lost their abilities." I started strapping on weapons. Lots and lots of weapons. "Or at least they stopped being able to access their abilities, which eventually became dormant. The amulet was created by the last high priest of Atlantis not only to store all the technological and quantum knowledge the Atlantean people had gained over the millennia but to make contact with those of Atlantean blood until it found a member of the royal bloodline."

He gave me an aggrieved look. "Yes, I know this. I am the guardian for a reason."

"What you don't know is that, when the amulet comes into contact with a member of the royal bloodline of Atlantis, it will reawaken all the power and abilities of the people of Atlantis within that person."

"Of course, that's the whole point." He was starting to sound annoyed. "But Darroch isn't a member of the bloodline, or he'd have accessed the amulet a long time ago."

"Exactly."

"So, we're fine," he insisted. "No need to rush around like headless chickens."

I smirked at him as I slid my sword into its sheath. "That's where you're wrong." I did a quick mental weapons check. "The power of the amulet can be accessed by *anyone* with Atlantean blood. Warrior, priest, royal, or commoner—doesn't matter. It's simply the level of power and type of ability that changes. The amulet will allow only a descendent of the bloodline to fully tap into the knowledge and power contained within."

My favorite stiletto knife needed sharpening, so I yanked out a drawer and grabbed a whetstone before continuing. "That's why you have become as strong as you have, Jack. The amulet allowed you to tap into your latent abilities and gave you the information you needed to understand your mission and survive the centuries, not to mention make you freaking immortal. The problem is that even a commoner can access at least some of the power of the amulet, and with that power and knowledge combined without the proper wisdom..."

Jack looked a little pale. "With the Church losing power day by day and the economy in a mess, the world is ripe for the picking."

"Darroch could become more powerful than the Templars ever were," I agreed. "He doesn't even need to find the bloodline."

"But that doesn't make sense." He shook his head. "If he could access the amulet himself, he would have done so already. You've got to be wrong about that."

I shook my head. "Not necessarily. Maybe he isn't Atlantean at all. Or if he's descended of a common line, he's not strong enough to access the amulet's full power on his own. But there is another way. He has to perform a very specific ritual to release the power. Even members of the priest and warrior lines can access only a tiny fraction of power unless they perform the ritual." I did a mirror check. "That is why the amulet chose you in the first place.

That was always the plan. A descendant of one of the original half-blood warriors should be the one to find and deliver the amulet to a royal descendant, presumably so that the royal descendant could access both the full knowledge and power contained in the amulet without having to perform the ritual. Theoretically, the amulet would also imbue the royal descendant with wisdom to not abuse that power."

"So that pretty much proves you are descended of the warrior priest class as well. Since the amulet has been talking to you. It would explain your other abilities," Jack pointed out.

I mulled it over. "I guess that makes sense. Once I got close enough to the amulet at Darroch's house, it must have sensed me or something like that. That's why I keep getting the dreams. Obviously, it wants us to rescue it."

Even to me, that sounded like a bit of a stretch, but the amulet was starting to feel almost sentient. That old high priest must have had some serious magic mojo to create it.

"Anyway"—one last check to make sure everything was in place—"we need to get it back so that you can do your job and find the right royal person to give it to."

Except something was bothering me about those dreams, something I couldn't quite put my finger on. Unfortunately, it was escaping me at the moment.

"Well, come on, then. Let's go save the world." He opened my bedroom door and waved me outside.

I shoved aside my doubts and flashed him a grin. "And kick Darroch's butt."

His answering grin was frighteningly feral as he followed me out the door. "And definitely kick Darroch's butt."

Chapter Twenty

I was not entirely stupid, so before Jack and I did the whole break-ing and entering thing, I sent a text to Kabita and Inigo to let them know where I was and what I was doing. Jack is one of the best fighters I've ever seen. Possibly the *best* fighter I've ever seen (nine hundred years of experience would do that), but Darroch has a lot of goons. Backup is never a bad idea.

"Doesn't look like anyone's home." His voice was low in my ear as we sat in the car across the street from Darroch's. His breath tickled my skin and sent shivers through my body.

"We still need to be careful. He's got an alarm system and lots of hired muscle. Unless they're out for the evening too." I scanned the grounds. Sure enough, two of the big black cars I'd seen on the day of the barbecue were gone. Then again, I wasn't discounting the possibility they were in the garage or something.

"How many times have you broken in?"

I shrugged. "This is only the second time. And lucky you, I know how to get in."

"Good. You know where the amulet is kept."

"Um. Not so much," I admitted.

"So it could be anywhere." Exasperation was clear in his voice.

"Well, excuse me. I only had time to search the bedroom before he came home," I sniped.

"It wouldn't be in the bedroom." He sounded very sure of himself.

I gave him a look. "What do you mean, it wouldn't be in the bedroom? Wouldn't he want to keep it close?" I guess I had a few things to learn about the fine art of burglary. Is it my fault I am better at killing things than stealing them?

Jack shook his head. His eyes glinted silver in the moonlight. "No. That's the first place a burglar would look. There's no way Darroch would allow that amulet to accidentally fall into the hands of some petty thief." Now it was his turn to give me a look.

"I am not a petty thief." I couldn't help it if my voice came out a little snippy. "I was trying to get the amulet back for you. So it's *your* fault."

He laughed softly. His face was awfully close to mine. It wouldn't take much for him to lean over and kiss me. Despite the slight chill in the night air, I suddenly felt decidedly warm.

"Hey." He reached out and stroked one finger down my cheek, leaving tingles in its wake. Oh, good lord, I was going to melt into a puddle right then and there. "When this is over, I'm taking you out for dinner. How do you feel about Italian?"

Did he just ask me out on a date? "I…uh…I love Italian."

He flashed me a grin. "Great. I know this fantastic little spot just outside Rome. Very romantic."

I think maybe I squeaked. The guy hadn't even slept with me except in the literal sense and he wanted to take me to dinner in Italy? *Holy crap, wait until Kabita hears about this.*

"Guess it's now or never," I said, playing it cool instead of blurting something stupid or, even worse, begging him to throw me to the ground and have his way with me. "Let's go."

I slipped out of the car, shutting the door behind me as quietly as possible. Jack did the same, then came around to join me. He grabbed the back of my head and pulled me in for a quick, hard kiss before taking my hand and heading off across the lawn. Great. Now all I could think about was how warm and strong his hand was, and how soft and full his lips were. How they made certain parts of me sit up and take notice. How much I wanted to kiss him again, strip him naked, climb on top, and…

Honestly, had it been *that* long since I'd been with someone? Come to think of it, yeah. It had definitely been that long.

I led him around to the side of the house where the laundry window was. Unfortunately, this time it was locked up tight. *Dammit.*

"Thought you said you knew the way in," he hissed at me. I just glared at him and moved around to the back, where I knew there was a nice big sliding-glass door. If push came to shove, a rock could accidentally make its way through said door. Though, no doubt the thing was alarmed.

Fortunately for the door, there was no need for mysterious flying rocks. Jack tested it and it slid open easily. Call me crazy, but while I could accept an open mudroom window, a big-ass sliding-glass door left open was another story entirely. "Jack," I hissed at him, "I don't think—"

It was too late. The light inside snapped on and Brent Darroch sat there in all his creepy Julian Sands glory. He looked for all the world like some kind of wannabe king, with his velvety high-backed armchair, surrounded by his neckless goon squad, minus Clive and the scrawny guy. Only, instead of a scepter, he held a very large pistol. Freaking fantastic.

I wondered vaguely if he'd been sitting there since I dusted Kaldan. Frankly, I wouldn't put it past him.

There was no point in running back the way we came. A quick glance over my shoulder revealed Clive and Scrawny lurking behind me, Clive with a smug look on his face and a really big gun in his hand. *Damn.* He ushered us inside with a wave of his gun for an audience with his majesty. Scrawny took up the rear.

"Welcome back, Miss Bailey." Darroch's oily voice sent chills down my spine. Not the good kind, either. "I didn't expect to see you again so soon. And my old friend Jackson Keel, how lovely to see you. It's been, what, at least ten, fifteen years?"

"Twenty," Jack growled. I could see the muscles working in his jaw. If he weren't careful, he would grind his teeth flat.

Darroch waved his hand airily. "Has it truly been that long? Well, six of one, half dozen of the other. Isn't that how the saying goes, Miss Bailey?"

I ignored him.

"I really must thank you both for being so accommodating. I'd been worrying about how to deal with you, and then there you were, sitting right outside my house." He smirked at us.

"You've got the amulet, Darroch. You've had it for twenty years. Why do you need us?" Jack snarled. "You took it the same night you..." He broke off.

"Yes, the same night I killed your little plaything. It was such a pity. I wouldn't have minded having her to myself for a while."

He didn't make a sound, but the expression on Jack's face made my blood run cold. There was so much hate and anger. He launched himself at Darroch, but Clive threw himself in front of Jack and slammed him across the head with the butt of his gun. Damn, that looked like it hurt.

The goon holding me obviously expected some kind of damsel in distress, because my sudden move took him by surprise: I jerked out of his hold, gave him a nice hard kick in the shins with my heavy boots, and took off toward the other side of the room where Jack and Clive were slugging it out, praying Darroch wouldn't shoot me in the head.

Scrawny, who'd obviously seen one too many Jet Li movies, did some complicated flip thing and dropped down in front of me, blocking my path. I got in a few good punches before he got me in a headlock. I could barely breathe, never mind move.

Jack slugged Clive a good one, sending the large man staggering into the heavy curtains around the window. They crashed to the floor, sending Clive sprawling, but there was no time to applaud. Darroch waved at one of the other goons with his gun.

Next thing I knew, a couple more meatheads waded into the fray, throwing kicks and punches with far too much glee. Clive managed to get himself untangled and knocked Jack on the head with the butt of his gun again, dazing him. The other goons made short work of tying Jack up and propping him against the nearest wall.

Jack may have been stunned, but he wasn't out, and he was still pissed. "Darroch, you fucking…I will kill you for what you did."

"Don't be ridiculous, Keel. You don't have a chance in hell of touching me. So stop being so melodramatic." He waved his hand airily and Clive kicked Jack viciously in the ribs, sending him toppling sideways.

"Darroch, you jackass, what did you do that for?" I snapped. "He's already tied up. What *do* you want us for, anyway?"

"Well, that's the thing, you see." Darroch flicked an imaginary piece of lint from his pant leg before crossing one leg over the other. "I've been trying to access that damn amulet for *years*, only to discover—and this will amuse you, Jack—that I am not strong enough!" He threw his head back and laughed uproariously. "Can you imagine? Me! Not strong enough! Me, not *pure* enough. Me, a member of one of the richest and most influential families in the United States of America, a descendant of nothing more than a *commoner*! I can't access more than a mere smidgen of the amulet on my own; I need to perform the damn ritual. Can you believe the injustice of it?"

"Proof positive that money doesn't buy breeding." I couldn't help it; it just came out.

"Oh, Miss Bailey, you have no idea!" He seemed delighted. "All these years I've been searching for the pieces I need to complete the ritual and now"—he clapped his hands together—"now I have them!"

"Why don't you get on with it already instead of talking our ears off? We know you're in control of the local vampires. We know you had them watching me. You've already got the amulet. So why the hell do you need us?" I was getting really pissed off.

"Why, my dear Miss Bailey, you are so feisty today." He beamed at me. I scowled back. "You are right, of course," he continued, unfazed. "I have taken control of the local vampire clans. The clan leaders were weak and ineffectual, so it was really quite easy. I promised them power and human slaves. In their greed and hunger, they were delighted to do whatever I asked of them. All I needed was for the master to willingly exchange a little blood with me and the entire clan was bound to do my bidding. They've been so tremendously useful finding the ritual pieces."

"So that was why their eyes were red. You're not a vampire, so your control of them changed their physiology."

"Yes, I believe so. I'm not sure entirely why their eyes changed, specifically. Something in my DNA, I imagine." He chuckled. "No matter. I lied, of course, about giving them power. I have no use for the undead, certainly not ones with any power. I had no intention of keeping my promise. I just needed Kaldan to take my blood willingly. I simply wanted them for one purpose. They were a means to an end, so to speak."

"To kill me."

"No, no, Miss Bailey, you mistake my meaning. I did not want them to kill you." He leaned forward in his chair, almost eagerly. "I sent them to test you. Kaldan took it a little too far, I admit, but I had every confidence you would prove yourself, and I needed to make sure."

Jack and I gave each other a look that was entirely full of bafflement. "Test me? Why?"

"I had to be sure, of course. I had to know if you were the one. You see, don't you?"

Jack shook his head. "Stop beating around the bush, Darroch," he snarled from his place on the floor. "What 'one'? What is Morgan to you?"

"Why, she's the one I've been looking for all these years, of course."

"Excuse me?" I was running very short on patience. "What the hell are you talking about?"

"You should be delighted, Miss Bailey." He leaned back and did the finger-steeple thing. "You are the last piece of the puzzle, a puzzle that's millennia old. The last piece I need to perform the ritual that will allow me to access the power of the amulet and my own latent abilities. You, Miss Bailey, are the key to the treasure of Atlantis."

Well, shit.

ശ

"Are you crazy? Never mind. I already know the answer to that. Me? A key? You've got to be kidding." I gave Jack a sideways look. He just shrugged.

Darroch gave me a toothy smile. "Not *a* key, my dear. *The* key. I need the blood of a royal descendant of Atlantis as part of the ritual."

That made no sense. If blood was the key, how would that help Darroch? Wouldn't the royal get the knowledge instead of him? "I thought the whole point of the ritual was so you didn't need a royal."

"Ah, but that is the whole problem. The ritual only works if there are no royals left alive. As long as there is a living royal Atlantean, the ritual won't work. However, I mix the blood of a royal into the ritual..." He spread his hands as if to say *voilà*.

"And you think I'm a royal? Are you nuts?"

He didn't answer, just smiled that annoying smile of his.

At last, it made sense. If Darroch thought I was a descendant of the royals—which was completely insane—he would need my blood for the ritual. Which made me wonder why, if he thought I was a member of the royal bloodline, he hadn't just killed me so he could perform his little ritual in peace without needing any of my blood.

"Of course, killing you would have been so much easier," Darroch continued as if he'd read my mind. "But the last high priest was a crafty one. He built in a safety. Anyone who murdered a royal and then tried to gain access to the amulet would be denied. Of course, I could have had one of my boys do it, but... Well, I couldn't take that risk."

"Because the amulet would *know*, and then you'd never get the damn thing to open," Jack snarled.

"How did *you* know about the amulet?" I asked. It isn't like they teach ancient Atlantean history in school.

Darroch gave me a pleased smile, as though I'd said something really smart. "Why, the knowledge has been passed down through my family for generations, of course. From father to son since the beginning. Many commoners survived, surprisingly."

It hit me. "You are a descendant of Atlantis too."

Anger slid through his eyes before he caught himself and gave me a smile. "Very good. Unfortunately, while the amulet is designed to wake latent genetic knowledge in *all* descendants of Atlantis with whom it comes into contact, only the blood of a royal can open it fully. And there aren't many of them around. It is a most annoying quandary."

"I still don't get it. If a royal touches the amulet, it's the royal who will get the knowledge and power, not you."

"Ah, but not if the royal dies immediately after." His smile was decidedly unpleasant.

He was planning to use my blood, then kill me. Wonderful. "Killing me isn't going to do you any good, Darroch. I am not a royal."

Darroch looked smug, flush with victory at outsmarting a long-dead priest. "Oh, you shall see soon enough."

I hoped not. Our backup was on its way—if they managed to get their asses here before Darroch chopped me into little pieces, or whatever it was his ritual required.

Darroch waved to his goons, and they hustled across the floor toward where Scrawny still had me in some kind of Vulcan nerve pinch. I guessed I was going to find out sooner rather than later. They stripped me of my weapons, then dragged me back to Darroch. They even got the ones in my wrist sheaths. *Dammit.*

"Stop!" Jack bellowed. "She isn't a royal. Her blood will do you no good. If you must sacrifice someone, sacrifice me."

Sounded like a good plan to me. Except for the whole part where Jack would probably die. Jack could survive pretty much everything, from what he'd told me earlier, but I wasn't sure massive blood loss coupled with the activation of the amulet was one of them. And I really didn't like the thought of Jack dying. But I shouldn't have worried, because rather than taking him seriously, Darroch roared with laughter.

"Who said anything about sacrifice? Oh, you stupid, pathetic man. How weak you've become since I saw you last. No longer the proud warrior of legend." He leaned forward, right into Jack's face. I wondered how Jack managed not to head-butt the man. I would have found it an irresistible temptation.

Then I felt something cold and hard pressing against my temple. Clive had stepped up beside Scrawny and me. Oh, yeah, goon with gun threatening to kill me. That would put a damper on things. Jack might be willing to risk himself—he'd spent the last nine hundred years immortal, after all—but I knew without a shadow of a doubt he wouldn't risk their hurting me.

Darroch tilted Jack's head up as Clive yanked my arms back and tied them behind me. "How can you not know, Jackson? How can you have been so blind? Do you not even know who you've been sent to protect?"

Say what? What made Darroch think he knew anything about me? I didn't have time to figure it out. I had a murder to prevent: my own.

Darroch shook his head in mock pity. "I almost feel sorry for you. Almost." He let go of Jack and, surrounded by his goons, headed toward the hall with me in tow.

"Darroch!" Jack roared, yanking against the rope. "Don't you dare harm her. Take me!"

Darroch turned around. "I don't want you. Your blood isn't strong enough, either. Otherwise, I would have killed you years ago. Instead, you kept me entertained until I found what I needed. I found her." He stroked my face, and it took all I had not to throw up on his shoes. "I wasn't sure when we first met, but he was right about you. Blood calls to blood, after all."

"What does that mean? Darroch! What does that mean? Who was right about her? Darroch!" But Darroch didn't answer him. Instead, he swept out of the room with his entourage and me behind him.

∽

Darroch left a couple of his guards with Jack and dragged me toward the front stairs, which I already knew led up to his bedroom and whatever else was up there. The amulet, obviously. I fought him every step of the way, dragging my feet until Clive hoisted me up over his shoulder like a sack of potatoes. Resistance was futile, apparently.

Clive followed Darroch down the hall, the other five goons, including Scrawny, trailing behind. Each stomp of Clive's enormous feet jostled me, sending my head knocking into his back and his shoulder digging deeper and deeper into my stomach. Not the most comfortable mode of transport.

We finally reached what appeared, from my upside-down position, to be the gate to a castle. Seriously, there was one of those black wrought-iron accordion gates, which Darroch unlocked, then pushed back. Underneath that there was a thick wooden door that just needed some cast-iron hardware to complete the look. Instead, the hardware was ordinary cheap brass, but the lock was some serious business.

Once we were inside the room, Clive finally put me down. It was a good-size bedroom with a nice view of the backyard, but it was completely empty of furniture other than a couple of small chests against one wall next to a closed door. Even the floor was just plain under flooring. No carpet. No hardwood. Nothing. Symbols were chalked in a circle on the floor like wiccans would use a pentagram. I recognized the symbols from the pictures I'd seen of the amulet: ancient Atlantean.

"Put her in the center of the circle," Darroch commanded.

With a nod, Clive dumped me, still trussed up like a chicken, into the middle of the circle and then stepped back, gun trained on me. Darroch joined me there, looking very solemn and somber, while the goons rummaged about in the chests, bringing out random objects.

"This is ridiculous, Darroch."

He ignored me as Scrawny placed a tattered leather-bound book in his hands. He nodded to Scrawny, who then began placing incense braziers around the circle, carefully lighting each one. Great. There went my allergies.

As the other goons moved to form points around the circle, still holding whatever objects were needed for the ritual, Darroch began chanting. I had no idea what the language was, but it sounded like it might have been pretty if spoken by someone who had an actual ear for languages. Darroch was not such a person.

This was it. Now or never. I could try to break the ritual and risk Clive shooting me in the head or wind up a zombie or whatever Darroch had planned. Not much of a choice, if you ask me.

I kicked out, sending one of the burning braziers skidding across the room to slam against the wall. I made sure to swipe my blue-jeaned leg against the chalk marks, blurring the symbols on the floor.

"Stop her!"

Clive lifted his gun. Took aim.

"Don't shoot her, you idiot," Darroch snarled. "Not yet."

With a shrug, Clive stuck his gun into his waistband and strode into the circle. I lashed out, kicking him with both feet right in the kneecap. He didn't even flinch. Instead, he scooped me up, then hauled off and slapped me across the face, snapping my head back. Then he dropped me back down in the middle of the circle. I swear I actually saw stars.

Scrawny set up the brazier again and Darroch returned to his chanting. My head was throbbing, but I had no plans to lie down and take it. This time I kicked out, knocking Darroch off his feet. He crashed to the floor nearly on top of me, sending the book flying.

"You stupid bitch," he snarled, cocking his fist back.

"Hey, Morgan. Got yourself an interesting situation, I see."

I glanced over toward the doorway. A woman dressed all in black with midnight hair in a long plait behind her stood in the doorway, a silver dagger in one hand. Her smirk was nothing if not sardonic.

I grinned back. "Hey, Kabita. How's it shakin'?"

Darroch snarled as he struggled to his knees. "What the hell is this?" He waved his goons forward.

Clive raised his gun and fired. I was sure Kabita was a goner. I screamed her name as the bullet grazed her shoulder. Clive fired again, only this time the bullet stopped in midair.

We all stared at it in confusion as it dropped to the floor with a little thunk.

What followed was a barrage of bullets, the sound nearly deafening me. Not one found its mark. Instead, they all slammed up against some sort of invisible shield before falling harmlessly to the ground. I had no idea Kabita has such power. It was extremely cool.

Finally, the shooting stopped. Either the bad guys were out of bullets or they'd finally realized bullets weren't going to work.

Kabita may not have been very tall, but her anger made her formidable. "Do you know what I hate?" She twirled the dagger between long, supple fingers. "I hate liars. I hate people who try to use me. And I *really* hate people who try to hurt my friends. I'm your worst nightmare, Brent Darroch. You do *not* mess with me or my friends and get away with it."

Before the goon squad could grab her she'd whipped out a long knife and slashed one across the face, while nearly taking a hand off the other one with her dagger. I wanted to jump up and down and clap my hands like a little kid, but they were still tied, and I was still lying in the middle of that stupid circle.

Instead, I whirled into a kick, catching Darroch right in the solar plexus and knocking the wind out of him.

He went down with a gasp. I just laughed. Brent Darroch and his minions had one or two things to answer for.

Kabita twirled toward the center of the room, knives slicing and dicing as she went. She paused long enough to toss me one so I could cut myself free off the bindings.

I jumped to my feet, just catching movement from the corner of my eye. With a quick backward thrust, I stabbed the guy coming up on me from behind so fast he was on the floor holding his stomach before he could even think about firing his gun, if he had any bullets left. I looked around and discovered Inigo had popped out of nowhere and started thrashing goon ass. Awesome.

That was when I realized Darroch had used the distraction to slip away from the fighting. I caught him hurrying through the closed door I'd noticed earlier. Shit, I'd bet anything he was going after the amulet. If he got to it, we were screwed.

"Morgan!" It was Jack, shouting from downstairs.

I didn't have time to answer him. I slashed at another goon as I fought my way to the door. I made it up a few steps before Scrawny, who was on the floor with a nasty-looking slash across the abdomen, grabbed my ankle and tried to haul me back down, so I kicked him in the face. I felt something crunch under my shoe, and blood spurted up my jeans leg as he howled in pain. *Ew, gross.* I probably had blood all over my shoe now too.

I scrambled through the door, ignoring the fighting behind me. Kabita and Inigo seemed to have things well in hand. Stopping Darroch was paramount. I couldn't let him get away with the amulet.

I popped my head through the door. Nothing. It was an ordinary closet—and completely empty. *What the...?* Then I noticed a little light spilling across the wine-red carpet. Light that wasn't coming from the room behind me.

Doh! False wall, of course. The amulet wasn't *in* the closet; it was in a tiny safe room *behind* the closet, and Darroch was inches away from it.

Without so much as a thought, I gathered the darkness in the room all around me. I gathered the darkness of the house and of the night outside and pulled it into me. Everything took on edges of purple and silver, like looking through some weirdo night-vision goggles. My breathing slowed, my heart calmed, everything grew still. And the darkness roared...

Chapter Twenty-One

I don't know how I did it, but one minute I was at the closet door, too far away to stop Darroch from grabbing the amulet. The next I was across the room, ripping him away from the pedestal in the center. Not about to go easily, Darroch punched me in the stomach, doubling me over.

Anger flooded me, cold and hard. My hands closed around his throat. Then he was clear across the floor, smashing into the wall and then sliding down into a motionless heap. The darkness was screaming at me. Screaming for blood and for death. My fingers closed around the knife Kabita had thrown to me. The one I'd nearly forgotten.

I paced toward Darroch, the bloody blade raised.

"Holy hell, Morgan!"

It was Jack. My weird night vision picked him out in rich blues and sparkling silvers. His eyes glittered in the darkness with an eerie greenish hue, more like a cat's eyes than human. I wasn't sure if that was a sunwalker thing or a side effect of my vision.

The darkness didn't care. The darkness wanted blood. I started for Darroch.

Jack reached out and grabbed my hand, and I blinked. It was like waking up from a dream. I could feel the darkness ebbing away slowly, like a wave after it hits the shore, while reality crept in to take its place, returning my vision to normal.

I glanced around at the room. The amulet lay nestled in a bed of black velvet on a small pedestal in the center of the floor. The walls, carpet, and even the ceiling were solid black, the amulet the only thing of color in the room. A single light shone overhead, bathing it in a golden glow. *Oh, my.*

"I need to find a safe place for this." Jack quickly wrapped the amulet up in the velvet and tucked it away in his pocket.

"No kidding. Um…I think we'd better get Darroch out of here and see if Kabita needs any help." It was lame even to my ears, but it was all I could think of. I was starting to scare myself with this whole crazy kissing the darkness thing. I couldn't imagine what Jack was thinking. Eddie was right: I needed to get this ability or whatever it was under control or figure out a way to stop using it. Each time I did, it was increasingly reluctant to leave.

Darroch was out cold, so Jack grabbed his shoulders, I grabbed his feet, and we hauled him out of the secret room and through the closet to the bedroom, where Kabita and Inigo had pretty much cut a swath of destruction through the goon squad. There was blood everywhere, and the rich copper tang made my stomach turn over.

"Oh, good, you got him." Kabita was an oasis of calm in the middle of the wreckage. She didn't sound any more ruffled than if she'd just had afternoon tea with her grandmother, but I could see something else in her eyes. Something that said the violence hadn't really been that easy.

"Uh…yeah. How are we going to explain this one to the cops? These aren't vampires or demon spawn or anything. These are humans." I didn't have a whole lot of experience fighting humans, strangely enough, but I knew the cops wouldn't be terribly thrilled with us. Somehow, I didn't think they'd be impressed if we told them we were trying to save the world. Getting locked up for murder was a distinct possibility. The government doesn't give us *that* much leeway.

Kabita shrugged. "That's what our government liaison is for. He's not going to be happy, either, let me tell you." She seemed ridiculously gleeful over that fact.

I guess I was wrong. The government *does* give us that much leeway, which is disturbing.

She gave me a look. "The amulet?"

"Jack's got it, safe and sound."

"Better make it disappear or it may become a little more safe and sound." She pulled out a travel pack of wet wipes from her back pocket and started cleaning the blood off her hands. That's Kabita for you, always prepared.

She had a point too. The government likes to make artifacts disappear permanently. Research, I guess.

"Sure thing. What about Darroch? Won't his muckety-muck friends be pissed about this?"

Her features hardened. "I've got friends in high places too, remember."

That she does. "Good. Long as he gets locked away from the rest of us, I'm fine with it. You take care of the Darroch situation, and we'll meet you back at the office." I grabbed Jack's hand and pulled him out of the room before he could argue, leaving her to it. I knew he wanted to deal with Darroch himself, but some things really are better left to the government. Jack would probably kill Darroch, but our little secret government agency? Oh, they'd make him wish he'd never been born. Thanks to the Supernatural Terrorism Act, they could do a whole lot of nasty things with complete impunity.

"Can I see it?"

Jack pulled a parcel of cloth out of his pocket and unfolded it, revealing the Heart of Atlantis.

"It's beautiful," I breathed. So this was what we'd fought for. Bled for. Nearly died for. The amulet was a wide, slightly convex gold disc about four or five inches across, with strange symbols carved around a round blue stone set in the center. The stone glowed softly in the low light, the color of deepest sapphire.

Jack picked it up and gazed at the amulet in his hands, turning it over as though to make sure Darroch hadn't damaged it. "Yes. This is the Heart of Atlantis. It carries all the knowledge and power the people of Atlantis gained over thousands of years of existence. So much power in so small a thing." He cradled it to his chest, sorrow welling in his ocean eyes. "And it is useless."

"Useless? Excuse me? We just went through hell to get that thing back, and it's useless? What about that whole blood-sacrifice bullshit? And Darroch claiming I'm a royal?"

"If you really were a royal, I'd have sensed it long ago. The Heart would have told me." He shrugged. "Unless I can find a member of the royal bloodline, I can access only fragments of the knowledge. Just enough to keep myself alive and it safe until the rightful owner comes to claim it. Without the bloodline, the information will be lost forever."

"Well, obviously the rightful owner was not Brent Darroch. But what about the original ritual? If you can't find a royal, can't you access it yourself?"

"I tried. Years ago. It didn't work."

"So you're telling me that the priest screwed up?" I found that hard to believe.

"Either that or Darroch was right, and as long as there's a living royal, the original ritual won't work."

"He was trying to use *my* blood. He seemed to think I was a royal. Why would he think that? Why would he want to kill me?"

Jack gave me a look. "Well, he might have just wanted to kill you, but for entirely different reasons."

I punched him in the shoulder. He just smirked.

"Come on, be serious."

"I don't know. Maybe he thought your unusual abilities would do what his own blood couldn't do."

"How would he have known about my abilities?"

He shrugged. "You said he had Kaldan watching you, so obviously the vamps must have seen something and reported it to Darroch."

"So, what now? Are we going to find someone from the bloodline?" I asked. "Do we just keep protecting this thing until someone pops out of the woodwork? Because these dreams are going to drive me nuts if they don't stop."

"So far, in over nine hundred years, I've not met a single survivor of the royal bloodline."

"How would you know you'd met a royal?"

"The amulet would tell me, like it has with everything else over the years." He shook his head. "More than likely their DNA is so diluted it can no longer activate the Heart. I don't hold out a lot of hope for finding a survivor."

I glared at him. "So I'm still going to be dreaming these stupid dreams? I swear, I haven't gotten a good night's sleep since I met you." Technically, the dreams had started the day I met Darroch and learned about the amulet, but I wasn't going to point that out. More fun to blame Jack. "This is so not good."

He smiled, his slightly longer canines glinting in the soft light. "No, not so much." He reached out and took my hand. I laced my fingers through his. It felt nice. Better than nice.

He wrapped the amulet gently in the velvet lining and then tucked it away in his pocket. "I've never seen it activated, but there were drawings in the cave where we found it. It must have been a sight to behold."

"At least we have it now, though, instead of some whacked-out lunatic. That's good, right?" I pointed out. He lifted my hand and kissed it. I guessed I could take that as agreement. "Better go meet Kabita back at the office or there's going to be hell to pay."

He nodded, so we headed outside to the car. The ride to the office was quiet, each of us lost in our own thoughts. I didn't even turn on Tom Petty.

∽

When we got to the office, we walked into bedlam. Kabita and a man I'd never seen before were having an almighty shouting match. I think Kabita might have actually been losing. Scary thought. Kabita doesn't lose shouting matches.

"You are way beyond your purview with this, Ms. Jones." The stranger's voice was as elegant and smooth as melted chocolate, deep and terrifically sexy, but the tone was all kinds of nasty, as was the cheap suit he was wearing. Definitely government issue. "You had no right to detain Mr. Darroch…"

"I had every right," Kabita snapped back, interrupting him— something he didn't take very well, if the scowl on his arrogantly handsome face was anything to go by. I'd never seen her so pissed off before. Wow, the guy must really have gotten under her skin. "Not only is he responsible for the deaths of several civilians, the unbalancing of power within the local vampire clans, the kidnapping of one of my agents, *and* the theft of a priceless artifact, he was also the mastermind of a plot to enslave the human race. I think that gives me the right to lock his ass up. That's why you pay us, isn't it?"

The leather chairs that normally sit in front of Kabita's desk had been shoved aside so the combatants could snarl at each other without obstruction. Inigo was lounging on the matching leather sofa, looking amused. Jack didn't look like he was going to step in, either, so I did. It took a good minute or two of throat clearing and "excuse me's" before I finally gave up and shouted, "Oi! You two. Shut up!"

Their twin expressions of surprise at the interruption were priceless. The man recovered first, a smooth mask sliding into place, ever the bureaucrat. Oh, he was good, but I could smell a company man a mile away.

"Ah, you must be Morgan Bailey. It's a pleasure to make your acquaintance at last. Trevor Daly. I am your government…" He hesitated. I'll just bet he'd planned to say "handler," but my glare made him think better of it. "I'm your government liaison."

He held out his hand, so I took it. He had big hands, smooth but strong, with a slight callus on his right index finger. I bet he spends a lot of time on the firing range. His grip was just the right balance between strength and gentleness. It was the sort of hand-shake that said, *Look, I can crush you with one hand, but I'm not going to unless you give me good reason.*

Of course, he didn't know what I was. I mean, he knew I was a hunter and that I was stronger and faster than most humans, thanks to my attack, but he didn't know about the darkness. If anyone's hand got crushed, it wouldn't be mine.

Trevor Daly might be a pain in Kabita's ass, but I had a feeling he'd be a good man to have behind you in a fight, if you could ever convince him to join your side in the first place.

"Nice to meet you, Mr. Daly."

"Trevor, please. Call me Trevor." He flashed me what I could only assume was his most charming smile.

"Look, Mr. Flirtypants." I almost laughed out loud as his eyes widened in surprise and a dull flush spread under his dark skin. "Don't you start that bullshit with me. I take it you're the asshole I can blame for this fiasco."

"Excuse me?" He was practically spluttering with outrage. He clenched his hands into fists so hard his knuckles turned white before he regained his composure, that bland mask slipping back into place. Interesting. They'd trained him well, but underneath, he was pure fire and heat.

"Morgan." There was a warning in Kabita's voice, but I ignored it.

I propped my hands on my hips and thrust my chest out. "You heard me. I hold you personally responsible for this fubar situation. Brent Darroch as a client? A 'magical' artifact? Really? Did you expect me to fall for that bullshit? I don't know why you want some supposed 'sunwalker' dead, if sunwalkers even exist, and I don't care. Next time you want your dirty work done, do it yourself. Don't expect us to do it for you, and don't use some bullshit story to cover it up, 'cause we ain't buyin.'"

I turned my back on him and spoke to Kabita, who was pretending to look stern, but I could tell she was howling with laughter inside. "Darroch? The goons?" I asked.

"Daly called in a cleanup crew for the dead ones. I don't think we need to worry about the ones who are still alive. They're just hired muscle, but we're...debriefing them, just in case. We don't exactly want them telling the police what happened. Darroch"— she nodded at Trevor, who was still gaping at me—"the government will take over. They've got a nice cell for him out at Area Fifty-One."

I am fairly certain Area 51 in the Nevada desert doesn't have anything to do with aliens. It's where the government sticks felons whose crimes are of a supernatural nature, when a public trial and imprisonment in a regular jail cell are out of the question.

"We don't call it that," Trevor interrupted.

Kabita ignored him. "And his government friends?"

Trevor's smile was tight. "Trust me. They won't be causing a problem."

"Good." Kabita gave a quick nod. "As far as I'm concerned, we're done. Job finished."

"Wait a minute." I watched Trevor pull himself together. "Did you find the sunwalker?"

I shrugged. Showtime. "There is no such thing as a sunwalker. My sources tell me they died out hundreds of years ago, not long after the

Crusades. The so-called 'sunwalker' we were supposed to hunt was just a powerful vampire Darroch wanted out of the way so he could control the local vamps. I took care of it." I knew there was no way Trevor Daly could follow up on my story. Vamps don't leave corpses.

Trevor brushed it aside. "And the artifact you mentioned. The one Darroch hired you to find. Where is it? It needs to be secured immediately."

Ah, so that was what this was about. The government didn't care one bit about a possible sunwalker threat or Brent Darroch and his friends in high places. They wanted the artifact, pure and simple. It was what they'd wanted all along. I wondered whether they had any idea what it was, what it could do.

"We didn't find it," Kabita broke in, her face every bit as bland as Daly's. "It probably doesn't exist. It was most likely just another of Darroch's stories to gain influence with the local vampire clans and to justify the hunt."

"But you said he had a plot to enslave humanity. How could he do that without the amulet?" Trevor wasn't giving up that easily. It was now obvious he had some idea of the amulet's power, and he was definitely suspicious of our story.

"He did. He was planning to unite the vampire clans. Do that and you can enslave humanity, turn us all into a bunch of sheep. At least on a local level. Who knows what his ultimate goal was. He's not exactly sane." Her face was completely deadpan. I swear, if I didn't know her as well as I do, I'd have totally bought it. I really hoped Trevor Daly did.

Trevor turned to me.

I shrugged. "I searched Darroch's place top to bottom. Never found any artifact. A few antique knickknacks, but nothing like what he claimed he had." I gave him a look of pure innocence.

Trevor looked from Kabita back to me, mistrust written all over his face. It was obvious he didn't completely believe us, but what could he do? Hold us down and frisk us?

Inigo made a sound suspiciously like laughter. I glared at him. He just smiled back blandly. If I didn't know better, I'd have said he'd read my mind.

"Fine," Trevor snapped, slamming his fist down on Kabita's desk. Temper, temper. "If that's the way you want to play it. Just remember, Ms. Jones, what I mentioned earlier? That isn't going away."

Kabita's normally dusky skin looked a little pale, but she stood ramrod straight and didn't give an inch. I was so proud of her. Of course, that is Kabita through and through. When she decides on a course of action, she follows it to the end. Damn the torpedoes and all that. I wondered what on earth Trevor Daly had on Kabita to make her so upset.

I'd no doubt that he was reminding her of whatever it was he'd threatened her with to get our cooperation in the first place. Whatever it was, it must be something big. I made a note to ask her about it later in private. My estimation of Trevor Daly dropped way down to scumbag. You do not threaten my best friend and get away with it.

Trevor snatched up his leather briefcase and, with barely a nod to me, stormed out of the office. But not before he paused in front of Inigo and gave him one long, very dirty look.

"You OK?" I asked Kabita once he was gone. She still seemed a little shaky.

I watched her visibly pull herself together. "I'm fine, Morgan. Thank you. Trevor Daly is just one of those nasty little things we have to deal with in our line of work. Unpleasant, but a fact of life."

"Right up there with Zagan demons, huh?"

That made her laugh. She turned to Jack. "The amulet?"

"Safe. And I'm going to make sure it stays that way."

"Good." She nodded. "I don't want to know where it is, either." Plausible deniability. I guess if it's good enough for the government, it's good enough for us.

"No problem," Jack agreed.

"I'm headed home. Want a ride?" I asked Jack.

"Yes, thank you."

"I'll talk to you tomorrow," I promised Kabita. She nodded as we exited her office, followed by Inigo. Then she shut the door behind us with a firm click. I hoped she wasn't staying in there to brood. I could tell Trevor Daly had upset her.

"Don't worry, she'll be fine." Inigo leaned against the reception desk in the outer office, well-worn jeans sculpting well-toned legs, but he reached out and took my hand. I felt guilty as a shot of pure lust hit me. How could I be drooling over Inigo and still be into Jack? Not to mention that Jack was standing right next to me. Was my libido that out of whack? Maybe there was some truth in Cordelia's catnip theory.

I gave Inigo's hand a quick squeeze, then dropped it. I didn't know what else to do with Jack standing right there watching our every move. It wasn't like either of them was my boyfriend or anything, but still.

"I'll make sure Kabita gets home OK," Inigo promised, his sky-blue eyes twinkling at me as though he could tell what I was thinking. "Pour a few mojitos down her. She'll be right as rain tomorrow."

I nodded. "Jack, could you give me a minute?"

Jack hesitated. He narrowed his eyes a little at Inigo before heading out the door.

"Listen, Inigo…"

In one swift move, he was beside me. Gone was the laughter, the twinkle. Instead, his expression was dead serious as he cupped my face in his hands.

"Morgan. I know you're freaked out about what happened between us. I know you're confused about me and about Jack."

I was surprised he was so perceptive, but I guess I shouldn't have been. He's clairvoyant, after all.

I opened my mouth to speak, but he shushed me. "You may not understand why I'm doing this, but I'm letting you go right now." There was sorrow in his eyes as he caressed my cheek with his thumb. "And the reason I'm letting you go now is because I know, when the time is right, you're going to come back to me."

His confession hit me like a ton of bricks. We flirted, yeah. But I'd never had any idea he felt this way about me. And even though I've always been attracted to him, I wasn't sure how I felt about his confession. Why hadn't he told me before? Why had he waited?

"You're right. I don't understand it. Letting me go? What the hell does that mean? I wasn't yours to begin with." The words came spilling out of me, laced with confusion and anger. I didn't know whether to be amused or angry or what.

Inigo swallowed hard. "I hate this. I hate that I have to let you go, but it's the only way you're going to know for sure that we are meant to be. Just remember, I'm still here when you're ready."

And then he kissed me. Hard and deep and thoroughly. The heat that is never far from the surface where Inigo is concerned came roaring back.

I jerked away from the kiss. I didn't know what to say. Confused didn't even begin to cover it. I opened my mouth to say something, anything, but nothing came out.

In that moment, I had no idea what I was feeling. If he'd said something even a week ago, things might have been different. But now there was Jack. My emotions were a whirlwind, and I felt trapped inside.

Finally, I took a step back, turned, and followed Jack outside. But before I shut the door, I gave Inigo one last look. For just a moment, his eyes glowed gold, then turned back to blue. It unsettled me to no end.

I hesitated, then finally said, "Night, Inigo."

"Good night, Morgan."

Chapter Twenty-Two

Instead of taking me back to my house, Jack drove to his. He pulled the car into the drive, but left the motor running. "You... ah...You want to come in?"

I hesitated.

"I think we have things to talk about."

He wasn't kidding. I had a few questions for my own personal sunwalker. "Yeah. OK."

I followed him into the house and waited while he switched on a couple of table lamps. "You want something to drink?"

Was he stalling? "Sure."

He disappeared into the kitchen, so I wandered over to the bookshelves. I pulled one off the shelf. It was a first-edition Mark Twain. Signed. Holy crap. I carefully turned the pages, loving the feel of the old paper between my fingers.

My mind kept playing over the scene with Inigo. His confession. Part of me was sad, and part of me was strangely angry. Angry that he'd waited so long to say anything. Sad about what could have been. Was I making the right choice? Was I even making a choice?

"Interesting man, Samuel Clemens." I hadn't heard him reenter the room. Jack's voice jarred me away from thoughts of Inigo. He set two mugs down on the coffee table and the scent of cardamom wafted under my nose. I really love his special blend of tea. "He was kind enough to sign that for me."

"I'm not sure I'll ever get used to the fact that you personally knew people who are, for me, ancient history." I definitely wasn't sure I'd ever get used to the fact I might very well be the same, experiencing centuries of history firsthand. I curled up beside him on the couch. He handed me one of the mugs, then slid his free arm around me. It felt really good leaning back into all that muscled warmth. I took a sip of the spicy tea and let out a sigh of contentment. I could get used to this.

"But you work with vampires nearly every day. Surely this is nothing new."

I shook my head. "I *kill* vampires nearly every day. It's not like I sit down and have a conversation with them before I do it. Besides, vampires wouldn't have had conversations with famous historical figures; they'd have sucked them dry."

That made him laugh. He had a good laugh, all rumbly and deep. It made my thighs quiver and other places go all tingly.

"Morgan Bailey, you are one hell of a woman." His fingers played with my hair.

"Why, thank you, kind sir."

We were quiet, enjoying the moment. Adjusting to this new thing between us, whatever it turned out to be.

Stupid me, I had to go and shatter it. "What did Darroch mean, 'Blood calls to blood'?"

Jack shook his head. He set his mug down and then wrapped his arms around me. Damn, that felt really good. "I'm not sure. Maybe he meant that descendants of Atlantis could sense one another, and maybe somehow he recognized that we are both sunwalkers. He is part Atlantean, after all. Maybe his forefathers taught him to recognize the signs."

I so wasn't going to go there. I wasn't ready yet to admit that I am a sunwalker, though obviously both Jack and Darroch think I am. Still, I wasn't sure I'd ever be ready for something as life changing as that.

"Did you know the first time you met me? That I was like you? Part Atlantean, I mean."

"Of course I did."

"Well, I suppose it could be that. Maybe it has something to do with the amulet, or maybe he and I are from the same genetic line," I speculated. Though the thought of being related to Brent Darroch, no matter how distantly, sent shudders down my spine. And not the good kind.

"That's as good an answer as any. We could have Trevor ask him, though I doubt he'd tell us the truth anyway." He hesitated.

"What?"

"I might have a theory, but"—he shook his head—"I need to think on it some."

I sighed. There were still so many questions, and it was doubtful we'd ever get all the answers. But there was one particular question I'd had ever since Jack had told me about his past with the Templars—and if things were going to move in the direction they were headed between us, this one I needed an answer to.

"Tell me about her. The woman who saved your life back in France. Lydia."

He let out a sigh. "That's the name I knew her by. We all change our names over the centuries, and she was more than a thousand years old when I met her.

"The Heart had shown me that the Templars needed to set up safe houses and that things were going to change, not in our favor. Many of our safe houses were run by civilian sunwalkers, and Lydia was one of them. She took me in and hid me until she could smuggle me onto a ship bound for Scotland." His voice held a distant, dreamy quality that sometimes happens when a person recounts old stories. I supposed most of his stories would be old.

"I convinced Lydia to come with me. If Phillip's men found her, they would execute her too."

"Why?"

He shrugged. "Collaboration. Spite. Revenge. He didn't need a reason; he was king."

"Were you and Lydia lovers?" I couldn't help it. I had to know.

Jack grinned a little. "Jealous?"

I just shrugged. No way was he getting that confession out of me.

"Not at first, but over time we grew to love each other deeply," he admitted. "She was my family, my world. The only one alive who knew what I was. Who understood."

I admit I felt a tiny twinge of jealousy toward the woman who'd been so important to him. How can a girl compete with a relationship where "long-term" meant centuries?

"Jack?"

"Yeah?" He was still playing with my hair, letting the red strands slip through his fingers.

"What is this?"

"What do you mean?"

"This." I waved at both of us. "You and me."

I felt him go deadly still, and I held my breath. I wasn't sure what answer I wanted to hear, but I knew it was important.

He didn't answer right away. Instead, he turned me around in his arms so I was facing him, my legs straddling his muscular ones and his ocean-blue eyes staring deep into my green ones. My heart was thumping so loudly in my chest I was sure he could hear it.

If he did, he didn't mention it. Instead, he leaned over and kissed me with those gorgeous velvety lips of his. He hadn't exactly answered my question, but for one moment, I stopped breathing, stopped thinking. I just held on for dear life and kissed him back for all I was worth.

He pulled back a little and I nearly whimpered at the loss. He didn't let me go, though. "Morgan." His voice was a little ragged, which made me feel better. I wasn't the only one affected by our kiss. "I'm more than nine hundred years old. I'm not sure I know how to love anymore. It's been so long. But I want to try—"

I cut him off with a kiss. I didn't want to hear any more than that. I wasn't ready to talk about love or commitment. I was OK with here and now and seeing where this thing would take us. I didn't need more. Not yet.

I wrapped myself around him and kissed him with everything I had. My hands slipped under the soft fabric of his T-shirt to lose themselves in the feel of his hot, velvety skin underneath. His fingers were working their magic with the hooks on my bra.

His tongue slipped into my mouth as I squirmed in his lap, trying to get closer. He pushed me back a little and I made an irritated sound, but it was only so he could rip my shirt and bra off. The look in his eyes when he saw my naked breasts was enough to have me smirking. What is it with men and boobs?

He dipped his head so he could take first one nipple in his mouth, then the other. I could feel the hard length of his erection prodding my stomach. I couldn't help myself; I rubbed against him until my panties were soaked and I was practically out of my mind with want.

Jack growled low in his throat and yanked down the zipper on my jeans. It took a bit of aerobics on my part, but we managed to get them off. He got rid of my panties too. I tried to pull the tab down on his zipper, but there wasn't enough give. Swearing, he managed to get the thing down and shrug his jeans off.

Oh, Lordy, he'd gone commando. My hand found the smooth, hot length of him, and I stroked. "Morgan," he hissed.

I just grinned against his lips, nipping his lower lip with my teeth. Most effective.

Not to be outdone, Jack slipped his own hand down until he found my slick folds. His finger rubbed over my clitoris and I nearly came then and there. I couldn't take it anymore. I jerked his hand away from me.

"I want you now. Inside me," I breathed in his ear. "Do you have anything?"

He nodded. "Wallet."

He hissed out a breath as I slid the sheath on him; then he grabbed me by the hips, lifting me a little. I positioned him at my entrance, the tip of him teasing me with pleasure. In one smooth move, I lowered myself on him until he was inside me. Filling me. I arched over him. Gods, it felt so good. I thought I might burst with the sheer pleasure of it. "Jack."

He nipped my ear, then kissed me hard, his tongue tangling with mine even as I found my rhythm. The thrust of our tongues mimicked the thrust of our bodies, the pressure winding tighter and higher, building until, in one moment, pleasure burst over me like a wave. My muscles contracted around him, milking him with my orgasm.

Jack groaned, his face taut as he flipped us over so I was on my back with him on top. I wrapped my legs around him as he thrust into me again and again, the tension twisting tighter and tighter. His last thrust sent another orgasm rippling through me, and this time he joined me.

For a while, we just lay there, wrapped in each other's arms, limbs slick with sweat. I nuzzled his neck and slid my hand down to squeeze his delectable backside. I loved the salty taste of him, the feel of him against my skin.

After a while, he shifted a bit. "You thirsty?"

"I could use some water, thanks."

"Stay here, OK? Don't move." He gave me a quick, hard kiss before pulling on his jeans and answering his cell. As he moved out of the room I watched his positively delectable backside with no small amount of glee.

Still lost in the afterglow, I just gave his back a dopey smile and sank back into the soft couch cushions. I'd probably kick myself for my sheer lunacy later, sleeping with a guy I barely knew, but for right now, I was living in the moment.

As he disappeared into the other room, my gaze shifted back to the amulet, which he'd left in its velvet cover sitting on the coffee table. Curiosity got the better of me, so I wrapped myself in the throw we somehow managed not to dislodge from the back of the couch. Then I reached out and gently lifted the folds of cloth away from the amulet, the Heart of Atlantis. I wondered vaguely why Darroch had called me the key. I couldn't understand it. The idea was ludicrous. Jack had said the amulet would tell him when he found a royal, and it never had, so obviously, I couldn't be it.

It might be next to useless without the bloodline, but it was still pretty. A sudden urge came over me, that same urge you get when they offer you free samples in a chocolate shop. I couldn't help myself. I reached out and caressed its surface, smooth and cold under my fingertips. As my fingers brushed the center stone, a blaze of rich blue light suddenly shot out of the gem, bathing the room in blue fire.

I jumped back a good ten feet.

"What the heck? It's glowing!" I gasped as Jack returned. "Why is it glowing? Is it supposed to do that?"

Jack just stared at me, face white and eyes wide. He opened his mouth, closed it, then fell to his knees. "My lady," he whispered, his voice gone hoarse. He bowed his head and placed his right fist over his heart in the same salute I'd seen in my dreams. "My lady, I am yours to command, now and always."

I glanced from Jack kneeling on the wood floor to the glowing amulet in my hand and I suddenly understood. Or thought I did.

Apparently, Jackson Keel, former Templar Knight, immortal sunwalker, guardian of the Heart of Atlantis, had finally found a member of the royal Atlantean bloodline. And she was standing in his living room.

There was really only one thing I could say.

"Oh, shit."

Acknowledgments

Thanks to my fabulous critique partners Lois and Tamra.
You made this novel shine.

Don't miss Morgan Bailey's next exciting adventure in
Kissed by Fire!

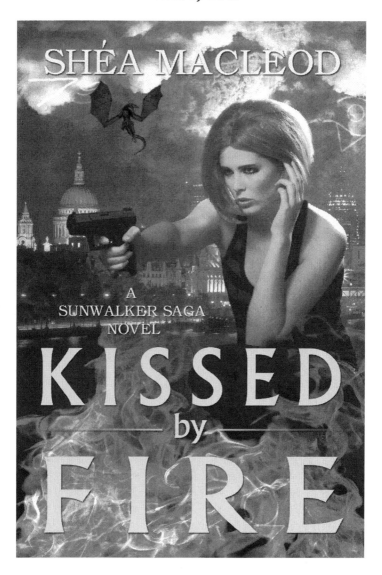

Available now on Amazon.com

About the Author

Shéa MacLeod spent most of her life in Portland, Oregon, before moving to an Edwardian townhouse in London located just a stone's throw from a local cemetery. Such a unique locale probably explains a lot about her penchant for urban fantasy post-apocalyptic sci-fi paranormal romances, but at least the neighbors are quiet. Alas, the dearth of good doughnuts in London drove her back across the pond to the land of her birth. She is the author of the Sunwalker Saga and Dragon Wars series.

14809821R00148

Made in the USA
Charleston, SC
03 October 2012